Shall We Dance?

NEW YORK TIMES BESTSELLING AUTHOR

SHELLEY SHEPARD GRAY

Shall We Dance?

BLACK STONE
PUBLISHING

Published in 2020 by Blackstone Publishing
Cover and book design by Alenka Vdovič Linaschke

Printed in the United States of America

First edition: 2020
ISBN 978-1-9826-5852-6
Fiction / Romance / General

1 3 5 7 9 10 8 6 4 2

CIP data for this book is available
from the Library of Congress

Blackstone Publishing
31 Mistletoe Rd.
Ashland, OR 97520

www.BlackstonePublishing.com

For Tiffany, a great dancer and even better friend.

"Take more chances. Dance more dances."

Letter to Readers

Have you ever had a hobby that you really enjoyed but weren't very good at? That was me and dancing. I first started taking ballet, tap, and jazz lessons around sixth grade. My best friend Tiffany took dancing lessons, and I wanted to spend time with her.

I also wanted to be a graceful dancer, too.

For years, I took dance classes three times a week. I spent hours in the studio and eventually became fairly strong, somewhat flexible, and was even able to do a couple of time steps. However, I never was anything more than fairly proficient. Later, I joined the high school's dance team. I began to spend my summers sweating in the hot Houston heat at dance camps and most of each fall doing high kicks on a football field. I loved it. I loved the nerves before each performance, the camaraderie, the music. Other girls were much better than me—Tiffany even became the team's drum major. I was okay with that, though. I never measured my enjoyment of dancing in terms of awards or compliments. For me "success" wasn't what dance was about.

It's been a very long time since I've put on a ballet slipper or a tap shoe. Maybe that's why I was so excited about the opportunity to write this novel. It afforded me the chance to write about a character who liked dancing for all the same reasons that I did. But, because Shannon Murphy was made up, I was able to make her gifted and graceful and award-winning. That is a writer's prerogative, I think!

Writing about Shannon and her love of dance reminded me of how much pressure we now put on ourselves. We want success quickly and easily. We don't want to fail or to be embarrassed or made fun of. I can't help but be sad about that. I am now determined to step out of my comfort zone a little bit more and worry about being successful a little less. Yep, like the characters in this book, I really am going to try to "take more chances and dance more dances."

Thank you for reading my book, and I hope you'll think about taking a chance or two as well. I'd love the company!

Blessings, Shelley

PROLOGUE

November

They were supposed to arrive any minute. Pressing one hand on the slightly warped, freshly painted, white windowsill, Shannon Murphy looked out once again. And, just like she had every time before, she said a little prayer. *Dear God, please let this go okay.*

The seven words sounded hollow and awkward in the empty room. Since she'd never considered herself to be an especially religious person and didn't have a lot of experience praying, she was embarrassed about the clumsy demand. She was pretty sure there were rules to praying that she didn't know. However, she hoped God would give her a little leeway.

Especially since this was a pretty unusual circumstance. No, that wasn't the right word at all. It was a *special* circumstance. A terrific *occasion*. In just a few minutes, at age twenty-seven, she was going to meet her sisters for the first time.

Well, the first time that she could remember.

That was the kicker, wasn't it? Shannon felt a burst of pain slice through her insides. At least she had made *some* progress. Back when she first heard that she had two sisters she hadn't known about, she'd done some cursing and yelling about the injustice of it all.

Twenty-four years ago, their mother had died suddenly. She'd left behind a mess of bills, a web of lies, and three little girls. The social workers, and ultimately the folks at the private adoption agency, ended up separating her and her sisters. Each had grown up never knowing about their past or their siblings. Only taking a DNA test on a whim—and the shock of learning that her parents hadn't actually been her parents—had led to this moment. Well, that and a driving need to discover her past.

Now, after a flurry of emails and phone calls, the three of them had decided to live together for one year on the top floor of Shannon's recently purchased building on the edge of downtown Bridgeport, Ohio.

Amazingly, though they were essentially strangers, they'd all agreed to give up pretty much everything in order to give their relationship and their future together a chance.

Their leaps of faith hadn't come easy.

She had come from a small town in West Virginia. Her sisters Traci and Kimber were arriving from Cleveland and New York City, respectively. Back in Cleveland, Traci had been a big city cop. Kimber had lived a fancy life as a runway and print model in the middle of Manhattan. They'd both given up a lot in order to move to southern Ohio—and to help Shannon achieve her longtime dream of owning a ballroom dance studio.

Their sacrifices were humbling. Some would even say too generous. However, Shannon didn't think any of them had an ounce of regret. It seemed a common mother combined with a need to know more about their past could overrule most any other obstacle.

Now, though she'd been the instigator, Shannon was feeling at a distinct disadvantage. Kimber had flown to Cleveland, spent two days helping Traci get packed, and now was riding shotgun during their short trip from Cleveland to Bridgeport.

While Shannon had been busy trying to make the sprawling loft into a home, they'd had almost two days of bonding and catching up. What if they'd already formed a bond that was going to be hard for Shannon to penetrate?

She could see that happening. Both Traci and Kimber were also from big cities, and with demanding jobs. Shannon, on the other hand, was simply a small-town dance instructor. Bridgeport, Ohio, was double the size of her hometown of Spartan, West Virginia. What if they thought she was too country?

What if they were both used to fancy things and exciting lives, while a trip to the supercenter was sometimes the highlight of Shannon's day? As question after question rattled through her brain, she became even more agitated.

Frustrated with the direction of her thoughts, Shannon turned away from the window and looked hard at their living room. It currently consisted of a small, ancient fireplace that needed a good cleaning, a lumpy sofa, a rickety side table, and a lamp. Saying the space looked sparse was putting it mildly.

The open living room was connected to a galley-style kitchen that sported an oven and refrigerator almost as old as Kimber. On the other side was a bathroom that was bigger than any Shannon had ever had but now seemed woefully small for three women to share.

The only good thing about their third-floor loft was that there were three bedrooms. They were small and didn't even have closets, but they did give each of them a small amount of privacy.

When she'd told the other girls about it all, Shannon had been so excited. But now? She was afraid that they'd see it for what it was—a desperate small-town girl's attempt to make a vague dream into a home.

Even though she'd since tried to tone down their expectations, there was a good chance they'd be disappointed. Why, Kimber, especially, was probably used to fancy New York apartments and designer furniture.

Just as another wave of doubt crashed through her, a gleaming white Subaru Outback pulled into the parking lot on the side of the studio, accompanied by two sharp honks.

Feeling like her heart was in her throat, Shannon rushed down the stairs and opened the front door just as both women stepped out.

And . . . there were her sisters. Traci and Kimber. Traci, with her long brown hair clasped in a low ponytail and a far more athletic build than her own. Kimber, with her gorgeous cappuccino skin, statuesque height, perfect features, and large doe eyes. Both were so different from her. They were practically strangers who'd dropped everything in order to become family.

That was everything. Everything. Suddenly, nothing else mattered—not the shock of their circumstances, the anger at her parents, nor all the self-doubts and worries that she'd been holding close like long lost friends. All that did matter was that it had finally happened. She was seeing her sisters.

All that was why she did the only thing that she could—she promptly burst into tears. "I can hardly believe y'all are here," she said as she flew into their arms.

"Of course we're here," Traci said as she wrapped an arm around her. "Wouldn't miss it for the world."

The three of them clung together, holding each other close like lifelines in the middle of Kiowa Street. A light snow had started falling and it stuck to their eyelashes and sparkled against their dark hair.

Pulling back slightly to wipe her face, Shannon said, "You two are so tall! I feel like a shrimp next to y'all."

Kimber chuckled. "You are just a tiny thing."

"I think you're cute," Traci said. "And you have even a thicker accent in person than you did on the phone. I love it."

That little bit of affirmation only made her start crying again. "I'm sorry. I don't know what's wrong with me."

Kimber grinned as she wiped tears of her own. "Welcome to the club. Traci and I've been crying nonstop for the last two days," she said as she leaned in and hugged Shannon once more.

Shannon held her close, then pulled back slightly to see her face better. "Oh my goodness, but you're beautiful."

"Stop. You are beautiful, too." Smiling over her shoulder at Traci, she said, "And for what it's worth, over the last couple of years I've had the chance to see a lot of pretty things and people. But, I promise, nothing holds a candle to you two."

Pulling away from the both of them, Shannon smiled so big that her teeth were getting cold. "Having you two here? Knowing that I have sisters after growing up as an only child? It's a miracle. Definitely the answer to a lot of prayers."

Some of the warmth that had filled Traci's gaze cooled. "Prayers and a good DNA test, huh?"

Shannon nodded. "Absolutely."

Stepping away, she took another long look at her sisters. Both had dark brown eyes and brown hair like her. She tried to see if there was anything more that they shared. She couldn't see anything, though.

No, they were essentially strangers. Strangers that she had so many hopes for. Doubts filled her again as the three of them dropped their hands and simply stared at each other.

Taking her in. Taking in their new home, their new town. Their new life. Did they have doubts?

Worse, were they already regretting their decisions to give up so much for a bond they weren't even sure they would ever actually have?

"So, this is it," Traci said.

Kimber looked up at the three-story building and smiled. "It's just like I imagined."

They were standing on the street in the snow.

"Welcome home," she said, finally remembering what was important and what wasn't. "Come on in and get out of the cold."

Popping the trunk, Traci went over and grabbed a pair of duffle bags. "Lead the way, Shannon. I can't wait to see it all."

After Kimber grabbed her designer suitcase, Shannon steeled her shoulders and led the way in. It was time to move forward. To begin again.

CHAPTER 1

"Dancing in heels should count as a superpower."
—MOLLY W.

January, Two Months Later

When the set of bells chimed on the front door to Dance with Me, her finally finished dance studio, Shannon felt a burst of satisfaction. Her very first private client had arrived, and right on time, too.

After taking a quick glance at herself in the mirror, she smoothed her dress down on her thighs and strode forward to meet the man who was standing in the small lobby. "Hi, I'm Shannon Murphy," she said as she held out her hand. "Are you Dylan Lange?"

The man who looked like he could have played quarterback for the Broncos stared at her for a good long moment before clasping her hand in his. "Yeah, I am. It's nice to meet you."

His palm was gargantuan. She was sure two of her hands

could neatly fit inside it. Yet, he clasped her hand in a way that was both firm and gentle. That was no small feat, she reckoned. Most men either shook her hand so lightly it felt like she was holding onto a limp trout or with so much pressure it felt more like a vice than a hello.

Thinking that this simple handshake was a sign of good things to come, she smiled up at him. "It's real nice to meet you, too."

"Thanks for fitting me into your schedule on such late notice. I really appreciate it."

"Of course. I'm always happy to help someone learn to dance—especially when I hear that they're in a bind."

When he smiled at her, faint lines formed around his blue eyes. He really did have nice eyes. And, yes, she could admit it, she liked how the rest of him looked, too. He had dark-blond hair, a light tan, and those blue eyes . . . And his teeth? Perfectly straight and pure white. Immediately she switched her comparison from pro football lineman to Coppertone model.

As what she was doing hit her, she felt her cheeks heat. She knew better than to start fantasizing about her clients. She liked to keep things professional and organized. For her, it was a needed element since she spent much of her time in such close proximity with her students. Things could get out of hand fast if she allowed anything to become personal while fox-trotting or waltzing in her ballroom.

When she noticed that he was looking around the lobby and the large room off to the side, she knew it was time to get to business.

Walking toward the antique desk she'd bought for a song, and Traci and Kimber had helped her refurbish, she gestured to the pair of chairs next to it. "Dylan, come on in. We'll have a seat, get all the paperwork done and discuss your goals." Motioning to the neat line of antique silver hooks that lined the wall, she added, "There's a place for you to hang up your coat, too."

"Thanks." He shrugged out of his black wool peacoat and hung it on a hook. Looking more awkward, he shoved his hands into his pockets instead of sitting down. "It's pretty cold out, huh?"

"It sure is. There's no way around it—January is for the birds."

And, now she had succeeded in sounding like an old woman. What was wrong with her? She needed to get a grip.

Clearing her throat, she gestured to the chairs again. "Please sit down."

When he did at last, she pushed forward one of the packets of information she'd worked so hard on. She loved how the contents were comprehensive but not too overwhelming. She'd learned over the years that it was a mistake to pass on too much information to a student too quickly. "So, here's all the information about the classes and fees. We went over all of this on the phone."

He scanned the page. "Okay . . ."

"Here is a basic health form. If you could fill it out now, it would be helpful."

"I'm a cop. I'm in good shape."

Oh yes, he certainly was. Still a little embarrassed that she'd been ogling him, Shannon handed him a pen. "This is just in case you have a heart condition or something I need to know about."

"Is that really a concern?"

"It can be." Remembering Mr. Gerome back in Spartan and how he seemed to be last person to realize that he wasn't too steady on his feet, she swallowed. "It's just a precaution. I'm sure you understand."

"I understand that you take this dancing stuff pretty seriously." He smirked.

Ouch. She wasn't a big fan of his attitude.

She smiled tightly. "I know it seems unlikely, but some of our sessions might be more active than you realize." When he raised a brow, she shrugged. "All I really need from you is a signature saying that you are aware of the health risks associated with being here."

Dylan scrawled his name at the bottom, not even pretending to look at her carefully written warning at the top of the page. "Is that it?"

Suddenly her hot client didn't seem all that attractive anymore. "Almost. The last thing that we need to do is determine your goals."

He leaned back and folded his arms over his chest. "What goals do I need to have? I already told you that I wanted to learn to dance."

"Yes, I know, but most people have a reason for taking classes, such as a couple might sign up for classes so they can dance at a wedding or something," she replied in her most reasonable tone. "These private classes are expensive, and I don't want to waste your money."

He rolled his eyes. *Rolled his eyes!* "Honey, why don't you let me worry about how I spend my money?"

Never had being called "honey" irked her so much. "I'll gladly let you manage your finances on your own—after you let me know how many classes you'd like to take and what particular dance you'd like to learn."

"I have to take five classes, and I don't care which dances we learn." He winked. "You can choose."

This whole situation was getting curiouser and curiouser. And it was also beginning to get her pretty irritated. After reminding herself that she was trying to make money and not new friends, she asked, "I'm sorry, but I'm getting confused. Why five? And why don't you care what you learn?"

He kicked out a very large, tree-trunk sized leg. "Look, I didn't want to go here, but you're leaving me no choice. See, the truth is that I'm not actually here to get ready to dance at a wedding." Blue eyes zeroed directly on her. "I'm here because I lost a bet."

"Pardon me?"

"We had a pool with my fantasy football league," he explained. Sounding completely sincere, he added, "The winner got three hundred dollars but the loser had to do penance."

"Penance," she repeated, not even trying to hide her dismay.

"Yeah. Two of my key players choked, and another one got hurt. I couldn't believe my luck."

"Your luck?"

He nodded. "I went from eighth place to dead last in two weeks." Dylan exhaled, just like he was explaining something that was actually important. "I couldn't believe it. I still can't. I mean, I was sure the Raiders' defensive line was going to be pretty good this year."

Shannon stared at him. She was a girly-girl, but she'd grown up with a hunting-and-fishing dad in West Virginia, too. She was used to listening to him talk about all kinds of "typical male" things that he found interesting (and that her mother pretended to care about): Friday night high school games, deer blinds, and even wily trout.

But a bet based on made-up football teams? Well, that took the cake.

Not even trying to hide her irritation, she said, "So, if I understand you right, you're only here to take classes because it's your punishment?"

For the first time since he'd walked in, Dylan looked uncomfortable. "That's putting it a little harsh."

"But . . ."

"But . . . well, yes."

She was dumbfounded. Here she was, working seven days a week, stressing about her sisters, stressing about owing so much money to the bank, trying like crazy to get her business up and running—but he was treating it as part of his stupid game. "I can't believe you are wasting my time like this."

He held his hands up like he was fending off her attack. "Hey, now. I don't see how I'm wasting your time."

"You can't be serious."

"Yeah, I am. As a heart attack." He grinned like she was supposed to think his joke was original and cute. "You teach dancing and I have to take lessons. And I'm gonna pay you, don't worry about that. It's a win-win situation."

"Not really. You don't want to be here, and I have a strange desire to teach dance to people who actually want to learn. I don't think this is the right studio for you." She folded her hands over her chest. I think you need to leave."

He blinked, waited a beat, looked at her intently, and then spoke again. "Listen, I think you are taking everything the wrong way." He winced. "Or, heck, I think I've been explaining everything completely wrong. Maybe I should try this again. You see—"

Oh, no. There was no way she wanted to hear about the rules of his stupid fantasy football game again. "Please stop. I get it."

"If you're sure."

"Real sure. Believe me, it's clear. Crystal clear."

"What I'm trying to say is that while I might not have ever considered taking lessons before, I'm still going to do my best. I'm not a jerk."

He sure seemed like one to her.

But, just as she was about to shake her head and point her finger toward the door, she noticed a muscle jump in his cheek. There was a softening in his eyes, too—almost a vulnerability. He actually wanted her to give him a chance. And, if she wasn't mistaken, it wasn't because he just wanted to take care of his penance. There was something more going on. She was sure of it.

Maybe she was being stupid, but something about him made her want to give him a chance, too.

Plus, she could almost hear her sisters remind her that money was money. She had a mortgage to pay, furniture to upgrade, and a reputation to earn. None of that was going to happen if she started judging who wanted to take classes.

She wasn't changing lives here. She was simply trying to teach people to dance.

Smiling tightly, she decided to get off her high horse and do her job. "You know what, it doesn't really matter what your reasons are for coming here. I'm sorry I got all defensive."

"So, we're good?"

"Yes."

"Can we get started now? Not to be rude, but I've to get home soon."

"I understand." Even though it sounded a little cheesy, she held out her hand. "All right, Dylan. Shall we dance?"

Folding his own around hers, he grinned. "Shannon Murphy, I thought you'd never ask."

CHAPTER 2

"Forget your troubles and dance."
—BOB MARLEY

It was Friday night and he was sitting in Kurt Holland's garage an hour before the rest of the guys started to arrive for the Bridgeport Social Club's monthly poker game. Kurt was nowhere around—likely spending a few minutes with his wife before joining the guys for the next five hours.

But that didn't stop the rest of them from enjoying a beer and catching up before the cards and the chips came out.

Of course, if he had realized he was going to be grilled about his first dance lesson, he would've arrived *just* before the tournament began and skipped the interrogation.

"Dude, you were supposed to get pictures together," Meyer complained after Dylan filled him in on his first dance class. "We need documentation."

Thinking about how he'd almost gotten himself kicked out of dance school before he'd even taken his first box step, he grimaced. "Yeah, well, I don't think she was really up for a photo op. Maybe next time."

"But how are we going to be able to be sure you were there?"

"Because I'm not going to lie about it. I agreed to take five lessons and I am. I took one, and now I've got four more to go. End of story."

"I saw his Jeep outside the place," Ace Vance said. "It was there when I got to Meredith's studio for lunch, and it was still parked there when I went back to work."

"See?" Dylan said to Meyer. "You now have confirmation."

"Maybe."

"No, *definitely*. Stop giving me crap."

"Now that we have that settled, how did it go?" Ace asked.

How did it go? Yeah, that was the question, he supposed. Thinking about Shannon, thinking about that old building with the gleaming white woodwork and the smooth wooden floors—and how he'd had to do some fancy verbal footwork in order to get her to still accept him as a student— he wasn't sure he had words. So he settled for a reply that was the universal guy-speak for when there wasn't much to say. Or for when he wasn't sure what to say.

"It was all right."

"All right?" Meyer rolled his eyes. "No go, buddy. If we don't get pictures, you're gonna have to give us more info."

"What are you after?"

"Details. What was your dance instructor like?" He wagged his eyebrows and grinned. "Just how old was she? Old enough to be my grandmother or yours?"

Though it was tempting to hide Shannon's youthful good looks from Meyer—which made no sense, except maybe opening the door for more teasing—he said, "Neither. She was in her late twenties, I think."

Ace sat up. "Really? I wasn't expecting that."

"Yeah. Me, neither." He hadn't been expecting anything about Shannon—he hadn't expected such thick, long brown hair, or big brown eyes framed by thick eyelashes . . . or that fabulous figure set off by a pair of killer legs in nylons. Or that she would be wearing a pair of three-inch heels that put her almost to his chin.

Or that, even though there was so much about her that he found attractive, not a bit of it compared to the way he'd admired her spunk.

And none of that could compare to the way he'd felt when he put one hand on her waist and attempted to move around the room per her directions. For a few moments there, he hadn't thought about anything else. Not the case he was working on, not his sister, not anything but holding her a little closer, if only for a little while.

"So, did you actually dance?"

He blinked. Returned to the conversation at hand. "We did."

"Well, what was it? Swing? Fox-trot? Samba . . . ?"

Ace laughed as he continued to shuffle a deck of cards. "Meyer, how the hell do you know those things?"

"Annie loves *Dancing with the Stars*."

Ace grinned. "I get that. But are you saying that you sit around and watch it with her?"

For the first time in memory, Meyer looked uncomfortable. "Not every week, but sometimes, yeah."

Dylan was tempted to give him crap for that, but then he realized that he didn't have a single thing to give the guy a hard time about. Meyer was going on thirteen years of marriage and had two kids. He loved his wife enough to watch reality dancing programs on TV.

He, on the other hand, had yet to keep a decent long-term relationship going for more than a year.

Thinking about his sister, he realized that if Jennifer ever dated a guy who cared enough about her to watch one of those singing reality shows she loved so much, he'd buy the guy a beer. Shoot, he'd do more than that. His little sister needed a hero in a bad way.

"We waltzed today." Thinking about how most eighth-grade boys at their first school dance probably looked better, he amended his report. "I mean, Shannon attempted to teach me how to count and guide her around a dance floor without knocking her down or stepping on her feet."

Ace raised his eyebrows. "Her name's Shannon?"

"Yep."

"I'll have to ask Meredith if she knows her."

"I don't know if she would. Shannon just moved here from West Virginia."

Ace leaned forward. "She's from West Virginia, too? No way. What part?"

"Some little town." Dylan tried to remember. "I don't know. Something with an *S*." He thought some more. "Sperry . . . ? No, Spartan! Does that ring a bell?"

"Uh, yeah. I'm from Spartan."

"That's crazy!" Meyer exclaimed.

Ace nodded. "Really crazy. Spartan's barely got two stoplights Hey, Dylan . . . wait a minute. What's her last name?"

"Murphy."

Ace gaped at him for a full thirty seconds before whistling low. "Your dance teacher is Shannon Murphy from Spartan? No way!"

Meyer raised his eyebrows. "Don't tell me she's part of y'all's group, too. I've never met so many people from someplace so small."

Dylan knew what Meyer was talking about. A couple of years back, several guys from the same Podunk West Virginia town moved to Bridgeport. Later, even more came, each for a variety of reasons. Dylan didn't blame the guys for coming—Bridgeport was a really great place to live, and all of the guys were good people.

But it really was becoming a case of small world.

"I wouldn't call her a good friend. Not really. She's a couple of years younger than me," Ace said to Meyer. "But I know her. Shoot, probably everyone in Spartan does."

"Because it's such a small town, right?"

"Well, yeah. But that's not the only reason," Ace said, still musing. "Shannon Murphy was a pretty popular girl. And her parents were always running her around for all kinds of dance competitions. Everyone followed her progress."

Though he was trying to act cool, Dylan was intrigued. "Really?"

"Oh, yeah. Her picture was always in our town's paper, winning this award or getting some kind of big trophy." Ace leaned back. "Dancing wasn't really my thing, but I do remember that some of them were a pretty big deal."

"Huh." Which pretty much summed up the extent of how much he was thinking.

Meyer grinned at him. "Maybe we should put the word out that these dance lessons aren't going to be the punishment all of us were expecting."

Dylan shook his head. "Don't even think about that, man. Besides, the bet had to do with dance lessons. I'm doing them."

"Yeah, but nobody thought you'd find a young, hot dance teacher."

Ace grinned. "You would've done the same thing, Meyer. We all would have."

* * *

Dylan was still grinning about the conversation he'd had with the guys when he got home late that night after the game. He hadn't seen that coming, but he couldn't deny that he was happy about the way things were turning out. Ace's information about Shannon had been illuminating, to say the least.

Now, he realized that *of course* Shannon had been a professional dancer in the past. No one opened a dance studio without some kind of success as a dancer.

But he couldn't help but wonder what had happened. How did a girl like her end up giving dance lessons in an old, remodeled building in Bridgeport, Ohio? There had to be a story there.

"What has you grinning like that?" Jennifer asked as she walked into the kitchen.

He noticed that she had her hair up in a messy knot that shouldn't stay on top of her head but somehow did. She also wore her glasses and one of his old sweatshirts from college. More importantly, she looked like she was in pretty good spirits.

He breathed a sigh of relief. His little sister had had another good day.

Returning his head to the subject at hand, he replied, "Oh, I was just thinking about some of my buddies. They were all interested in my first dance lesson, and it turns out that Ace Vance is from the same town as my teacher. Small world."

She raised her eyebrows. "Boy, that is pretty amazing. What were the chances?"

"I'm starting to think *pretty good* now. Spartan, West Virginia, needs to keep hold of more of its citizens or they're all going to move here."

"At least they're all nice, right? I mean, you said the guys you know from there are nice."

"They are. Stand-up guys. Shannon seems real sweet, too." He sat down on a barstool. "I think you'd like them all, Jen. Maybe you should think about letting me introduce you to some of them. Who knows? Maybe they'd turn out to be a good friend."

Her open expression turned guarded. "Dylan, you know I'm not ready to start meeting strangers."

He was tempted to remind her that everyone was going to be a stranger until she was willing to talk to them, but he didn't dare. He knew she was trying.

And every time he thought about how far she'd come, about the way she'd been two years ago, it felt like someone had just knocked him in the gut. Every time he thought about what had happened to her, either he felt like he'd been punched . . . or he had the overwhelming desire to punch his own fist through a wall.

"Let me know when you are, okay?" he asked lightly.

"I will." She smiled.

He smiled back, liking that, for once, she wasn't as self-conscious about the scar on her face that prevented half of her mouth from curving.

"So, what do you want to do about dinner? Any ideas?"

Looking pleased, she opened the refrigerator and pulled out a casserole dish. "I made a casserole."

His little sister, all of twenty-one, cooked like she was Betty Crocker circa 1952. It was awesome. "What is it today?"

"King Ranch Chicken Casserole."

"Which is what, exactly?"

"Chicken, green chilies, cheddar jack cheese. All kinds of good stuff." Turning on the oven, she said, "It'll be ready in forty minutes."

"Perfect. I'm going to take a shower."

"We can eat when you get out. I made a salad, too. Oh, and I got bored, so I made you some brownies!"

"Did we have brownie mix? I could've sworn we used the last box a week ago." Chocolate was his weakness. Actually cookies and brownies and any kind of dessert was.

"I made them from scratch."

"Of course you did."

"It wasn't a big deal. Don't make it one."

"I won't, then." He pushed everything he was thinking about how a girl like her shouldn't be playing happy homemaker to an older brother. Her counselor had cautioned him about doing things like that. "How about this? Thank you for supper, Jen. I really appreciate it."

"It's nothing. You know that. Not compared to what you did for me."

She walked out of the room too soon to see him wince.

Since he was alone, he closed his eyes and said a little prayer for small favors. Life wasn't fair, but every once in a while things got easier.

At least there was that.

CHAPTER 3

"Every day brings a chance for you to draw in a breath, kick off your shoes, and dance."
—OPRAH WINFREY

"Did anybody cook tonight?" Traci asked as she walked in the door.

Shannon looked up from her dinner of bagged salad, crackers, and a slice of leftover pizza from two nights ago. "Nope."

"I was afraid of that." After taking off her badge and locking up her holster in the cabinet she had installed in the corner of the living room, Traci walked over to the kitchen. She was wearing dark fitted jeans, and a fitted oxford shirt with the Bridgeport Police Department logo embroidered on the chest pocket. As usual, she looked like the woman she was—someone organized, neat, and devoid of a lot of frills.

She was also looking like she'd lost her best friend as she started opening and shutting cabinets. "I had to sit in on a community meeting. It was full of a lot of hot air and nothing to eat. Not even a bowl of pretzels."

"Bless your heart."

Traci didn't even roll her eyes at Shannon's comment. "I'm starving. Like, I could seriously even eat whatever it was you made three days ago."

Their current conversation wasn't anything new. Soon after they'd started living together, the three of them had learned that they had something in common besides brown hair and brown eyes. Not a one of them could cook. Nothing of worth, anyway.

But that said, Shannon was feeling slightly offended. "Traci, you said you liked those black bean burgers I made."

"That you *kind of* made," she corrected. "And, sorry, but I also *kind of* lied. They were edible, but that's about it."

"Here." Shannon pushed her big bowl of salad across the table toward Traci. "Grab a fork. Eat some veggies."

Traci grumbled but did just that and joined her at the table. "Where's Kimber?"

"She's on the phone in her room."

"Who with?" Her voice darkened. "Oh, no. Is it her agent?"

"I don't think it's Brett. I'm not sure though." Shannon hoped it wasn't. Every time Kimber got off the phone with her fancy New York modeling agent, she seemed upset and then didn't eat for two days.

After taking another bite of lettuce, Traci pulled out her phone and started swiping. "I'm going to get on Door Dash and get something delivered. Do you want anything?"

"I'm okay."

"I wonder what— Oh, great you're here," Traci said smiling at Kimber. "What do you want to eat? Chinese or Thai?"

Kimber popped a hand on one slim hip. "Oh, girl. You and your love of Asian food."

"I can't help it." Giving Shannon a look, she said, "It's tasty, and good for you, too. So, what do y'all want? My treat."

"Nothing for me," Kimber said. "I'm not too hungry."

"Is everything okay?" Shannon asked.

Kimber shared a smile with Shannon, but it didn't reach her eyes. "Sure."

Shannon didn't believe her, but she wasn't eager to push. They all deserved their privacy.

Traci was obviously not of the same mind. "What Shannon was too polite to ask is, Did that agent of yours make you worry about your looks again?"

"What? No. It wasn't Brett."

"Good. I hate when he calls. All he ever does is make you stress."

"You give him too hard of a time. I'm a model, honey. My career is based on my looks. It's nothing personal."

"I guess I don't understand it then," Traci retorted. "You're one of the prettiest women I've ever seen in person."

Shannon almost choked on the water she was sipping. "In person? The things you say, Traci."

"I know. I have no tact. I'm working on it, though."

Traci's cheeks were flushed, which Shannon was fairly sure would shock anyone on Traci's police force. Traci put up such a strong front that not a bit of insecurity ever seemed to seep through.

Kimber sat down. "Just to end all the speculation, I was on the phone with my mom."

"How did it go?"

"About how it always does," she replied with a look of regret. "Mom's hurt that I moved here. She doesn't understand why I want to know two women who mean practically nothing to me."

"Ouch," Traci said.

Kimber continued. "What else? Oh, yeah. She worries that I'm hurting my modeling career by living in the middle of Ohio, which she considers only slightly more sophisticated than, say, Tibet."

"So, she's good," Traci said.

Kimber raised one perfectly arched brow, then started laughing. "Yeah, Trace. Mom is great." After a pause, she said, "You know what? Order me up some veggie lo mein."

"Will do." Traci picked up her phone again. "Shannon?"

Looking at the dregs of the salad in her bowl, she said, "Beef and broccoli, please. With brown rice."

"On it."

As Traci started swiping screens on her phone, Kimber walked to the refrigerator, pulled out a sparkling water and joined them at the table. "You want to know the best thing about that conversation?"

Shannon nodded. "Yep."

"I told Mom that I had to get off the phone because you girls were waiting for me." Her smile widened. "I love, love, love having sisters."

"You and me both," Traci said. "Dinner's on the way, girls."

Feeling all the tension dissipate, Shannon sat back against her chair and simply enjoyed the moment. Sure, they had a long way to go before they had the type of relationship she'd dreamed of . . . but even after a couple of months things were good.

She'd take that.

CHAPTER 4

"Life is short and there will always
be dirty dishes, so let's dance."
—JAMES HOWE

Friday Night

Another week had gone by, and here she was again, waiting for her least favorite client. Did it help that he also paid more for her time than almost anyone else?

No, it did not.

Especially since he was late.

Feeling grumpier than usual, Shannon sat down on the velvet sofa in the lobby. It was a new purchase, paid for by Kimber, who seemed to have an unlimited supply of money to spend on their new building. After putting up a token argument about Kimber not needing to spend her money on Shannon's studio, she'd given in. Kimber assured her that she had more money from her modeling jobs than she knew what to do with.

Besides, the couch was gorgeous. It was a dark emerald green, and it was all curves and carved wood. Kimber had chuckled when she'd seen it online, saying it looked like something out of the Addams Family.

She hadn't been wrong.

But even if Shannon hadn't needed something for her students to sit on before and after class, she would have coveted it. It was that beautiful.

Another five minutes passed . . . making her aggravation spike.

Maybe Dylan was going to blow her off. And wouldn't that just be something he would do? He was self-centered, and that was a fact.

Still stewing, she decided that she wasn't going to lie to any of his fantasy-football buddies about tonight's class—if they just so happened to stop by and ask questions. She was going to make him pay for this wasted hour, too. Just like every other student.

Deciding to wait five more minutes, Shannon kicked off her three-inch heels. Boy, her feet hurt. She'd had a two-hour tap class with her new class of sixteen-year-olds—which wasn't for sissies.

Though they were all still getting to know each other, she was impressed by some of their skills. The girls were talented and had a ton of energy. They also were absorbing everything she could teach them like sponges. She was pretty sure that before long they were going to be able to dance circles around her.

Shoot, today after class, they'd started making up their own dances, laughing and squealing and doing what girls do. She'd watched them with affection . . . while sitting on her new favorite couch.

When had she gotten so old?

Feeling a bit melancholy, Shannon closed her eyes and allowed herself to do something she tried very hard to never do. She let her mind drift back to when she was sixteen and practicing twenty to thirty hours a week for competitions.

She'd switched to ballroom after she'd realized that she was never going to be a good enough ballerina to dance in New York.

With that new goal, she'd driven herself even harder and given up so much. Dates. Friends. Even a decent grade point average.

All she'd wanted was to dance and win a slew of ballroom competitions.

And her parents? Her father had worked overtime to pay for the extra lessons, and her mother had practically lived in her car, driving Shannon everywhere. At the time, she'd taken it for granted.

Most of the time, all she'd ever thought about was winning competitions, impressing a bunch of judges, and using those first-place trophies to propel her to bigger and better things.

She'd dreamed big, too. International competitions in Europe. Being paired with a famous partner. Broadway. Everything.

But then, in the preliminary round of one of her most important competitions, she'd been injured. Within seconds, all those years of dreams and goals had vanished. After a painful surgery, all that had been left was for her to go back home, head back to high school on crutches, and face the fact that everything she'd done had been for nothing.

"Hey, sorry I'm a little late," Dylan called out as he opened the door wide, trailing a burst of frigid air in his wake. "I had some trouble with a guy we brought in."

Realizing she'd almost been asleep, Shannon popped to her feet and then blurted out, "I'm not sure that being twenty minutes late for an hour-long class is just 'a little late.'"

He'd just shrugged off his coat but paused before hanging it up. "Yeah, you're right," he said with a grimace. "I'm real late. Better?"

She took a moment to appreciate the fact that the dark khakis he was wearing fit like they were tailored for him, and his dark green sweater showed that he obviously worked out. Like, a lot.

Realizing that once again she was thinking inappropriate

things about one of her students, she got to her feet. "You know, I should make you reschedule the lesson but charge you for the missed class. Just like I do for everyone else."

A good bit of the humor that had been in his expression when he entered vanished. "By all means, why don't you do that?" he said, giving her feet a pointed look. "Since, you know, your napping time is so valuable and all."

Her toes curled. Yep, she was standing practically barefoot while berating him about how busy she was.

Maybe she was overreacting . . . just a little.

Avoiding his gaze, she sat down quickly on her pretty couch, unbuckled one of her shoes, and did her best to ignore the twinge of pain that reverberated from a fresh blister on her toe.

"Hey, you're bleeding."

"Huh?" Looking at the oozing blister on the side of her big toe, she frowned. She fished out an old tissue from the pocket of her dress and tore it in half. "It's no big deal."

"You sure about that? Don't you want a Band-Aid or something?"

She had on nylons. Bandaging a toe meant taking them off, putting on the bandage, and then putting them back on. Which, of course, sounded like torture. "It's no big deal."

But he was already sitting next to her and staring at her feet. Her very ugly, very beat-up feet. After wrapping the piece of tissue around her toe, she pushed her foot into the shoe.

After slipping on the other shoe and buckling the strap, she got back on her feet, steadfastly ignoring the sting of discomfort. "Dylan, I'm sorry for the way I spoke to you when you came in. You didn't deserve it."

He looked surprised, then those eyes of his lit up. "I've been trying to figure out what was different about you tonight. Now I know." His lips curved into a matching smile. "You've got your accent on tonight."

She pressed a palm over her lips. "Sorry." Her accent was always worse when she was emotional or tired. On evenings like this, she practically sounded like she'd just sprung from the backwoods.

"Why are you sorry? I like it. It's cool."

"I sound like a hick."

"I didn't say that. All you sound is different, yeah?"

Now she felt even worse. He was being so nice and all she'd done so far was act high and mighty. Or maybe even worse than that. Clearing her throat, she said, "Are you ready to waltz?"

"You still up for it?"

"Absolutely." She led the way into the classroom and turned on her Ballroom Beats program on her iPad. Skimming through the choices, she selected "Moon River." The song was her favorite for beginning waltzing students, thanks to the slower pace and steady beat. She enjoyed thinking about Audrey Hepburn, too.

Turning to him, she smiled. "Shall we dance?"

He nodded and placed one hand on her waist and took her right hand with his left. "Let's do this," he said, looking like he was about to go into battle. She bit her lip to stop herself from grinning but he caught it anyway. "What's so funny? Did I mess up already?"

"Not at all. You just look so serious."

"I've got to be. All this counting means I've got to concentrate or I'm going to step on your toes."

"You let me worry about my toes."

"You're already in pain. I don't want to make things worse."

Glancing into his eyes, she realized that he was being completely serious. He really was worried about hurting her. "My toes are used to abuse. Now, stop worrying about me and just relax. Once you let your body take control, everything comes easier." She started guiding him through the basic steps, counting under her breath as he followed her directions.

When the song ended, she stepped backward. "Let me put on another song and we'll try a turn."

"I'm game."

Deciding he didn't need another classical arrangement, she put on "Come Away with Me" by Norah Jones. As she'd hoped, Dylan first looked taken aback, then slowly smiled.

"I like this better."

"I thought you might." When he took her in his arms again, she reminded him to lock his elbows. "No noodle arms, Dylan."

"Yes, ma'am."

She chuckled and adjusted the position of his hand on her waist.

And so it continued. They moved, she reminded him to count, and they twirled. She changed songs, and she coaxed him to stand a little closer and to hear the music's beat.

He hesitated, then curved his hand around her waist a little more firmly. Right away, she was aware of his height. Of the way his hand warmed her skin through the thin fabric of her dress.

Looking into his eyes, she smiled. "You're doing great. We're dancing, Dylan."

"Yeah?" He actually looked pleased.

"Yep."

"I'm still afraid of stepping on your toes."

"If you did, it wouldn't be the first time." She smiled. "And look up at me. Your feet are doing just fine."

After another ten minutes, she said, "This will be our last pass across the floor. I've already kept you fifteen minutes late."

He looked so surprised, he stumbled. "No way."

"I'm serious. Now focus."

He laughed, then spun her in a circle. Surprised, she started laughing too. "What was that for?"

"I don't know. Maybe because this has been a lot more fun

than I thought it was going to be. I needed this tonight, and I would've never guessed it."

He was right. She'd been so tired and tense, but now she felt exhilarated, almost like she used to back when she was a teenager. "I was just thinking the same thing."

"Yeah?"

"It was a long day. But this? Well, you ended it on a good note. Thanks."

Dylan's eyes lit up just as the front door jangled.

Surprised at the late visitor, Shannon turned her head to see who it was.

Then she kind of wished she hadn't, because Traci walked right in, her blue uniform bringing a dose of reality to the room.

"Shannon, what's going on? Wait, Dylan, is that really you?"

Dylan glanced over her shoulder, blinked, then slowly grinned. "Hey, Lucky."

His voice had lowered an octave.

Shannon turned to face her sister, who was still dressed for work, in her dark jeans, boots, button down, jacket, and her badge still in its chain around her neck. She also had her shoulder-length straight hair in a neat ponytail.

And . . . she was staring at Dylan like he was a perpetrator.

"What's going on?" Traci asked.

"We're finishing up a lesson," Shannon said.

"You're taking dance lessons from my sister?" Looking at how close they were standing to each other, Traci's eyes narrowed. "*Private* dancing lessons?"

Dylan took a step away from Shannon, like she'd contracted rabies.

Leaving Shannon more confused than even before.

CHAPTER 5

"Opportunity dances with those already on the dance floor."
—H. JACKSON BROWN JR.

Traci was staring at the two of them like they were fooling around behind her back. Shannon didn't know whether to tease her about that outraged expression or apologize—since she kind of *had* been feeling something toward Dylan that had nothing to do with dance steps.

But just as she was about to say something . . . Dylan held up his hands like he an innocent man who'd been caught in the wrong place at the wrong time. "I didn't know Shannon was your sister, Traci."

Why was he apologizing? And what did it matter if she was Traci's sister or not? Feeling thoroughly confused, she said, "So, I'm guessing y'all know each other."

"We were just assigned to be partners," Traci explained, her expression hard.

"This doesn't mean anything. I only have three more lessons left."

It doesn't mean anything. He only had to be here three more times.

Well, that put her in her place, though she wasn't exactly sure what place that was. Feeling kind of like she just got dumped in the middle of a dance, she said, "I'm sorry, but I don't understand how these dance lessons interfere with y'all working together."

"It doesn't and it won't," Dylan said.

Shannon studied her sister. "Traci?"

After a pause, Traci blinked . . . and then turned shame-faced. "Sorry. I'm not used to having my personal and professional lives intersect like this. It caught me off guard, walking in to see Dylan with his arms around you and "Come Away with Me" playing."

Dylan winked at Shannon. "My arms were absolutely not around you, were they? They were holding you properly and with the right amount of tension, too."

The comment made her chuckle. "That's right. We've, uh, been working on noodle arms tonight."

Traci smiled as she tossed her backpack toward the corner of the room. "Dylan, you do look better. Boy, maybe I should have been dancing tonight. I could have used some stress relief."

Now that she wasn't feeling so defensive, Shannon noticed that her sister didn't just look surprised about her and her partner. She looked exhausted. "Traci, are you all right?"

"Yeah." She rolled her shoulders, obviously trying to lessen some tension. "Sorry. It's been a heck of a day, hasn't it, big guy?"

Dylan nodded. "You could say that."

"Did Dylan tell you how he took down that perp and almost got shot?" Traci asked.

Feeling more and more confused, Shannon shook her head. "No. We . . . we didn't talk about work."

Traci raised her eyebrows. "You didn't tell her about how you almost got shot, Dylan?"

"No. And I'm fine."

"Not really," she retorted. "Your arm was grazed."

"Grazed?" Shannon whispered.

Both of them ignored her.

"It wasn't grazed." His voice was hard. "It's just a little banged up. No big deal."

While Shannon was gaping at the two of them and trying to process *shot*, *grazed*, and *a little banged up*, Traci fired off another comment.

"I heard the lieutenant tell you to go get checked out. Did you?"

"There wasn't any reason to do that. There was no way I was heading to the hospital. I'm fine."

Shannon finally interrupted. "I'm sorry, but you were hurt today? Your arm got hurt and I was giving you grief about noodle arms? Why didn't you say anything?" Yes, her voice had risen, and yes, her accent was back in full force.

Looking increasingly uncomfortable, Dylan shrugged off her questions as he walked to her side. "Don't worry about it. I'm fine."

He'd spoken soft. Sweet. Shannon looked into his eyes. "I can't believe you let me give you a hard time about being late."

"You didn't know."

If they'd been alone, she knew she would have reached out to him. Maybe pressed a palm to his chest. Maybe ran her fingers across his cheek. Anything to let him know that she cared.

Which had kind of just come from nowhere.

Traci cleared her throat, bringing them back to the present. "It was his right arm."

"You're right?" She moaned. "And here I've been telling you to hold it out steadier."

Dylan lowered his head so his mouth was just inches from her ear. "I promise that I'm fine. Don't worry."

"As long as that graze doesn't get infected," Traci said. "Since, you know, you refused to get checked out."

Dylan looked back at his partner. "Stop. You're scaring Shannon."

Traci looked from him to her. After a couple of seconds, she held up a sack of fast food that Shannon hadn't even noticed in her hand. "All right then. Changing subjects, I brought home burgers, Shannon."

"That's so nice of you. Thanks, I'll be right up."

"'Kay." After taking a few steps, she looked over her shoulder. "See you tomorrow, Dylan."

"Yeah. See you at eight, Lucky."

When Traci was out of sight, Dylan pulled out his wallet. "Traci was right, this is something, huh? Talk about a small world."

"I guess so."

"I can't believe you two are sisters," he continued as he handed her two twenties. "You don't look anything alike."

"We both have brown hair and brown eyes." Traci was also persistent and loyal—two qualities she knew she had in spades.

"That might be it, though. You're such a little thing."

"I'm five foot three."

He grinned. "Little."

"For the record, I can't believe you're my sister's partner on the force either. I was just as caught off guard as the two of you."

"Crazy, huh?" Stuffing his wallet back into his back pocket, he said, "Seriously, Traci is a good cop. She's got quite the reputation back in Cleveland. Bridgeport is lucky to have her."

"Wow. I guess I better ask her for some stories."

"If she gives you more than a couple of shrugs and 'I was part of a good squad,' I'll be surprised. She's pretty closed off." He winked. "My mother would call her a little prickly."

"My momma would have called that gumption." Thinking back to the way she'd greeted him when he'd first arrived, Shannon frowned. "Prickliness might be a genetic thing, I'm afraid. I'm sorry about giving you so much grief when you got here."

Dylan's eyes warmed. "You had reason. Being late is rude. I could have called or texted."

Yeah, when he wasn't getting shot at or avoiding the hospital. "Maybe, but I still feel bad. I could've been nicer."

"Hell, I could've been a little less honest during our first lesson. I didn't need to put that bet out there like an unwanted gift." Gazing down at her, the corners of his lips turned up. "So, any suggestions for getting into Traci's good graces?"

"I don't really know her all that well. But so far, food always helps." She smiled, hoping her little joke would encourage him to ignore her statement. But it didn't.

"Do I want to know how it is you don't know her well?"

"It's not a secret, but it's going to take a while to explain. Traci might want to do that."

"That sounds cryptic."

She smiled. "And you sound like a policeman: so suspicious." When he studied her carefully, she said, "So, class number three next Friday night?"

After a pause, he nodded. "Yeah. I'll be here."

"Have a good week, Dylan," she said as she opened the door for him.

Just as he was about to step out, he turned to her. "You know what? This dancing thing has been a lot more fun than I thought it would be."

She laughed. "Those are words to warm a girl's heart. I'll see you in a week, officer."

After he gave her another searching look, he walked through the door.

She locked it behind him but couldn't help but watch him leave. He'd been right. Their session had been a lot more fun than she'd expected, too. And the feel of being in his arms? Well, there'd been something there between them.

It seemed that old adage was true. Nothing really was what it seemed to be. Not the situation and not people.

CHAPTER 6

"Those who can't dance say the music is no good."
—JAMAICAN PROVERB

Saturday

She wasn't sure if she was going to be able to finally do it.

Gazing at the front door of Backdoor Books through her windshield, Jennifer Lange sighed. Backdoor Books was simply the cutest place. Well, she thought it was—she'd only seen pictures of it online.

The quaint bookstore was housed in a remodeled three story building right off Broadway in Montgomery, the next town over. There was a fireplace on the first floor where visiting authors did talks and signings. The children's area in the basement looked like a scene from "Hansel and Gretel." Wooden cutouts of trees and bushes and houses were everywhere. They looked perfect for six-year-olds to hide behind. There were also three little playhouses that the managers had outfitted with books, stools, and lots of windows for kids to peek out of.

The second floor was divided into fiction and nonfiction sections. Each genre section was large and filled to the brim with hardcovers and new paperbacks.

But the third floor was what interested Jennifer the most. It housed the self-improvement, crafts, travel, and cookbooks. Lots and lots of wonderful small-town cookbooks. Her hands practically itched to get hold of them.

The only problem with any of this was the fact that she was afraid to get out of her car. Almost petrified, thanks to the fact that she'd been attacked two years ago on her way from class, back to her car.

It had been bad. They'd robbed her, broke her arm when she'd struggled. And when they'd forced her down on the pavement, her face had been smashed into a shard of glass—a thick, jagged piece that left a deep scar, even though the doctors at the hospital had repaired it as best they could.

Chill bumps grazed her arms as she recalled everything else. Everything she hadn't been completely coherent for. Everything that the doctors at the hospital had said had happened.

Since then, a lot of things had changed. She'd become almost afraid of her shadow. Her brother Dylan, whom she'd always been close to, had become more stressed than usual. Their parents had tried to get her to move with them to Hilton Head. Some of her friends had drifted away when their sympathy ebbed and their confusion about her fears of men—and to a smaller extent, the whole world—increased.

She'd ended up moving from downtown Cincinnati to Bridgeport, where Dylan had gotten a job in the police department. And because he was so busy, her fear had reached a dangerous point.

That was when she'd finally started counseling. She'd been going for fourteen months now and had made a lot of progress. Now she could actually admit that she'd been attacked by three men, raped by one of them, and was never going to be the same for the rest of her life.

Melissa, her counselor, had smiled the first time Jennifer had said those statements out loud. But no matter how much better it was for her to face the truth, Jennifer had only felt sick.

Now Melissa had given her homework to work on in between appointments—assignments to go out into the world. She could now visit a few restaurants and public places if Dylan took her.

But *this* was a big deal. She was finally going to go someplace by herself. And not just "go" there, either. She was going to get out of the car, walk into a store, and even speak to a stranger.

That was why she was sitting in the parking lot. Yesterday, at the end of her session, she'd promised Melissa that she'd go to Backdoor Books. Not only that, she was supposed to go to the cookbook section, pick out a book, and purchase it.

Two years and two months ago she wouldn't have even been able to imagine doing any of that.

Could she do it now?

She was petrified. But did she really want to tell Melissa on Tuesday that she'd chickened out? Imagining the conversation, she knew that her counselor would nod, look her in the eye, and say she understood . . . but that she was disappointed.

Jennifer didn't want that.

More than anything she wanted to be able to tell Dylan that she had left the house and was trying to get better. Remembering her breathing exercises, she opened her car door. It was maybe thirty-one degrees out. Gray sky, old snow on the ground. Damp and bitter cold. The air clung to her skin, seeping in—making the warm lights shining through the bookstore's windows look even more inviting.

She looked around. There were only around eight other cars in the parking lot. It was also the middle of the day. She wasn't in danger.

But still, she hesitated.

The front door of the shop opened. A man who had to be in his seventies walked out. In one hand he held a paper coffee cup. In his other a packed shopping bag. He looked both ways, then crossed the parking lot. She watched him walk to one of the handicapped spaces near the front, get in his car, and drive away.

It was time.

Picking up her purse, she stood and closed the car door, but kept one hand on the roof of her car. She wondered if her therapist would think she'd done enough.

She wouldn't. She'd only look at Jennifer, lean back in her swivel chair, and ask if standing against her car in the cold was the same as walking into the bookstore and looking at cookbooks.

No. No, it was not.

She started walking. Barely remembered to stop and wait for the SUV that was zipping too fast through the parking lot. Then got to the door.

"Hey, hold that open for me, would you?" a man called out.

She froze. Looked behind her.

It was a guy about her age holding a squirming black-and-tan puppy and a large cup of coffee. He had sunglasses on even though it wasn't sunny.

"Do you mind?" His voice was more impatient.

"What?" Realizing he was about to be by her side, she yanked open the door.

"Thanks," he smiled at her just as the puppy squirmed again and yipped.

And . . . his coffee cup flew out of his hand and sailed toward the ground at her feet. They both stared in dismay as the lid popped off, as if in slow motion, and the hot liquid splattered out onto her legs.

"Oh!" She jumped back.

"Crap. I'm so sorry." He went down on a knee. The puppy scampered free as he reached out a hand.

Afraid he was going to touch her, Jennifer stepped back.

"Sorry!" Looking embarrassed, he picked up the fallen cardboard cup just as the puppy trotted closer and gave the spilled coffee a tentative lick.

"Jack?"

He looked up. "Hey, mom."

Obviously excited to see a friendly face, the puppy ran toward the woman.

She bent down and picked it up. "What is Harvard doing here?"

"You know I couldn't leave him home," the guy said as he got to his feet. "Not yet, but that's not the issue." He turned to Jennifer. "Miss, are you hurt? Did you get burned?"

Her leg was wet but nothing hurt. "I'm fine."

Still holding the puppy, the guy's mother turned to face her. "What happened to you?"

"My coffee just spilled all over her, Mom. Miss, are you sure you're not hurting?"

"I'm fine," Jennifer said again.

"Oh dear. Come on in, honey." As Jennifer stepped in, the lady put the puppy back down. It yipped, smelled a stack of books, then circled back to her. When she looked down, it wagged its tail.

It really was too cute. The dog didn't look like it was any sort of particular breed, more like a mishmash of a half-dozen. But seeing its sweet brown eyes and gentle personality, Jennifer decided it was a combination of all the best parts.

Ignoring the coffee spill on her leg that was now just more of a bother than anything, Jennifer knelt down to give Harvard a pat.

The dog wagged its tail some more.

"He's really soft," she said, looking up.

"He's a mess, but he's a keeper, for sure," the guy said as he knelt down next to her.

Then, suddenly, her body responded. He was too big, too close, and his proximity to her on the ground triggered far too many reactions.

Mainly, panic.

Feeling off-kilter, she pulled away from him.

"Hey, are you okay?"

She couldn't talk. Could barely get to her feet.

The woman hurried to her side. "Honey? What happened? Did you get burned after all?"

She shook her head. Suddenly, it felt like her cheeks were frozen. No, it felt like all of her was frozen in place. Hating herself for not being able to do more, she whispered, "Sorry," before turning back to the door.

Feeling like the whole world was buzzing, she pushed on it hard.

Rushed outside and tried to remember all of the coping exercises Melissa had taught her for panic attacks.

Just as the door was swinging shut behind her, the guy stopped it. "Mom, watch Harvard!" he called out.

The door closed with a snap behind them.

The air was still cold. But now, instead of yearning to button up her coat more, she was tempted to pull it off. To let the air revitalize her. To do *something*.

"Hey."

Now that she'd finally gotten her bearings, Jennifer turned around. He was standing about three feet away. His hands were raised like he was afraid of making any wrong move. Boy, she was such a mess.

"What did I do?" he asked.

What could she say but the truth? "Nothing."

His eyes skimmed her cheek. She knew he noticed her scar. Was probably now wondering what it was from. But he didn't say anything more.

Which made her feel like she could finally speak again. "My problem isn't with you. It's . . . it's me. I . . . Well, I sometimes get panic attacks." Okay. She sounded pitiful, but at least she was talking.

"I spilled hot coffee on your leg. That had to hurt. Will you come in? At the very least, you can go to the restroom and wash it off."

She couldn't go back in that store. "Thank you, but I'm fine."

"I feel terrible. Are you sure you aren't burned?"

"Don't. Like I said, a lot of what's going on is me, not you." Which sounded like a bad line from some Lifetime movie.

"I feel like I've ruined your day." Frustration was thick in every word. "If you want, I'll stay away from you in the store."

She wanted to be normal so badly. She wanted to be normal and easy going and the way she used to be. "I'm just going to go." She turned toward her car and started walking.

"Can I at least know your name?"

She turned around. "Why?"

"Because, at the very least, I'd like to know the name of the pretty girl whose day I ruined."

Before she realized she was doing it, she smiled. "You didn't ruin my day."

"I'm Jack. You already met my dog. He's Harvard. And my mom, her name is Camille." He gazed at her longer. Patiently waiting.

"I'm Jennifer."

He smiled. "I promise that I'm not here all the time. Come back another day, okay?"

"Okay." After noticing again that his eyes seemed kind, she turned back and started walking again. Behind her, she could hear the door open and whoosh shut.

By the time she got into her car, locked the doors, and put on her seatbelt, she almost felt okay.

* * *

"God, I'm not sure what just happened there, but I'm just going to go with it."

Of course she didn't hear a reply as she pulled out of the parking lot. But she did feel a strange, almost-forgotten feeling of satisfaction.

She might not have accomplished her task, but at least she'd done something. And even though it felt like everything that could have gone wrong actually had, she had survived.

She was a survivor.

CHAPTER 7

"Every time I dance, I'm trying to prove myself to myself."
—MISTY COPELAND

Saturday Night

"How did it go?" Jennifer asked Dylan when he walked into their house a little after nine that evening.

Dylan thought about the last twelve hours as he unbuckled his shoulder holster. "Pretty good. All in all, I think my first full shift with Traci went okay. At least, I think so.

Jennifer lifted an eyebrow. "You think so?"

"Bridgeport might take a little bit of getting used to for Traci." He'd been hoping for a quiet night so the two of them would have time to drive around the small town and do a little surveillance, but mainly have time to simply get to know each other. That didn't happen. "Right off the bat, we got called to a house smack in the middle of Symphony subdivision."

Jennifer raised her eyebrows. "Fancy."

She didn't lie. Symphony was a relatively new neighborhood with large million-dollar houses on one-acre lots. Usually, the most anyone on the force ever saw of the area was when one of them was asked to do private security for a party when they were off duty.

This time, though, the party they'd visited had been anything but fancy. A concerned neighbor had called about a bunch of teenagers having a party. When he and Traci had knocked on the door, they'd discovered that those kids had been doing their best to put a dent in the home's liquor supply. They'd all been underage.

But the worst part had been that the parents were home. They'd decided to let their daughter host a party, turning a blind eye to what was going on in their basement and on their front lawn. He and Traci had ended up having to call all the kids' parents, who'd either yelled at the parent hosts, their kids, or him and his new partner. It had been a long afternoon.

"The house was fancy enough. The parents who'd been letting a bunch of underage kids drink? I'm hoping they'll be thinking something different now."

"Are the kids okay?"

He finished locking up his gun then joined her at the island. Taking a seat, he accepted the IPA she handed him with a grateful smile. He didn't like to get drunk, but every once in a while, a good beer sure hit the spot.

"I think the kids will be all right. I mean, as well as they can be after they sober up."

"How did Traci do?"

That was where he was a little confused. "She was good, I think. She knows what she's doing, and I have to say that she was great with the kids . . ."

"But . . ."

"But, I think she's got a chip on her shoulder about Symphony."

"What, it was too nice?"

"I think everyone had too much money. She wasn't a fan."

"Well, those houses are enormous. I know a lot of people are surprised to see families with so much money in Bridgeport."

He shrugged. "Maybe." After taking another sip, he looked at his sister. Then he remembered her big day. She'd been planning to go buy a cookbook at a store. That was huge. And he'd forgotten all about it until just that minute! "Jennifer, I can't believe I didn't call you. How did your outing go?"

"Well . . . it could have gone better."

Again, he wished he would have remembered to at least text her. "What happened? Wait, did you choose not to get out of the house?" *Choose* had been a deliberate choice. Her counselor had cautioned him to do his best to not sound judgmental or overbearing.

It had definitely been a learning curve. It was in his nature to take charge. He'd absolutely had to learn how to choose his words carefully and remember to let her be the one guiding her progress.

"No, I left the house. And I did drive over to Backdoor Books. That went fine. And I even got out of the car. So that was a win, too."

"Good girl." He looked at her carefully. "And . . ."

She sighed. "And then, right when I was entering the store, I kind of ran into a guy."

"What do you mean? Jen, what did he do?" He inwardly winced. Looked like his attempt to choose his words carefully had already gone out the window.

"He was holding a cup of hot coffee and a puppy . . . and the puppy squirmed and the coffee spilled." She held out her leg.

He just then noticed that she was wearing shorts with a thick sweatshirt and socks. And that she had a three- or four-inch burn on her leg. It was bright red and had blistered.

She was hurt. Again.

Every bit of helplessness and fury that he'd felt when she'd been attacked two years ago came back tenfold. "Who the hell was this guy? Do you have a name?"

"It was no one to worry about, Dylan. He was just a guy trying to manage a puppy, a door, and a hot cup of coffee."

She was right. He needed to calm down and not make things worse. "Okay. So, what happened when he knocked into you?"

"He felt bad and called for his mom."

"His mom? How old was this guy?" Again, his mind went jumping from one conclusion to the next. Wait, it was a kid?"

She laughed. "No, the guy was about our age, but it turned out that his mother owned the shop. The dog plopped down on the floor and he wanted his mom to help me get cleaned up."

"Oh. So, did you let her?"

Twin spots of pink appeared on her cheeks. "Not exactly. When I knelt down to pet the puppy, he got on his knees, too. Jack was trying to make sure the puppy didn't jump on my calf, but being on the floor with him . . ." She looked stricken.

"You had a flashback," he finished for her. He'd gone through quite a few of those with her during the first four or five months after her attack. Little noises or movements would set her off.

She nodded. "Yeah. He was too close. I thought he was going to touch me. Or, at least it seemed like he was. I freaked out and ran out the door."

"Oh, Jen."

"I know. I had all these grand plans, but all that happened was I got burned by hot coffee and made a fool of myself in public."

"I'm really sorry." Her big day had been a fiasco. "How about I take you on my next day off?"

"No."

"Jennifer, I won't crowd you or anything. If you want, we can even go in separately. I'll just be there in case something happens."

"Like I freak out when I'm on the floor petting a puppy?" She rolled her eyes. "Yeah, I don't think so."

So, it was done. She was going to give up. Even though the counselor's voice was ringing in his ear and offering all kinds of advice, he couldn't hold back his thoughts. "I think you have to try again."

"I'm going to. One day soon."

He nodded, still trying real hard to say the right thing. "I know it's going to be hard, but it's like riding a bike, you know? You've got to get back on."

Jennifer waved a hand in front of his face. "Dylan, did you hear me? I've already decided to go back."

"Really?"

She nodded. "I promised Jack I would."

"Jack, as in that guy?"

"Yes." She smiled.

Well, this was new. Treading carefully again, he murmured, "He made an impression on you, didn't he?"

"I don't know. Maybe." She hopped on one of the barstools. "Or . . . maybe it's that his mother was nice. For some reason, after I, you know, got burned and freaked out . . . I wasn't as scared."

"That's awesome."

"Well, I don't know about that. But I do know that I can't give up. For a few minutes, I was almost happy, Dylan. That counts for a lot."

His insides felt crushed. His little sister had a big day today. For a few minutes she'd been almost happy. It broke his heart. But, looking at her face, he noticed that there was something new lurking in her eyes. She was determined to do better. Determined to get better. "I'm proud of you."

"You know, the sad thing is that I think you actually are."

"Of course I am. I love you."

"Do you ever resent me living here?"

"No." When she looked skeptical, he repeated himself. "I don't resent you being here. Not ever."

"Come on. Are you certain? I know we both thought I'd be back to normal by now."

"I promise you, everybody has something. I don't know what 'normal' is anymore."

"I'm pretty sure it starts with someone not being afraid to leave the house."

No, he was pretty sure that normal meant that a person wasn't assaulted on their way to their car. "Don't act like you're a burden. You do all the grocery shopping, cooking, and cleaning. Half the time I feel like I'm the one taking advantage of you."

"I don't feel that way."

"If you don't, then you've got to know that I don't feel that way either. All I want for you is to be happy."

"I want the same thing for you, too, Dylan."

"Then we don't have a thing to worry about, right?"

"Right." She hopped off the barstool. "I made a chicken enchilada casserole today. Are you hungry?"

"I wasn't until you mentioned that. How did it turn out?"

She gave him a look. "Good."

"Of course it did. I don't know how you do it, Jennifer. It's like you can make any dish amazing."

She laughed. "Go get cleaned up, and I'll heat some up for you."

He was ready for a shower. "Hey, want to watch something while I eat?"

"Sure. I'll even let you pick."

"No reality dance shows? Thank you, Lord. Meet you in the living room in ten."

As he went down the hall to the small bedroom, he thought again about being almost happy. Right then and there he vowed to do his best to edge his sister toward that point.

She needed it, and he needed it for her.

CHAPTER 8

"Take more chances. Dance more dances."

Wednesday Night

"Good class, ladies!" Shannon called out to her country line dancing class. "I fully expect to hear that all of you have gone out line dancing before I see you next."

Emily, her cute twenty-two-year-old student, walked up to her. "Travis is going to take me tomorrow night."

"Good luck. Maybe you'll be teaching him a thing or two."

"Maybe! We'll see." Throwing on her fuzzy North Face jacket, she waved. "Have a good night."

"You too."

After saying goodbye to the rest of the ladies, Shannon picked up a stray water bottle that someone had left. Then, just as she was about to turn off the lights, she caught sight of herself in the mirror.

Then she stopped and really looked.

Memories came flooding back. Being a little girl and standing so carefully at the barre. Later, wearing out ballet shoes. Then toe shoes. Then deciding to switch to ballroom dancing in an effort to save her feet. Hours of learning how to do all kinds of dances that she'd thought were boring as a teenager but whose complexity she had learned to appreciate in her early twenties.

But it had all started with one class and looking into the mirror. Before she could stop herself, she took off her shoes and did a pirouette. Then another one. Then another. Muscles flared to life as they remembered what to do, almost of their own volition.

The movement felt good. She began doing part of an old recital piece she hadn't thought about in over a decade. Laughing when it became obvious that she wasn't nearly as strong or as flexible as she used to be. But she wasn't nearly as bad as she sometimes thought she was. She did another turn, then an extension, and finally did a little leap.

"Hey."

She skittered to a stop and looked at the doorway. "Hey Traci. Sorry, I didn't hear you come in."

"I was upstairs. What were you doing?"

Remembering. "Oh, nothing."

"It looked like something." She tilted her head to one side. "You looked like a ballerina in a blue dress."

Shannon grinned. "That sounds like it should be either a song or a painting."

"Or my sister." Traci smiled, walking closer. "You know, I've watched you teach your students from time to time, but I've never seen you dance like that. You were a ballerina?"

That made her smile. "Well, I used to take ballet."

"For a long time?"

"Yeah. For years and years." She didn't like bringing it up, because she knew all those dance lessons had been expensive and time consuming. Traci hadn't had access to the money for such things or even anyone to really care enough about her to give up their time to take her.

But seeing Traci's look of interest, she knew she simply couldn't shrug it off. Haltingly, she said, "I started taking ballet and tumbling classes when I was four."

"You were only four years old?"

Smiling at how incredulous she sounded, Shannon explained. "My mom said that I was always flitting around the rooms, climbing on things, singing. She said she had to put me in something or I would drive her to drink. I loved it."

"Can you do handsprings and stuff?"

"Not really. I quickly realized that I didn't like gymnastics but I loved to dance. By the time I was eight, I was taking ballet, tap, and jazz classes."

"Three of them?"

"They started out just an hour class three times a week, then I dropped jazz and just did ballet and tap. And then I moved to a better dance academy and started competing."

"Whoa. You were serious."

Shannon nodded. She paused, not knowing whether to continue or not, but Traci motioned with her hand. "Around the time I was seventeen, a senior in high school, I started having some problems with my feet and some of my thigh muscles. Because the thought of not dancing made me so upset, I gave ballroom dancing a try when the physical therapist suggested it."

"And you became just as focused on that."

"Yeah. I don't seem to be able to do anything halfway."

"Thank goodness for that, huh?"

Shannon smiled then looked at Traci a little more closely.

There was something more there than just a cute comment. "What do you mean?"

"What if you hadn't tried so hard to discover your past after that DNA test? What if you hadn't reached out to Kimber and me again and again?"

"We wouldn't all be living together. Or maybe we would. I don't think I'm the only sister who is determined."

"I'd like to think I would have done as much for you two, but I don't know."

Well, there was honesty. "Traci, I do. I think you're doing yourself a disservice. You are as determined as I am."

She looked embarrassed. "Anyway, I'm really glad that you were in here dancing. You've been doing so much for all of us and this business, I haven't seen you do much for yourself."

Was this what she did for herself? The thought caught her off guard. Did she still love dance and not just teaching other people to enjoy it? She made a mental note to consider that some more later.

"Are you ready to go upstairs?"

"Actually, I came down to see if you wanted to go grab something to eat at Paxton's. There's nothing upstairs."

"Sure. What about Kimber?"

"She's in sweats and eating a pint of some kind of diet ice cream."

"Is she okay?" Shannon asked as she started turning off lights.

"I think so. I asked if she wanted to go out, but she said that she was all into some Netflix show."

"Gotcha." She considered going upstairs to put on a pair of jeans, but it sounded like too much trouble. Instead, she slipped on her long eggplant-purple wool coat and picked up her purse. "Let's go grab a burger."

* * *

When they got to Paxton's, it was just as crowded as ever. Luckily, though, they found two seats at the bar. Shannon noticed that Traci was receiving more than one double-take. She wondered if it was because of her looks or the fact that she was the new cop in town.

After they ordered a pair of drinks and two burgers with fries, she brought up the new job. "So, how are you liking small-town police work?"

Traci chuckled. "It's good. I'm still trying to figure out who are the movers and shakers in the department."

"It's not the sergeant and lieutenant?" She didn't know much about police stations, but they seemed like the logical people.

Traci thanked the bartender when she delivered their drinks then answered. "Oh, they count, but it's just like any other office. There are the gossips, the negative influences, the people who make everything easier. It's better to just keep your head down, you know?"

Shannon took a sip of her chardonnay. "How are things going with Dylan?"

Traci smiled. "I wondered when you were going to ask me about him."

"What? It's a legitimate question." She was also probably doing a poor job of acting like she wasn't thinking of Dylan at least two times a day.

She took a sip of her draft. "Sure it is."

But Shannon noticed that Traci still didn't answer her question. "If you don't want me asking about work, just let me know."

"I don't mind talking about work. But I'm not sure if you are really all that interested in learning about the traffic stops I did yesterday."

"All I wanted to know is if y'all were getting along."

"Sorry. I know I've been teasing you. We are. He's a good guy, decent. He's fair, too. Some guys are still living in the eighties and pretending that I'm only there to fill a quota. Dylan, though, he acts like he's glad I have his back."

"Speaking of your record, he said that you were kind of a big deal back in Cleveland."

"I wasn't." She looked away. "I just did my job."

"He said you received some commendations. Were you upset to leave?"

"I didn't lie, Shannon. I really am happy to get out of there." Shadows filled her eyes. "My job in the city . . . well, it was hard. I dealt with a lot of folks who didn't have much to lose. Some days I wondered if they were going to get so desperate that I would become just another one of their losses."

That sounded terrifying. "What happened? What did you have to do?"

Traci shook her head. "Nope. We're not going there. Not tonight."

"I'm tough. You can tell me anything."

"I'll remember you said that." Just as she was taking another sip of her beer, she sighed. "And, speak of the devil, here he is." She raised a hand. "Hey, partner."

Shannon turned to see Dylan approaching. He was wearing what she was beginning to think of as his usual uniform. Snug, faded jeans, a long-sleeved T-shirt that was also well fitted, and boots. His hair looked like he'd run his hands through it a dozen times in the last hour.

He also looked as confident as ever.

Shannon's smile faltered when she realized he wasn't alone. A very pretty blonde was walking by his side.

"Hey, Trace. And Shannon, too." He smiled warmly. "Hey, I've got someone for you to meet. We just got a table. Do you want to join us?"

"Sure," Traci said.

As they stood up to move to the empty table Dylan had pointed out, Shannon felt her stomach turn to knots.

Maybe this was a mistake. Dylan's date didn't look very happy to see them. Not at all.

CHAPTER 9

"This is my dance space. This is your dance space.
I do not go into yours. You do not go into mine."
—DIRTY DANCING

Tuesday Evening

"You don't mind that I asked them to join us, do you?" Dylan asked Jennifer as they watched Traci and Shannon pay the bartender and then head their way.

The look she gave him could've frozen boiling water. "It's a little late to be asking, don't you think?"

"So, you do mind." And yes, he knew that was a stupid statement.

"I don't know what you want me to say, Dylan," she muttered under her breath. "You know that even being here in the middle of a crowded restaurant is difficult for me."

He knew. And he also knew that he'd never intended to ask Traci and Shannon to join them. But the moment he saw Shannon the invitation just came out of his mouth. "I'm sorry." He wasn't lying. He really was sorry.

But was he going to change his mind and take back the invitation? Not a chance.

Ignoring Jennifer's obvious exasperation with him, he stood up as the women got to their table. "Traci, Shannon, this is my sister Jennifer."

Shannon blinked then smiled brightly. "I didn't know you had a sister." Turning to Jennifer, she held out her hand. "I'm Shannon. Shannon Murphy. Nice to meet you."

After a second's hesitation, Jennifer held out her hand. "Nice to meet you, too." Looking at Traci, she kind of waved. "Hi."

"Hey," his partner said as she took the chair across from him. "Traci Lucky."

"Thanks for asking us to join y'all," Shannon said as she sat down.

"No problem." Dylan held out her chair and helped get her settled, to both his sister's and his partner's obvious amusement.

Shannon seemed not to notice their smirks. Instead, she smiled up at him.

Still standing behind her, he fought an urge to curve his hands around her shoulders. Just as if they were a couple and he couldn't resist touching her.

"Do y'all eat here very much?" Shannon asked after he sat down. "All I've ever gotten here is a burger."

"Burgers are a good choice. What else do you like, Jen?"

She swallowed. "Everything is pretty good, though I don't eat here all that often."

"I'm getting chili and a chicken sandwich," he added.

"I'll have to try that soon," Traci said. She took another sip of her beer and grinned. "So, buddy, have you recovered yet from today's big adventure?"

"Yep." Boy, he'd hoped she wouldn't go there, but the moment he saw both Jennifer's and Shannon's looks of interest, he knew it was a hopeless wish.

"What happened?" Shannon asked.

He gave Traci a warning look. "Nothing."

"Oh, it was something, all right," Traci said. "My partner here got his butt kicked by a poodle."

Shannon giggled.

He was just about to give Traci a pretty fierce look when he realized that his sister had chuckled as well. Traci's teasing had helped Jennifer settle down. He couldn't remember the last time that had happened in public.

It was totally worth the loss of a little bit of pride.

"It wasn't that big of a deal. It was just a matter of miscommunication."

"Between?"

"Between me and the dog's owner."

"The octogenarian who couldn't hear all that well." Traci grinned. "Dylan and I had to keep raising our voices so much that Snookie got freaked out."

"Snookie?" Jennifer said.

Dylan rolled his eyes. "I didn't name the thing."

"He only ran from it," Traci added, her eyes bright.

Oh, brother. "We were yelling so loud, the dog thought we were screaming at the lady," Dylan explained.

"She'd called for assistance. She thought someone was trying to break into her place, but the wind had just caused a broken shutter to clap against the house," Traci supplied. "After we ascertained that there was no danger, Dylan here went to talk to the lady. But that little dog went into attack mode. It was quite the sight."

Jennifer's lips twitched. "I wish I could have seen it."

"I'm glad you didn't," Dylan said. "Snookie was dangerous."

"All fifteen pounds of her," Traci said.

"Come on, Lucky. You know it was bad. I had no idea poodles

could be so vicious. That dog almost bit off a piece of my um, rear end."

Shannon's eyes were dancing. "How did you stop it?"

"I had a piece of beef jerky in my pocket," he said. "Thank God."

Jennifer made a face. "Oh, Dylan. How old was that?"

"Not too old," he said. "But don't give me grief about it. If I didn't have that, it could've been a real mess. I could've gotten injured."

Traci snorted. "He isn't lying. That jerky saved his hide."

"Good pun!" Shannon high-fived her sister.

"Now I'll never be able to convince you to get a dog," Jennifer said.

"Jen, that's the last thing we need."

"That might be the last thing you need, but I would love one. One day you're going to get home and there will be a puppy greeting you at the door."

Shannon looked from him to his sister. "Y'all live together, just like Traci and I do?"

Smiling at Jennifer, Dylan nodded. "Yep. She's a good roommate. She cooks like Betty Crocker on steroids."

"No way. You can cook?" Traci asked.

Jennifer nodded. "I enjoy it."

"She's phenomenal. I'm not kidding," Dylan said, more than happy to talk up his sister's talent. "Jennifer can make anything."

"My brother's a little biased. I just have a way with casseroles."

"They're terrific. And she does all the cleaning up, too."

"It's the least I can do."

"Why?" Shannon asked.

When Jennifer hesitated, Shannon added, "I mean, since I live with my two sisters, I'm confused why she feels like she needs to do all of the cooking and cleaning."

Just as Dylan was about to share that it wasn't her business, Jennifer said, "I don't work, you see. And I'm agoraphobic. I only started going out to eat with Dylan a couple of months ago. Before then, I'd hardly leave the house."

After darting a quick look in his direction, Shannon smiled. "Oh. I see."

Jennifer looked down at her hands. "I know. It's odd."

"It's fine," he said. He hated when his sister put herself down. "Jennifer has her reasons."

"I'm sure," Shannon said quickly. "Please, you don't need to explain anything to us."

"No, I don't mind," Jennifer said. "I'm working with a therapist. I've gotten a lot better, but it's a work in progress. Things like this are good for me to try, but it's not easy. I know I can be a little awkward. I'm trying to get out of my shell."

"That's really hard," Traci said in a softer tone than Dylan had realized she was capable of. "I actually became a cop because I'd been working through some things myself."

Dylan noticed that Shannon looked stunned by that news. Again, he wished he knew more of the story about Shannon and her sisters. He was especially intrigued by the sense that she was eager to ask about it but didn't. He had a feeling the problem wasn't because he and Jennifer were sitting there.

"Here's your order," the server said to the ladies, putting two large cheeseburgers in front of them. Turning to him, she added, "Your meals should be out in about ten."

"No problem. Thanks."

"These look so good, Shan," Traci said. "I'm starving."

He and Jennifer exchanged smiles. He already knew that Traci didn't shy away from eating a decent meal but Shannon looked so elegant. For some reason, he had thought that she would have only eaten a salad.

Shannon looked at her plate. "Sorry that our meals came out so much earlier."

"Go ahead and eat."

Five minutes later, his chicken sandwich and Jennifer's soup and salad arrived. He'd just taken his first bite, when Traci grinned.

"Since we're all here together, I might as well ask how the dance lessons are going."

Jennifer popped her head up. She remained silent but her lips twitched as she glanced his way.

Shannon frowned at her sister. "We don't need to discuss this now."

"Why not?" Traci asked as she picked up a French fry. "You said you were really enjoying it." She raised her eyebrows in such a fake look of surprise, Dylan realized that it was a good thing she'd gotten into police work and not theater.

Shannon picked up her glass of wine. "That doesn't mean we need to put Dylan on the spot like this." Turning to him, she said, "You don't need to say a word."

"I can take Traci's ribbing, Shannon. Don't worry."

"See?" Traci asked.

Before Shannon could get more upset, Dylan started talking faster. "To answer your question, the classes are going real well. We worked on the rumba last class."

"The rumba, huh?" Traci leaned back in her chair. "That sounds, um . . . intimate."

"It wasn't *that* intimate," Dylan said.

Jennifer coughed.

"It's a natural progression after one learns to waltz, Traci," Shannon said.

"Good to know."

Remembering how he'd held her when she'd been counting in his ear, Dylan glanced her way. "Shannon's a great teacher. I've enjoyed the lessons. They're a lot different than I thought they would be."

"Huh," Traci said.

"Is it always like that?" Jennifer asked. "Do you always find the lessons go smoothly?"

"Oh, no." Shannon put a napkin to her mouth to stifle a laugh. "Though this my first studio of my own, I've taught a lot of lessons. Each partner and student has his or her own pros and cons."

"Sounds hard."

"No, they're a lot of fun. I love meeting new people and love making them feel more at ease on the dance floor. But that doesn't mean we always have as good a time as Dylan and I do."

Traci and Jennifer both looked his way, but he was prepared for the looks this time. Instead of reacting too strongly, he simply smiled.

The conversation moved on to other topics. But the damage had been done. He couldn't seem to do anything but think about Shannon and reflect how she was right. There was something significant between them.

After they all paid and were walking to the door, he was pleased to see that Traci and Jennifer were conversing and Shannon was walking by his side.

"This was fun," she said with a smile at him. "Thanks for inviting us to join you."

"Thanks for joining us and especially for being so kind to my sister."

"She's nice. I'm glad we met."

He turned to Jennifer. "You ready?"

"Yes." Eyes shining, she smiled at Traci and Shannon. "Nice to meet you."

"You too, Jen. See ya, buddy," Traci said.

"Be careful tomorrow," Shannon said.

"I will. Thanks." He guided Jennifer to their right where his Suburban was . . . and tried not to think about how if they'd been alone he probably would have kissed Shannon.

Right there on the sidewalk.

CHAPTER 10

"Life isn't about waiting for the storm to pass; it's about learning to dance in the rain."
—VIVIAN GREENE

Saturday

She was back. Sitting in her white Altima, Jennifer took her time checking messages on her phone, retouching her lipstick, and pulling on her favorite gloves spun with alpaca. All of that took ten minutes.

It was time.

Grabbing her purse, she opened the driver's-side door and winced as a burst of snow grazed her face. The snow was a surprise. The forecasters had mentioned snow arriving after six o'clock that evening. Not at two.

Well, she assumed the meteorologists were human, too.

If there was a plus to this, it was that the cold and snow helped her stop making excuses. She hurried into the bookstore, closing the door securely right behind her.

"You came back."

Turning, she saw Camille standing next to a cart near a cute sign that announced they were in the *Mysterious* section. "Yes, I guess I did."

"I'm so glad. Right after you left, I told Jack that you were a woman who I wanted to know."

Whoa. "Really?"

"Any woman who can put up with my son both throwing hot coffee on her leg and his dog being a general pest is a winner in my book."

Camille was putting a really kind spin on what had actually happened. She smiled at her. "I'll take that as a compliment."

"I hope you will. I'm a tough cookie. Not too easy to please, you know."

Somehow Jennifer couldn't see that. No, instead she looked like a sweetheart. "Is Harvard around?" And yes, she was kind of also asking about Jack, though she wasn't sure why.

Camille shook her head. "No, I'm sorry honey. Harvard is home with Jack. I bet you're sorry to miss him. That puppy is a cutie, isn't he?"

She nodded. She wondered if Camille was as complimentary about everything. She was kind of getting that impression.

"I came to look at the cookbooks."

"I know! I remember." Pointing to the stairs that were just to the right of them, Camille said, "You go right on up, honey. Have a good time."

"Thanks." She walked up the narrow stairs and then stopped with a gasp. She had to have stumbled upon cookbook Mecca. In a loft area that had a 1950s-style red laminate booth, shelves of gorgeous ceramic pie plates of every design and color, and a tree filled with copper cookie cutters. Next to it, in the corner, was a finely refurbished turquoise vintage stove, and a working

Coca-Cola bottle dispenser, and a pair of metal chairs with shiny white cushions.

And interspersed among it all . . . was the mother lode of cookbooks.

They were everywhere. On shelves. In stacks. On the Formica table. Some were arranged by subject. Others, by author. Still others looked like they'd been simply set down and forgotten.

Glad that she was completely alone, Jennifer felt tears prick her eyes. Oh, not because of the beautiful display, but because it had been there all along and she hadn't even known about it.

No, that wasn't right. She hadn't been brave enough to overcome her fears to even step foot here, a place that would give her so much pleasure.

Just as sternly, she shook off her doubts and self-recriminations. There was nothing she could do about the past. It was done. All she could do was move forward.

Even with something as simple as being in a favorite store.

Swiping her eyes, she pulled out her bifocals, walked over to the first stack, and sat down at the booth. Then she opened up her first selection with a happy smile.

* * *

Jennifer wasn't sure how much time had passed when she heard footsteps on the stairs. Her muscles tensed, preparing to flee, though her head was telling the rest of her to calm down.

"It's just me," Camille said. "Sorry to disturb you, but I thought you might want sustenance."

Jennifer noticed then that the proprietor was holding a tray with a black and yellow teapot and cup on it. It was a sweet thing—the cup was on top of the pot, making it look like Camille was holding an overgrown bumble bee. She also had a little plate of shortbread cookies.

"You brought all this up for me?"

Camille shrugged. "I was making myself a pot and thought you might be ready to take a break, too."

Curious to know just how much time had passed, Jennifer glanced at her watch and gaped. She'd been sitting in the same spot for over an hour. "Wow. I had no idea it had gotten so late."

"Did you find anything good?"

"Only five cookbooks," she admitted sheepishly.

"Only five, hmmm?" Camille sat down on the bench across from her and pushed the tray toward Jennifer. "Well, now you've got to tell me all about them. You can do that while you have a spot of tea." A worried frown suddenly marred her forehead. "That is, if you like tea?"

"I do. Thank you. This was so nice of you."

She shrugged. "It wasn't anything."

Realizing that the room had gotten a little chilled, Jennifer removed the cup from over the teapot and poured herself a steaming cup. After taking a fortifying sip, she smiled. "Peppermint."

"It's my favorite this late in the day. Bracing but not caffeinated."

She took another sip. Then nibbled on the corner of a cookie for good measure.

Then, like a woman in the middle of an antique market, she started talking about the treasures she found. "I'd been wanting to see this one in person forever."

"Julia Child's *The Way to Cook.*" Camille nodded. "Good choice."

Jennifer grinned. "There's a French onion soup in here to die for."

"When you come back, you'll have to tell me how it turned out."

"I will."

"Now, look at this one." It was a Junior League cookbook from Birmingham, Alabama. "Isn't it a gem? Next, I found these two baking books. And then, of course, I couldn't resist this one," she said, noting that it was from a recent winner of a cooking competition she'd watched on TV.

Camille stood up. "Have you seen this one from Nigella? She makes everything sound so sinful."

Jennifer giggled, but couldn't resist scanning the pictures with her.

And so it continued. They scanned cookbooks, talked recipes, and shared stories about their successes and epic failures. Only after a half hour went by did it occur to Jennifer that Camille was upstairs, which meant no one was watching the shop.

"Ah, Camille, I love chatting with you, but don't you have to worry about your other customers?"

She waved a hand. "Oh, no. No one is coming in on a day like today."

She was at a loss. "What's special about today?"

Camille looked at her strangely. "Um, the snow?"

Jennifer stood up and walked to the windows lining the front of the store. And sure enough, it was snowing like crazy, and there had to be at least four inches of fresh powder on the ground.

Panic set in. It wasn't that she *couldn't* drive in the snow, but this was a whole new level of mess. The road was covered and the sky was so dark, it was obvious that a whole lot more was on the way.

"Oh my word. I didn't even think. I've got to go." Picking up the books she'd chosen, she faced Camille. "I need to check out, please."

Camille got up far more slowly. "Of course. Um, honey, I just assumed that you lived close by. Is that not the case?"

"I live in Bridgeport."

Her eyes widened. "It's going to be a mess over in Bridgeport."

Jennifer nodded. Bridgeport was a picturesque town, filled with rolling hills, narrow, curvy streets, and a river that flowed through the middle of the town. All of it was beautiful to look at, no matter what the season. But it was hell in the snow. Everyone knew that, which was part of the reason the sleepy town had never reached the size of the other suburbs and outlying towns of Cincinnati. "Those hills are going to be really bad," she said softly.

"Now you have me worried, especially with you being out on your own. Is there someone you want to call?"

"There's no need." The only person she could call was her brother, and she knew he was going to have his hands full attempting to keep the people of Bridgeport from trying to kill themselves by driving like maniacs. "I'll be fine."

After she followed Camille down the stairs, she placed the books on the counter so they could be rung up. Just as she was pulling out her wallet, her phone started ringing. Though she would usually ignore it, she saw it was her brother.

And that he'd already called two other times. Boy, she really had been in her own little cookbook world!

After handing Camille her credit card, Jennifer said, "I'm sorry, I've got to take this. It's my brother."

"Of course you do," she said as she slid the card through the reader.

"Hey, Dylan," she said.

"Where are you?"

He never talked to her like that. Well, not since her attack. "I'm at the bookstore."

"I've been calling you," he said, sounding more irritated. "Jen, you didn't pick up."

"I know. I'm sorry. I got busy looking at cookbooks with Camille."

"Who's that?"

"She's the manager of the shop." She smiled at Camille, as she picked up her credit card and hastily signed the receipt.

"So you're still there?"

"Yes. I'm paying now."

"This is unbelievable. I can't believe you picked today to finally conquer your fears."

Finally? "Dylan, what is that supposed to mean?"

"It means that I took time off to go by the house and you weren't there. It means that I've been calling you and you didn't pick up. It means that now I'm going to have to drive over there to get you and take you home."

She might have some issues, but she really wasn't used to being babied or talked down to. "I'm not a child. You don't need to come get me. Not ever."

He let out a big sigh. "Jennifer, Traci and I just spent the last hour caring for a woman who slid off the road and needed an ambulance. There's no way I'm going to let you drive by yourself home in your Nissan. It doesn't even have snow tires."

He was starting to scare her, not that he needed to know just how much she was affected. "I'll go slow and I'll be careful," she said in a soft voice. "Don't worry about me."

"Jennifer."

"Um, excuse me."

Jennifer put her hand over her phone. "Yes, Camille?"

"I think I have a solution for you getting home."

"Yes?"

"Jack can take you."

"Jack?"

"Yes. He's a great driver. And before he became a remodeling contractor, he worked in the oil fields out in South Dakota. He's used to driving in snow."

"Thank you, but—"

"He just lives around the corner. And I know he's home because he called me just before I went upstairs to see you. He'll be happy to drive you home," she said in her sweet, comforting voice. "I know it."

She felt frozen. Everything Camille said made sense. But was she willing to get in the car with a strange man? "I . . . I'm sorry but I can't."

Hurt shone in Camille's eyes. "Are you sure?"

Jennifer turned her back on the woman. "Dylan? Sorry, I'm back."

"You sound different." Worry edged into his tone. "What happened? Is everything okay?"

"Yes." She walked a few steps away and lowered her voice. "Camille suggested that Jack could drive me because he has a big truck and used to work in South Dakota oil fields."

"Who the hell is Jack?"

"Her son."

"Do you even know his last name?"

"No."

"Well, don't you get in the car with him."

"Don't worry. I'll wait for you. Sorry about this. I really don't know what happened."

She heard him mutter something under his breath. "I'm on my way. What's the name of the store?"

"Backdoor Books." Feeling Camille's look of disappointment, she closed her eyes.

"Traci and I'll be there within thirty. Okay?"

"Okay."

"Now, don't you stuff that phone in your purse, okay? Keep it someplace where you can hear it. If we get sidetracked, I want you to know what's going on."

"I'll keep it handy. Thanks, Dylan." Her voice sounded small and unsure and she hated that. "Sorry for the trouble."

"No apologies. I'm sorry I sounded like such a jerk. See you soon," he added before hanging up.

After pushing the button on her phone, she reluctantly turned to Camille. "My brother is a cop. He's going to come out here to get me. He said he'd be here in about thirty minutes. I hope you don't mind if I stay here a little longer?"

Camille's blue eyes looked worried, but she smiled again. "Of course not, honey. You do whatever you need to do."

"Thank you for understanding."

"How about another cup of hot tea?"

"Thanks. That . . . well, that would be really nice." Finally relaxing, she leaned back against her chair and looked out the window.

The snowflakes were thick and heavy, clinging to the windowsills, the branches on the nearby trees, even on top of the mailbox. If she'd been home, she would be thinking about how it was beautiful.

Then she noticed a shadow standing next to her car. She blinked, sure she was seeing things. Obviously letting her imagination get the best of her.

But then the shadow moved, and she could have sworn she'd caught a glimpse of something familiar.

A chill coursed through her as all of her worst fears burst forth. She was probably letting every fear she'd ever had take control over her.

Because there was no way any of the men who'd made her life so miserable could have already gotten out of jail and started following her.

Was there?

She was afraid to find out.

CHAPTER 11

"I'd rather learn from one bird how to sing than teach ten thousand stars how not to dance."
—E. E. CUMMINGS

"Do I even want to know why the sergeant didn't even blink when you said you had to drive to Montgomery to pick up your sister?" Traci asked.

Dylan glanced her way and wished that he didn't feel so obligated to tell his sister's whole story. But a good partnership was all about trust, and that meant that they had to be honest with each other.

He also owed Traci, because she hadn't once suggested that he go on his own after the sergeant said that they could go get Jennifer but to make it back as soon as possible.

"A little over two years ago, my little sister was attacked by three guys on her way to her car. They beat her up good. That was where she got the scar on her face."

Too intent on the road—and his memories—to see Traci's

reaction, Dylan kept his eyes straight ahead. But he could feel the tension radiating from her.

"And . . . ?" she whispered.

He paused, trying to recover his composure. "And she was raped."

She pressed a hand to her chest. "Oh my word." After a brief pause, she said, "It was obvious that she'd been through some kind of trauma when we were at dinner, but I hate that's what happened. I'm really sorry."

He was too. "Jen's a lot better, but she still has a hard time leaving the house. And I . . ." He took a deep breath. "I have a tendency to be pretty protective of her."

"Again, I'm really sorry, Dylan."

Her voice was filled with compassion but not pity. He appreciated that. It enabled him to be even more honest than he usually was. "Jennifer's assault was really hard on the whole family, and that's putting it mildly. We all circled around her and pretty much didn't leave her side for a solid year. But her counselors encouraged us to give her space. She told us that we were only delaying her healing."

"I've dealt with my fair share of rape victims, Lange. It's all so bad—there's no one way to overcome it. I'm sure you feel the same way."

"Yeah." Traci was right, but she was speaking as a cop, not a sibling.

"Jennifer sounds really strong."

"I think so too, but if Jen was sitting right here, she would probably give you a hug for saying that. She wants to be strong. And she's come a long way. I'm proud of her."

"What happened to the perpetrators?"

He slowed as he took a left turn, reminding himself to keep both the vehicle and his emotions in control. "We got two of those bastards. They'll be in prison for a while." He didn't need to tell her that they weren't going to get any concessions given that they'd raped a cop's sister.

"What about the third?"

"He was sixteen."

"Sixteen?"

"The little brother of one of the others. Since he had only been there but didn't actually assault her, the judge recommended he only go to juvenile detention for a year."

"So he's out." Her voice was flat.

"Yeah." He rolled his neck, hoping to alleviate some of the tension that had settled in his jaw and shoulders. "I didn't agree, of course. My little sister was in the hospital for three days and pretty much a mess for weeks. Nightmares, wouldn't eat. For months, my parents and I weren't even sure she was going to be able to get over it." He slowed and put his truck in a lower gear as he made the way down a hill toward Montgomery.

"Anyway, all that is why both she and I are the way we are."

"And why she lives with you."

He nodded. "When Mom and Dad decided to move full time to their condo in Florida, I asked Jennifer to move in with me."

"That was really nice of you."

"It wasn't anything. I would've done anything. Anything to help her. But see, she is better, but she's only just now leaving the house."

"I bet she thought I was so rude at Paxton's. I'm sure I was staring at her like I didn't get it."

"To be honest, I don't know if she even realized. She's usually trying so hard to get through her outings that she can't do a whole lot besides survive." After signaling for Traci to call in a plate they just saw on a car that looked abandoned on the side of the road, he continued. "Today was just the second time she's ever gone someplace completely by herself and spoke to another person."

"And she got stuck in a snowstorm. What rotten luck."

"Yeah." Now that he was retelling Jennifer's story, he felt even worse about how impatient he'd sounded when he'd talked to her on the phone. She didn't deserve that. "She drives just fine. So this 'rescue' we're doing is on me. Obviously, I need to work on giving Jen more space, too."

"I get it, though. You can't lose her now."

"Yep. Plus, the owner of the shop was offering to have her son drive Jennifer home. Like she would ever get in the car with a stranger, let alone let him see where she lived."

"Right. Well, we'll be there soon."

As he pulled through another intersection, he braced himself for another round of questions or to listen to her tell him about how she would have handled things differently. But she didn't do any of that. She remained silent.

Realizing that the tension in his jaw had lessened, he said, "You know what? A lot of people would be acting like I was ruining their whole schedule by taking care of my sis. But you are taking it in stride. I think I got pretty lucky with you."

Sounding completely full of herself, she said, "Well, my name *is* Lucky."

He groaned at her joke just as he pulled to a stop in front of the shop. "I'll be right back."

"Sure thing. I'll call the sergeant and let him know that we'll be back in town in forty."

"Thanks."

Approaching the shop's front door, he opened it and looked around. To his surprise, he saw Jennifer sitting on a chair with another woman. They were sipping tea.

"Jen?"

She turned to him and opened her eyes wide. "Oh my gosh!" she called out as she jumped to her feet. "I didn't even hear the door open."

"No worries."

"Sorry again that you had to come out."

"You know I did this for me as much as you. I need to know you're safe."

She smiled at him, relief in her blue eyes. "Dylan, this is Camille, the owner of this bookstore. Camille, please meet my brother Dylan."

Camille stood up. "So nice to meet you," she said as she held out a hand right as the shop's door opened again and a muscled guy who was easily over six feet came in.

He looked at Jennifer and smiled. "Hey, I got here in time."

"Just in time to say hello before I left. This is my brother Dylan."

"Hey. Jack Patterson."

Not being shy about looking him over, Dylan shook his hand. "Dylan Lange."

"Good to meet you." Turning to Jennifer, Jack said, "I hope this doesn't mean you won't come back."

Dylan was just about to step in and tell Jack he didn't need to worry about his sister, when her face lit up.

"I did get five cookbooks, so I don't think I'll need to return for a while."

"Not for cookbooks, but maybe there could be other reasons?"

Just as Dylan was about to send the guy a look to back off, Jennifer added, "I think there might be. Your mother makes a mean pot of tea and then there's Harvard and the fact that I haven't even started looking at the mysteries yet."

Jack grinned. "Good to hear."

"Are you ready, Jen?" Dylan asked. "Traci's in the truck and we've got to get back."

"Yes, of course." She picked up her bag and handed it to him. "Thanks again for everything, Camille."

"Anytime, honey. Come back soon."

Dylan held the door open for her.

"Hey," Jack called out. "Do you want me to drop off your car to you tomorrow?"

Jennifer froze, giving Dylan the perfect excuse to intervene. "If you could drop it off at the station, that would be great," he said as he handed the guy his card. "Just ask for me."

"Thanks so much," Jennifer said as she fished her car key out of her purse.

Glad that there was only a car key on the ring and not a house key, Dylan nodded at Jack again then ushered his sister out into the cold.

The snow was falling fast again. "Careful, now," he murmured as Jennifer stepped onto the narrow walkway leading from the store's front to the parking lot.

"I'll be careful."

Traci got out as they approached, opening the door to the back seat so Jennifer could slide right in. "I've got the heat blasting."

"Thanks," Jen said.

As they buckled up, he looked at Traci. "We good?"

"Good enough. Sergeant wants us back as soon as we can."

He started up the engine and backed out. "Call in our progress, Traci."

"On it."

As he started down the unplowed road, he couldn't help but glance at his sister. She was buckled in tight and looking out the window. She didn't look worried or upset, though. No, she looked rather reflective, like she was thinking about something other than the roads.

"What's going on with that guy, Jen?"

"Hmm?"

"You heard me," he said after making a left turn and heading onto Columbia, the main street leading into Bridgeport. "Was he bothering you?"

Beside him, Traci coughed into her hand. When he glanced at her, she shrugged. "Sorry."

"No, he wasn't bothering me, Dylan," Jennifer said. "You heard how nice he was."

"Do you need me to check him out?" Of course, he was already planning on discovering everything there was to know about Jack Patterson, no matter what.

"I do not."

"How come? Do you like him?"

"Do we really need to talk about this now?" she snipped.

He knew what she meant. Jennifer was determined to keep her past private. Usually he did his best to honor that. But sometimes—like now—he felt like all their tiptoeing around didn't help her much at all. Instead, it just pushed her problems out of the way. "Traci doesn't care. Do you?"

Traci, who had been typing something on her phone, looked up. "Don't think it's me you should be asking, buddy."

Maybe not. But with the storm, there was no telling when he was going to get a moment to talk to Jennifer. Not for another twenty-four hours, easily. "Sorry. But Jen, you know I worry."

"I'm fine. He wasn't doing anything but being nice."

"I just want you to be safe."

"I was in the bookstore, Dylan. You can't get much safer than that."

"See, that's something you need to worry about. There can be problems just about—"

"Dylan, I can't believe you. You are actually having a problem with me liking someone when that has been the goal this whole time."

"Wait, you like him?" He tapped too hard on the brakes and the vehicle slid.

"Watch it, buddy," Traci said.

He quickly righted the steering wheel and got his head back on the road. "Sorry."

Neither Traci nor Jennifer said anything in reply, which made him want to both stew and ask more questions. But when he glanced back at his sister and saw that she looked even more pensive than usual, he kept his silence.

Fifteen minutes later he pulled up in front of his house. "I'll be right back, Trace."

"Take your time." Turning to look at Jennifer, she said, "Good to see you again."

Jennifer gave Traci a wry smile. "You, too. Thanks for rescuing me."

Dylan reached for Jennifer's tote bag of books and then walked by her side. When he murmured, "Careful," and reached for her elbow, she glared at him.

"Dylan, I'm not eight or even eighteen. You need to remember that."

"What are you mad about? Me picking you up or this whole Jack thing?"

"I'm trying to decide. Right now it's a toss-up."

"The streets are bad, and you hardly even drove at all last year. I would have wanted to help anyone I care about. Even Shannon."

Now, why had he mentioned her?

Jennifer smiled. "*Even Shannon*, huh? Now that sounds interesting. Why did you bring her up? Do you like her?"

He rolled his eyes. "I deserved that. And about this Jack guy. You know I just want to make sure you're okay."

"I know. But you need to learn to keep some of your opinions to yourself, Dylan. I may never see this guy again. I may never even want to. But for me to even think about it is a good thing. It's taken me two years and two months, right?"

She was still counting the weeks, and he was acting like a jerk. "You're right. I'm sorry. I'll be better."

"I hope so."

Practically feeling Traci's impatience reverberating from his vehicle, he motioned to the door. "I've gotta go. Get on inside, okay?"

She nodded, pulled out her keys, and stepped inside, quickly disabling the alarm.

"Be safe, Dylan."

"I'll try. I'm sure I'll be late. I'll try to text you later so you won't worry."

She leaned up and gave him a kiss on the cheek. "Thanks. Now, go—before Officer Lucky has a conniption."

He grinned and trotted back to his truck.

"Everything okay?" Traci asked.

"Yeah." As he backed out, he said, "I'm sorry to stick you in the middle of my drama."

"Don't worry. I get it. I find myself worrying about Shannon and Kimber all the time now, and I didn't even know they existed a year ago. Love's a powerful thing."

There it was again. A Shannon mention. He wasn't sure what that meant, but he decided that it was a sign that he was supposed to find out.

CHAPTER 12

"Any kind of dancing is better than
no dancing at all."
—LYNDA BARR

The snow just kept coming. Standing at the bank of windows at the front of the studio, Shannon watched some kind of foreign sedan spin its wheels on the street in front of her building. The intersection that the car was attempting to climb was tricky on the best of days, since part of it was on a steep hill. No one in a rear-wheel-drive car had any chance of climbing it in weather like this.

The guy should have been driving a good old Chevy.

Kimber, who had been doing some yoga in one of Shannon's empty classrooms, walked in beside her. "What's got your panties in such a knot?"

"I've been watching this guy in that foreign job spinning its wheels and causing a mess."

Kimber turned to watch. "That would be a sixty-thousand-dollar Mercedes, Miss Hick."

Shannon shrugged. "Whatever. All I know is that it keeps sliding down the hill like it's on Snowshoe Mountain."

"Uh, Snowshoe?"

"That's a ski resort in West Virginia."

"And, you've been there?"

"Sure. Everyone back home goes." Ignoring Kimber's amused stare Shannon continued to watch the Mercedes's efforts. Another minute later, she breathed a sigh of relief. "Oh, good. It's finally attempting to go into that parking lot on the right."

"About time, too. He's about to cause a bunch of accidents," Kimber said. "You know what? I would say that the cops need to come out to direct traffic, but that might mean Traci the new girl."

Shannon gulped. "I had forgotten that Traci's probably directing traffic out there. I always just imagine her investigating burglaries or something."

Pulling over two stools, Kimber hopped on one. "Come on, let's sit down while we watch the show." After Shannon hiked herself up—it really wasn't fair that Kimber was so much taller than she was—Kimber smiled at her. "So, you reckon that our Traci's out catching burglars, huh? Are you worried about the Bridgeport crime rate?"

"No. I mean, not really, Miss New York City. I just worry about Traci."

"Even though I sounded snobby, I promise I was only teasing a little bit. To be honest, I never thought about Bridgeport being anything but a quiet little town."

"I'm sure it's real quiet compared to New York City."

"Yes, but it's not in my nature to worry too much. I guess I just always assume I'm going to be safe."

That was kind of a surprise, given what Shannon knew about

Kimber's childhood. It was good enough, but she'd had her share of doubts and worries. Then there was the fact that Kimber was drop-dead gorgeous and often traveled to big cities all by herself. Shannon knew that she would be scared to death boarding a plane in New York City to Rome or Paris or wherever and then getting off and finding her way to her hotel.

"What are you thinking about now?"

"Oh, just that I'm such a small-town girl compared to you. I'm suspicious of foreign cars and I think Snowshoe is a fancy ski resort, while you're used to traveling all around the world by yourself."

"I was surprised you knew how to ski, Shannon. That's where my look came from. I sure don't know how. And I don't think you're all that much of a hick. I mean, you did all those dance competitions. I know you traveled for those."

"Yes, but I wasn't going to foreign countries. Mainly just places like Atlanta. Then, too, I was always with my mom or my dad and my teacher and friends." Thinking about how oblivious she'd been to anything outside of her dances and her friends, she shook her head. "I was a pretty self-centered girl. I never thought much about anything ever going wrong." Or how much her mother had given up in order for Shannon's dreams to become a reality.

"That's a good thing, girl."

She shrugged. "Do you ever think of Traci? She doesn't talk about much, but everything about her childhood sounds so tough. I feel guilty, and I didn't even know about it."

Kimber frowned slightly. "I feel guilty, too." She crossed her legs, somehow looking elegant while perched on an old wooden stool. "But that's how it goes, right?"

"What does?"

"Well, we're sitting here feeling bad and guilty that she had a crappy childhood, even though we had nothing to do with it.

Her parents, on the other hand, have probably never given her a second's thought."

Kimber didn't lie. Shannon rarely thought about their birth mother now. Beyond thinking that she missed out getting to know them, she tried not to think about her. It hurt too much. "I'm never going to be like our mother."

Kimber chuckled. "Of course you aren't. Our mother had all three of us before she was twenty-six. You're doing your own thing now."

"Thanks."

"Sure. Oh! Look at that. Now we've got ourselves a police officer to watch." She whistled low. "And he looks fine even bundled up like that."

Shannon turned to watch the cop in jeans, boots, and a thick police uniform jacket and hat. He was motioning a pair of cars to go up the hill. Then she realized that *fine* man was someone she knew. "That's Dylan."

Kimber's smile widened. "Your studly student?"

"Stop." She felt her cheeks redden. "Oh my gosh, Kimber, you have the stupidest expressions," she said, hoping that her comment might take some of the focus off of her embarrassment.

But from the way Kimber was still grinning, it was evident that her sister wasn't missing a single thing. "All to make you smile, sweetheart."

"Mission accomplished, then." Shannon smiled at her, then settled back in to watch Dylan direct traffic. She couldn't help but admire him. Oh, not because of his looks, but because of the way he seemed to command every driver's respect. And, well, he simply looked so assured. None of the drivers looked like they were even thinking about hesitating when Dylan told them to either stop or continue on.

Watching Dylan made her realize that she really hadn't given enough thought to *all* of him. He wasn't just a handsome guy who lost a bet in his fantasy football league and had a great smile. No, he was so much more—a police officer who constantly put his life on the line for other people.

As that sunk in, she began to feel more and more apprehensive as she watched him. What if a car didn't slow down? What if someone slid into him and Dylan got hurt?

She even started worrying about him getting home. Just because he was a cop didn't mean he was immune to folks like that Mercedes man sliding all over God's green earth.

After another thirty minutes, Shannon knew she had to do something for him. Even if it was only something small—at least he would know that someone cared. Getting to her feet, she turned to Kimber. "You know what? It's really cold out there. I'm going to go make a fresh pot of coffee and bring a cup out to him."

Kimber's eyes lit up, making Shannon realize that she might be trying to act all calm, cool, and collected, but she wasn't fooling her sister one bit. "That's a real fine idea. You know what? I'll make it. I was going to get a snack anyway."

"Are you sure?"

"Oh, yeah. You keep watch."

She was gone before Shannon could even offer a token protest. When Dylan blew his whistle and yelled at somebody who was going too fast, her heart clenched. What if someone lost control of their car and hurt him?

It would be so awful.

And, she realized, it just might render her heartbroken. Not just because he was a good guy, but because she was starting to think of him as *her* good guy.

Uh-oh. What in the world was going on?

CHAPTER 13

"Hand in hand, on the edge of the sand, they danced by the light of the moon."
—EDWARD LEAR

Dylan was sure that she was going to get herself killed. There was Shannon, all dressed up in some kind of fuzzy oversized jacket, black leggings, furry boots, and bright pink gloves. Her brown hair was down and floating around her shoulders as she tromped towards him in the snow.

She looked exactly like she was—a pretty girl with great legs standing in absolutely the wrong place.

When he saw yet another driver stare at her instead of watching him or the intersection, Dylan felt his heart rise up into his throat.

"Shannon, go back inside!" he yelled.

She paused on the median she was carefully walking on. Then she held up a white paper cup. "I will. But I brought you coffee. It's fresh!"

Of course it was. He was beginning to realize that Shannon was the type of woman to do everything as well as she possibly could. He couldn't imagine her serving anyone stale, cold coffee. Maybe it was her West Virginia upbringing. Maybe it was just her.

Whatever the reason, he was toast. He didn't think he was capable of hurting her feelings. "Wait a sec. I'll come to you."

Her eyes widened. "But—"

"No. Stay there." Yes, he realized he was ordering her around, but he was doing his best to keep from telling her to go inside where she could be safe and warm.

She bit her lip and watched as a van with nearly bald tires slid into a right turn.

Please, Lord, don't let the driver lose control.

After it made a successful right turn and disappeared out of sight, he walked over to Shannon. After scanning the roads, he relaxed slightly. Only a lone Subaru was nearby, and that driver was only going about ten miles an hour. It looked like the population was finally listening and getting off the roads.

"Thanks for this," he said, taking a tentative sip. The hot liquid blazed a trail down his throat, showing him just how cold he'd been. And yes, it also was strong and tasted terrific. "It's great."

She smiled like he'd just given her a real compliment. "I wanted to do something for you. You've been out here for a while."

After checking the progress of two plows about a hundred yards away, he smiled at her. "Want to tell me how you know how long I've been out here?"

"I might have been watching from my front window."

He raised his eyebrows. "You've been watching me direct traffic?"

"Yep. It was my sister Kimber's idea."

"Oh. Of course." He took another sip, draining the cup. "Thanks. This was real kind of you. I better get back to work."

She looked disappointed. "Already? How much longer will you be out here?"

He shrugged. "Maybe another half hour, unless people start acting stupid and coming back out on the streets."

"When you're done, if you want, you could come over. I could heat up some soup or make you a grilled cheese."

Even though they were standing out in the middle of an intersection and the snow was falling down around them, he grinned. "Grilled cheese, huh?"

She lifted her chin. "Everyone knows that nothing tastes better than a grilled cheese sandwich on a snowy day."

"You might be right about that."

"So?" She tilted her head slightly. Still watching him.

It was tempting. So tempting that he wished it were possible. "Thanks, but I can't. I've got to check in at the station house."

"Oh. Well, maybe another time . . ."

"That sounds good. After the station house, I need to see Jen. I've got a feeling that she's already made me something, and she'll be upset if I don't eat it. I'm sure you understand." Then, of course, was the fact that he and his sister were going to have to have a heart-to-heart about her trip to the bookstore, whatever was going on with that guy . . . and he was also going to have to apologize yet again for acting like a jerk.

"Oh. Yes. Yes, of course." She held out her hand. "Let me take the cup from you. Be careful out there, Officer."

"Always," he replied, his cocky smile faltering slightly as he realized that she had already turned and was walking back. What had just happened?

The sound of honking horns interrupted his thoughts. Turning back to the job at hand, he blew his whistle, reminding the guy in the four-wheel-drive Land Rover that he might have a lot of money, but he didn't own the road.

* * *

When he walked into the house two hours later, the first thing he noticed was the silence. Usually Jennifer had music playing and was busy in the kitchen.

But not only was the kitchen dark and silent, there was no sign of her anywhere. Or dinner made.

"Jen? Jennifer?"

"Yes?"

"Where are you?"

"Up in my room! Why?"

Why? Why was she up there? Why was he yelling up at her like he was a dad and she was his teenage daughter? "No reason. I'm going to go take a shower."

When she didn't reply, he bit back a sigh. He was a piece of work. Here he was always telling her that she didn't need to always cook and fuss over him, but when she didn't for the first time in a long time, he felt let down.

While he showered, he told himself to stop being so selfish. Jennifer needed him to be there for her, not to expect her to wait on him.

After pulling on an old pair of gray sweats, remnants from the police academy, he walked into the kitchen. Seeing it was still empty, he felt a burst of satisfaction. He was no cook, but Shannon's idea about grilled cheese sounded pretty good. At the very least, he could open up a can of soup and make them a couple of sandwiches.

Feeling good about that idea, he pulled out Jennifer's cast-iron skillet and then opened the refrigerator. Just as he was buttering the bread, Jennifer joined him.

"What in the world are you doing?"

He looked up and smiled. "Exactly what it looks like. I'm making us dinner."

Her eyebrows rose over the frames of her glasses. "You're cooking?"

"I do know how to work a stove top, Jen. Not like you of course, but I can make you a sandwich without burning it." At least he hoped so. He held up a can of soup. "Tomato soup okay?"

She nodded as she hopped up on a barstool.

Opening the can, he looked over at her. She was wearing a pair of black leggings and a soft-looking violet tunic sweater. In addition to taking out her contacts and putting on her glasses, she'd washed off her makeup. She looked almost like a kid again. "How are you doing?"

"I'm okay."

Walking to the refrigerator, he pulled out two Miller Lites and handed her one. "You know, I was worried about you today."

"I do know. And we already talked about this. I told you I was sorry for worrying you."

He poured the soup into the saucepan and added water. "I don't want to rehash it. I . . . well, you have to see it from my point of view. You being out on your own again . . . well, it's new for me, too."

"I know. But I think I need to do this, Dylan. I need to try new things and make mistakes."

"I hear you." Her therapist had even told him once that her mistakes might be the best thing that could happen to her. She needed to remember that it was okay to make mistakes—and he needed to remember that she wasn't made of glass.

As he was pulling out plates and bowls from the cupboards, Jennifer walked to his side and picked up the spatula. "Let me help you."

"I'm doing fine."

"You're about to burn them." She slid the metal spatula under the sandwich, peeked under it, and then flipped it.

"You know, this is good practice for both of us," he joked. "If you're going to be doing more things, I'm going to need to remember how to cook for myself."

Her expression softened, showing that she'd understood his unspoken meaning. "I agree, but your mistakes also affect my well-being, and I don't want to starve."

He sipped his beer and stepped out of her way. "Since we're cooking together and all, what's going to happen with that guy?"

"Jack?"

He nodded.

"Oh, I don't know. Probably nothing."

He glanced at her sideways. Was she upset by this? Glad? "What do you want to happen?"

She looked surprised he'd asked. "I don't know. Honestly, I'm not sure how I'm supposed to feel, Dylan. For the last couple of years . . . well, you know." She pulled out two spoons from a drawer.

He knew. She'd been wary and scared. All with good reason.

"I'm trying to remember what you were like before you got attacked, Jen." He stirred the soup even though it didn't need to be stirred. Just gave him something to do instead of staring at her. "Do you ever think about those days?"

"I didn't used to. But now I'm kind of wondering if it would be possible to get a little bit of myself back." Placing the sandwiches on plates, she looked at him. "One day I think I'd like to smile again at people without being scared . . . and to do something spontaneous without feeling like I'm about to have another anxiety attack."

"That's going to happen, Jennifer. I know it is."

Watching him carry their simple meal to the kitchen table, she nodded. "I think so, too. Actually, I think it's time I started dancing a little more and being scared a little less. I think I deserve that."

He knew she did. Actually, he thought that maybe they all deserved dancing more and worrying less.

That was a good thing, too, since he was becoming very fond of a certain lady who knew a thing or two about dancing.

CHAPTER 14

"What would life be like without a little tango?"

"One of us needs to learn to cook," Traci announced as she glared at the stove like it had offended her. "Which of you wants to take cooking lessons? I'll pay."

Shannon glanced at Kimber. She was leaning against the doorframe and not looking particularly pleased. "What do you think, Kimber? Are you up for cooking classes?"

Looking as haughty as all get-out, Kimber lifted her chin. "No, I am not."

Shannon chuckled. It had taken a couple of weeks of living together to learn the various nuances of Kimber's dry sense of humor. Kimber would probably be surprised to learn that she was far more big city than she realized.

Turning to her other sister, Shannon shrugged. "Sorry, Trace.

If you want better food made in this kitchen, you're going to have to do it yourself."

"I was afraid of that." She turned and opened the refrigerator. Then looked in the freezer.

"Are you looking for a chef in there?" Kimber asked.

"I wish. No, I was just thinking about Dylan's sister. He said she makes him dinner every night." She shut the freezer door and leaned back against the appliance. "Wouldn't that be something? We could come home and have a hot meal waiting for us."

"Sounds like you need a wife," Kimber murmured. "Like, one from the 1950s."

If Traci heard Kimber, she was ignoring her. "Maybe I could hire someone to make a couple of meals that we could freeze and then heat up," she mused.

Shannon was about to ask about how she was going to pay for that service when it all clicked together. "Wait, who are you talking about?"

"Jennifer, Dylan's sister. The 1950s cook," Traci said. "Dylan said she's real fond of casseroles. I haven't had a decent casserole in forever. Doesn't that sound so good? Something warm and hot with melted cheese on top and maybe crushed crackers or potato chips on top?"

Kimber looked horrified. "I've got a magazine shoot in two weeks. I can't go around eating casseroles with potato chips."

"That's too bad. You'll be missing out."

"I would be all about it, you know . . . if, after my shoot, we had a casserole like that in our future," Kimber replied as she stared into the empty freezer. "Which, we do not."

Ignoring the casserole talk, Shannon smiled at Kimber. "You didn't tell me about your new job. Congratulations! Is that the spread you were hoping to get?"

Kimber smiled. "Yep. I couldn't believe it when my agent called this morning. It's for a bathing suit and sportswear magazine. Five days in Cozumel wearing string bikinis and skimpy clothes."

"Better you than me," Shannon said, imagining how much she'd hate to be barely dressed in front of a bunch of people analyzing how she looked. It was hard enough dancing in front of judges. "Kimber, do you ever get tired of everyone judging you?"

"Sometimes, but then I remind myself that they're paying me a small fortune. That usually helps."

Traci grinned. "Do you need someone to carry your luggage?"

"Sorry, I'm not bringing much more than a backpack," Kimber said.

Shannon was fascinated. "Really? That's all you'll need? What about all your beauty products?" She and Traci had teased Kimber more than once about her forty-minute beauty routines—and the array of lotions and potions that took up half the bathroom counter.

"They'll have makeup and hair people and all the clothing. All I have to do is show up on time and look decent."

"But what about clothes for when you go out at night? I heard there are some great clubs in Cozumel."

"I'm not going to be clubbing." Kimber looked incredulous. "Honey, all I'll be doing is sleeping at night."

"Really?" Traci looked pretty disappointed. "I thought models partied all the time."

"Not this one. Plus, I can't risk getting bloated by beer. Those bikinis are tiny." She winked at Shannon. "Things do get awkward if I look like I've gained weight."

Shannon was starting to get a whole new appreciation for the pressures of Kimber's job. "I guess even a pound would show up when you're wearing practically nothing."

"Unfortunately, yes. That's why I'll be drinking bottled water in Mexico . . . and not eating any casseroles until I get back to Ohio."

Now that they were talking about food again, Shannon said, "Speaking of casseroles, I think I just made a really stupid mistake."

"What? Why?" Kimber asked.

"When I walked out to give Dylan a cup of coffee, I asked him in, but he said 'Jen' probably had a meal for him. I didn't put two and two together and got jealous."

Kimber smiled. "Here you thought he had a girlfriend and it's just a sister."

"Yes, which is embarrassing. We had a whole meal with Jennifer."

Traci opened the refrigerator again and pulled out a Dr. Pepper, which seemed to be her favorite thing in the world. "Backtrack a sec, Shannon. When did you see Dylan?"

"When he was directing traffic in front of our house."

"He looked good, too." Kimber snickered. "Just a little chilled."

"He was out there a long time."

"So you just decided to bring him a cup of coffee?" Traci looked incredulous.

"Well, yes."

"She met him on the median," Kimber supplied. "It was super cute."

"You shouldn't have gone out there. Vehicles were sliding everywhere. You could've gotten hurt."

"Dylan said the same thing."

"Because he was right. Some of those drivers are idiots."

"I was careful. And for the record, I can't say that I was real excited about watching Dylan stand in the middle of the intersection while cars and trucks were sliding around."

"We're trained, you know. You are not."

"Traci, I'm fine. I was only out there for a few minutes and then I got sent back inside."

"Good."

"Oh, please. Don't act like a grown woman can't deliver a cup of coffee."

"I didn't say that. But you have to be careful."

"I could say the same thing about you, Traci. Kimber and I were worried about you today."

Traci froze for a moment before an expression came over her face that told everything.

Shannon realized then that her spunky, brave sister wasn't used to have people looking out for her. Sadness gripped her hard, hating that she'd been so cosseted as a child while Traci had only known the opposite of that.

Even though Shannon knew she was making herself vulnerable, she said, "You two are just going to have to get used to being worried about. I don't know what I'd do if something happened to y'all."

Kimber blinked hard. "I feel the same way. For so long I wondered when I was going to fit in. You gals made me realize that I just had to wait for you two."

"I feel the same way," Traci said. She turned away abruptly. "But I'm going to eat my foot if we don't get something going."

"You know, since no casseroles are in our future, we really need to eat something." Kimber walked to her side. "We have lettuce. I could make a salad."

"We have ham, cheese, and eggs. How about omelets?" Shannon asked.

"That's perfect," Traci said. "And I'll make hot chocolate and cookies for dessert."

"You know how to make cookies?" Shannon asked.

"Well, I know how to make the slice and bake ones," Traci said.

"That's it. I'm going to call Dylan's sister and ask her to make some meals for y'all," Kimber said. "Unless you want to do the calling, Shannon?" she added with a gleam in her eye. "Who knows, maybe she'll give you some more information about Dylan."

"Or, I can give you more information. What do you want to know about him, Shannon? I'm great at interrogating," Traci teased.

Shannon knew she was turning bright red. "I appreciate that, but I'll take a pass. If I need any more information I'll ask him at our next class. I'll ask him about Jennifer making us a meal, too."

Kimber shared a smile with Traci. "Can't wait to hear about what you learn, girl. I have a feeling your conversations aren't going to center on speeders and breaking and entering."

Boy, she hoped not. "Let's eat before Traci gets hangry."

"Or hangrier," Traci murmured.

That was all they needed to hear before they got busy and the three of them started working side by side in the old-fashioned, small kitchen.

When Traci put on some music, they all started singing an old Maroon Five favorite together.

And they realized that they didn't need much else.

CHAPTER 15

"Life is like dancing. If we have a big floor, many people will dance. Some will get angry when the rhythm changes. But life is changing all the time."
—DON MIGUEL RUIZ

Three Days Later

Jennifer clicked END on her cell phone, set it on her kitchen counter, and then stared at the now blank screen.

What had just happened?

She'd been so surprised when Dylan had asked if he could give Shannon her phone number that she'd given permission without wondering too much about the reason behind it.

She'd been almost as surprised to actually get that phone call.

But the quick conversation that had ensued had completely taken her by surprise. Shannon had been all business, talking about how she and her sisters couldn't cook, how they couldn't live much longer on sandwiches, takeout and omelets. Then she'd gone into some kind of convoluted explanation about modeling, casseroles, and Traci's getting hangry.

Jennifer had found herself agreeing to bring over a meal that evening. In six hours.

Luckily, she already had a full pantry, so it would be easy enough to make a poppy seed chicken casserole, rice, and a lemon meringue pie for dessert. And then deliver it.

Her hands started shaking. Was she even ready for this?

What if she wasn't?

Then those girls would be wondering where their food was and Dylan would be forced to deal with the consequences, since both his partner and his dancing instructor were going to be affected.

In a panic, she dialed Dylan's number. He answered immediately.

"Jen, you okay?"

As it had so many times before, her brother's brusque, matter-of-fact tone calmed her down. "I'm sorry to bother you, but do you have a minute?"

"Of course." She heard him rustle some papers around. He was at his desk. "What's going on?"

"Shannon Murphy just gave me a call."

"She did? Hmm. What did she have to say?"

The warmth in his voice told her that she was the only one surprised. "After telling me all about how neither she nor her sisters could make much of anything that was edible, she asked me to make them dinner tonight. For money." She took a deep breath. "I told her I would."

"Really? Hey, Jen, that's great."

She could practically hear the smile in his voice. "I think I said I would do it before I even realized what I was doing," she admitted.

"You're a great cook. Why do you sound so nervous?"

"Oh, I don't know." But part of her couldn't help but dwell

on the man she'd seen by her car at the bookstore. What if she saw him again? What if he had been one of the men who'd attacked her?

She was almost tempted to ask Dylan to double-check that they were still incarcerated, but all that would do was make him worry about her yet again.

Almost worse would be if she did ask, he did double-check, and then discovered that they were still very much locked away. Then she would have to come to terms with the fact that her fears were causing her to see problems lurking in every corner.

After another few seconds had passed, she heard him click his pen a couple of times. "Do you want me to get you out of it, Jen?" he asked slowly. "Is that why you called?"

"No," she replied quickly. That was Dylan. Always ready to save her. Worse, she knew she'd probably started to rely on him saving her, too. Far too much. "I'm going to do it. It's just a big step, you know?" Yes, that was better. Far better for him to think that she just needed encouragement.

"It's a big step, but it's the right one. I promise." His voice warmed. "Jennifer, I promise. No one in Bridgeport, Ohio, cooks better than you. And from what Traci tells me, those ladies are desperate for your help. They're going to love everything."

Though she knew he was trying hard to boost her confidence, there was probably a bit of truth to it. "Shannon did say that they could barely heat up pizza without burning it."

"It's amazing that they haven't starved," he joked. "So, what are you going to make?"

"Nothing special."

After relaying the menu, he moaned. "I hope you're going to make some for us, too."

"Maybe, but don't you have your class tonight?" The last time he'd had a dance class he'd stayed downtown and gotten dinner at

Paxton's before heading over to his class.

"I do. Hey, how about I help you bring everything over? I could stop by the house and help you carry everything to the car."

She stopped herself just as she was about to accept. "Thanks, but I've got this."

"Sure?"

"I think so." She definitely needed to be able to handle this. "Thanks for picking up. I guess I just needed someone to talk this over with. Who knows? Maybe I'll see you over there tonight."

Dylan didn't say anything for a moment, then said at last, "I'm proud of you, Jen. I know you can do this."

"Thanks." When she hung up the phone again, she paced for a few moments, then started pulling out flour, shortening, lemons, and about another two dozen ingredients. Then she put on some music and her favorite apron and got to work. Right now, all she had to do was cook. If there was anything that she knew how to do, it was that.

When she started measuring, she repeated her brother's words over and over. "I can do this."

By the fourth or fifth time, she almost believed it.

* * *

She got to the dance studio five minutes before six. In a large canvas bag she'd found in a back closet she had loaded a hot casserole, a side dish of green beans with almonds, a loaf of bread, and a plastic cake holder with a really beautiful pie inside.

So far, the visit could be deemed a success, at least from her point of view. She got out of the car without having to convince herself that she was going to be fine.

She also hadn't even looked around the area much, just to be sure no one was watching her. That was something to be proud of.

Now all she had to do was ring the doorbell, deliver the food, and hope that Traci hadn't been lying when she'd said that she'd pay Jennifer right away.

But still she hesitated, wondering who was going to answer the door. What if it wasn't one of the girls? What if it was a strange man? What if . . .

A dog barked behind her. She turned, saw a man jogging toward her on the sidewalk, a yellow Labrador on a leash. When she met his eyes, she turned abruptly and pushed the button next to the door.

In this case, it seemed the devil she didn't know was better than the devil she did.

When the door opened, she was greeted by three women instead of just one.

Traci rushed forward and picked up the bag. "Jennifer! You're our hero! Come on in."

Smiling at the women, she followed Traci and then laughed as they all looked like she'd brought them a special gift.

"Hi again," said Shannon. "This is our sister Kimber."

Jennifer smiled at Kimber before turning her attention back to Shannon. The last time she'd seen Shannon, the woman had been wearing jeans and had her hair in a ponytail.

Tonight, she looked far more glamorous. She had on a dark-gray wrap dress that was slightly clingy and black heels. Her hair was longer than Jennifer had imagined and it fell to the almost the middle of her back in soft curls. No wonder she'd sensed something was going on between Dylan and Shannon!

Feeling all their eyes studying her and the tote bag, Jennifer focused back on her purpose for being there. "So, I have dinner for you."

"I can't wait to see it. It smells so good," Traci said.

Picking up the tote bag, Jennifer followed the other three up two flights of stairs to the living area. It was a combination of industrial and modern style, with a good dose of girliness mixed in. Purses, clothes, and shoes were scattered all over the floor.

Looking around, she said, "How is it living above a dance studio?"

"Really loud when all the squealing high school girls are here, but otherwise, we're getting used to it," Kimber said. "And used to living with each other."

Dylan had told her a little bit about how the sisters had recently discovered each other. And, how they'd all decided to relocate to a new place for one year in order to get to know each other.

"I moved in with my brother about two years ago. It's an adjustment, isn't it?"

"It is, but so far, so good," Shannon said. She handed Jennifer a glass of iced tea. "Especially tonight. We're going to eat like kings."

"Or queens," Kimber corrected.

Jennifer grinned. "You three are making me feel pretty good—and a little worried," she admitted as she pulled out the Rubbermaid container. "It's just a casserole, beans, and a pie."

Traci opened up the plastic lid. "Look at that pie. It's too bad you won't be able to eat any of this, Kimber."

"I decided I'd rather run on the treadmill for an extra hour instead of denying myself everything. I'm going to have a couple of bites." Looking at the dish of beans, she plucked one off the top. "I'll eat these, too."

"I hate to be rude, but I need to eat right away. I've got a class to teach in thirty," Shannon said as she pulled out plates. "Jennifer, would you like to join us? You're welcome to, or even hang out here for a while."

"Thanks, but I don't think Dylan is ready for me to watch him dance. I'm planning to be gone before he arrives." She wanted to show him—and herself—that she could do this errand just fine, too.

"So you know it's your brother's private lesson tonight?"

"I do." Though it was tempting to say something about how her brother had gone from complaining about his fantasy football bet to planning his Friday nights around his class, she didn't say any more.

"Does he talk about it much?" Kimber asked as she spooned a small portion of the casserole on her plate.

"Not a lot." Jennifer didn't want to embarrass Shannon or her brother. But she did smile at Traci, who looked like she was struggling to keep a straight face. "But some."

Shannon's eyes got big. "He does? What does—" She stopped herself abruptly. "Never mind. Forget I asked that."

"My lips are sealed." Knowing that Shannon needed to eat and wanting to be gone before her brother arrived, she took a step toward the door. "You know what? I think I'm going to head out."

"You don't have to," Shannon said. "I won't even talk about Dylan if you don't want."

"No, um, it's just that I wanted to do this right, you know? Be professional and deliver the food."

Kimber put down her fork. "Jennifer, I get that making us a meal was a job and all. But, as far as I'm concerned, you could move in here. This dinner is so good."

"I'm glad you like it." She picked up her tote bag. "Thanks for this. It, well, it helped me a lot. More than you can imagine."

Shannon walked to her side. "You're welcome. Here, I'll walk you out." She handed her an envelope. "Oh, and here's the money for tonight's meal. I almost forgot!"

Jennifer took the envelope gratefully and followed her down the narrow stairs, feeling like she was floating. She'd done it.

"I'm sure we'll be calling you again," Shannon said. "Actually, I'll get this ball rolling. How about you make us a meal one night a week?"

"I could do that."

"Great. I'll email you and we can devise some type of schedule and payment plan."

"I'll look forward to that," she said as they stopped at the door. "Night."

"Night," Shannon called out behind her.

Jennifer quickened her steps, got in her car, and then turned it on.

And she was feeling pretty good, until she realized that her car had been unlocked.

And that there was a note lying on the back seat with her name on it.

CHAPTER 16

"The only way to make sense out of change is to plunge into it, move with it, and join the dance."
—ALAN WATTS

Dylan couldn't get to the dance studio fast enough. He ran red lights, passed a vehicle in a no-passing zone, and pretty much committed another half-dozen traffic violations while speeding through Bridgeport.

The moment he arrived, Dylan double-parked in front of a red Suburban, and then ran over to his sister.

She was sitting almost motionless. The windows were up, the doors were locked, and the engine was off. It was hard to tell with only the streetlights casting light, but he was pretty sure she was crying. She was in a bad way.

He was going to need some help.

Looking up at the studio, he pulled out his phone and called Traci. She picked up on the second ring.

"Dylan, what's up? Aren't you supposed to be dancing with my sister?"

"Are you home?"

Her voice turned all business. "Yep. Do you need me?"

"Yeah. I'm in front of the studio. I need your help with my sister."

"I'm walking downstairs now. What happened with Jennifer? She was just here."

"Can you come on out?" He knew he needed to fill her in, but he wanted to get Jennifer out of that car. It was barely twenty degrees outside.

"Sure. Um, what about Shannon?"

He was definitely not used to mixing work with his personal life, and here his family, work, and Shannon were all intertwined. "Trace, could you tell her that I'm sorry and that I'm not trying to blow her off, but we've got a situation?"

"Sure. I'll be right down." Her voice was even more serious.

"Thanks."

She hung up right after, which he was appreciative of. Traci really was just like one of the guys.

Sliding his phone back in his pocket, he approached Jennifer once again. She was sitting stiff in the driver's seat. Now both of her hands were clenching the steering wheel.

Damn. She looked as bad as she did those first few days after her attack. What had happened?

Realizing he was feeling almost as stressed as he did two years ago, he reminded himself that she wasn't half-naked and bleeding on the floor of a concrete parking garage. Whatever had happened hadn't been that. And if it hadn't been that, then they were going to be able to get through this, too.

Feeling better, Dylan exhaled, rolled back his shoulders, and then gently knocked on Jennifer's window with two of his knuckles.

Jennifer flinched and closed her eyes.

His heart started racing. What the hell had happened?

"Jen?" he said. "Jennifer, it's me. It's Dylan," he added, knocking on her window again. "Unlock the door."

He was vaguely aware of the door to the dance studio opening behind him as he waited and watched his sister.

At last, she looked at him. Her pupils were dilated and she looked pale. Her lips were slightly parted.

She was in shock.

He crouched down and raised his voice. "Jennifer, open the door. You're worrying me."

When she looked just beyond him, her eyes widened.

He looked over his shoulder. Traci was standing at his shoulder. She was dressed in a loose sweater, jeans, and boots. He'd bet money that she had put her gun in the middle of her back. She was standing alert, looking both at him and the surrounding areas.

Just beyond her was Shannon. She had on a dress and heels and an open coat thrown over her shoulders. She was watching them, concern etching her features. Just beyond them was a man walking a dog. The man was bundled up in a hat, gloves, and ski jacket. There was no way to tell how old he was, but at this point, Dylan didn't want to worry about anyone in the perimeter.

"Come on, Jennifer," he said again. "Don't make me break into this car. We don't have money for that."

Finally, that did it. She slowly moved her finger to the button on the side of the door and pushed. It clicked right open.

With a silent prayer of thanks, he opened her door and pulled her into his arms. She remained stiff for a few seconds, then burst into tears. "Honey, what happened? What set you off? Did you get scared again?"

She pulled away, her eyes frantic. "No. *It's not me.*"

He ran his hands along her arms. "What happened, then? Are you hurt?" Grasping at straws, he murmured, "Did someone hit—"

"Dylan, one of them . . . one of them was here!"

Even though his body went on alert, he made sure to keep his voice easy. "Honey, you're going to have to help me out here. One of who?"

"There's a note! I locked the car, but it was unlocked when I got in," she continued, each word tumbling over the next. "And then . . . then." She hiccupped and pointed to the back seat. "I know it was one of them. I know it."

He stood up, looked at what she was pointing to, and then just about lost it. There really was an envelope sitting on the cushion of the back seat. JENNIFER LANGE was written in neat, dark block letters on the center of it.

"Lucky!" he yelled.

"Right here," Traci said. "What's going on?"

"We need a squad car. Fingerprints. Pictures. And I need Jennifer inside." Reaching out he clasped his sister's hand. It was ice-cold. "She's been out here for a while. I think she's in shock and needs to warm up."

"Okay . . . Hey, Shannon, come over here a sec."

When Shannon approached, Dylan felt her worry as much as he saw it shining bright in her eyes. Making a decision, he strode to her side. "Honey, could you do me a favor and take my sister inside? Maybe get her some tea or something?"

"Sure. Of course." She pressed a hand on his upper chest, right over his heart. "You okay?"

He wasn't. He was angry as hell and freaking out that the men who'd damaged his sister so bad could be back—*and* might even put Shannon, Traci, and their sister Kimber in danger, too.

But he had enough experience to keep his emotions held

down tight. "I'm just fine. Don't worry about me." He covered her hand on his chest with his own for a second, letting her know how much he appreciated her touch and concern before moving out of her reach. "I'll fill you in later about what happened."

Shannon nodded, giving him a shaky smile before leaning toward his sister. "Hey, Jennifer, how about you come in and have a slice of that amazing pie you made? I was just about to have a piece. I'll make us some tea, too."

Though she still looked to be in shock, Jennifer stood up. She was shaking but she stepped forward.

Though his heart wanted to do this later, Dylan's training kicked in. "Hey, Jen, before you go up. Tell me again what you noticed."

She nodded. "I got in the car. But as soon as I sat down I realized that I hadn't had to unlock the door. And you know I always lock the car. Always."

He nodded, well aware that both Shannon and Traci were listening to her account as well. "And then?"

"I was about to put on my seat belt, going over it again. It didn't make sense, but I started thinking that maybe I didn't click the lock hard enough because my hands were full or something."

"Makes sense."

She released a ragged sigh. "I thought so, too . . . until I saw that note. And then it all came together. I've been feeling like someone's been watching me the last couple of days. I'd told myself that it was just a natural reaction, on account that I'm finally going places by myself. And I thought I saw one of the men . . ."

"When was this?"

Traci stepped closer. "Get a handle on this, boss."

He clenched his hands but tried to contain himself. "Sorry."

"Dylan, what would you have done if I said that I thought I saw him? You know how scared I was. You would have thought

I was seeing things. I thought I was seeing things." She looked at Traci. "But seeing that note, I realized that I haven't been." Tears filled her eyes again. "I don't know what to do."

"Carpenter's coming," Traci said to him. "Hey, Shannon, you and Kimber help get Jennifer inside, 'kay?"

"Sure."

"One last thing, Jen. Did you touch that note? Did you open it?"

She shuddered. "No. No way was I going to touch it."

So, they had a chance for fingerprints. At least they had that.

After Shannon had escorted Jennifer inside, Traci spoke. "You're going to have to help me connect the dots when you can."

"I will. I just can't believe it's not over."

"What do you need me to do? Take the lead? Run interference?"

Honestly, he wanted her to do both everything and nothing at all. He wanted to be in charge of the case and walk away from any responsibility. Hell, a part of him wanted to turn around, go into Shannon's loft and simply eat a slice of pie.

Anything but open this case and risk hurting his sister again.

Then his discipline kicked in. He needed to stop wishing for what wasn't going to happen and concentrate on doing his job. "Let's go ahead and take this one step at a time." Gazing at the envelope with his sister's name on it, he added, "This might not even be connected."

"All right, then." She started toward Carpenter. "I'll fill in Mike and grab some gloves for both of us."

"Thanks."

Five minutes later, Mike Carpenter was taking pictures and he and Traci had on gloves. He opened the back passenger-side door and she picked up the note. "Ready to see what's inside?" she asked.

He could only nod.

Pulling out a Swiss Army knife, she popped out the small blade and slit the top of the envelope. After glancing at Mike, she pulled out the thin slip of paper and unfolded it.

Dylan noticed right away that there were only a couple of words on the paper. They were scribbled in the center and said everything he needed to know.

Reading the words again, he felt a chill settle into the center of his chest.

Jennifer had been right. This wasn't over. Not even close.

CHAPTER 17

"Dare, dream, dance, smile, and sing loudly! And have faith that love is an unstoppable force."
—SUZANNE BROCKMANN

It had been over an hour since Shannon had escorted Jennifer inside and had taken her upstairs, where Kimber had been waiting. Kimber had been watching what had been going on from their living room window, so she'd jumped in right away.

She'd started talking a mile a minute while she served Jennifer a slice of pie and put the kettle on to boil.

Shannon had been impressed. Kimber was by far the most reclusive and quiet of the three of them. Shannon knew she wasn't social by nature and could spend hours by herself simply reading a book.

But now she had a window on this new facet of her sister's personality. There was a reason Kimber was such a successful model, and it wasn't just her looks. It seemed that the girl could fake happiness with the best of them. She was as warm and chatty as a favorite grandmother. It was obvious that Jennifer wasn't sure how to react to that.

For her part, Shannon realized she was torn between concern for Jennifer and for her brother. Then there was the new, lingering interest in Traci's job. She hadn't ever seen Traci in her full cop mode and was curious about how she interacted in that role.

She finally opted for simply sipping tea and trying to make a soothing environment for Jennifer.

After they had a cup of tea, the three of them walked over to the couch. "Want to watch one of those home improvement shows?" she asked, sensing that Jennifer simply needed something mindless to focus on.

"Sure," Jennifer replied.

Kimber looked at her strangely, but sat on the couch, too, a hardcover library book on her lap.

Shannon turned on a show featuring a small-town couple down in Mississippi. They remodeled old houses for people who came back to their town. As she watched them tear down, scrape, and rebuild the house, she couldn't help but reflect that the work on those houses was an awful lot like what they'd all been doing. Repairing damage, trying to make something beautiful out of something that had been damaged and worn by abuse or neglect.

She was about to mention that, when she realized that Kimber had gone to her room and that Jennifer was sound asleep.

When she heard footsteps climb the stairs, she stood up and smiled at Traci and Dylan.

After seeing that Jennifer was asleep, Traci murmured to her that she was going to take a shower.

Which left Shannon and Dylan alone. He looked as exhausted as Traci had. And as stressed as Shannon.

He walked to her side. "Everything go okay?"

"Yep. We watched a home show on HGTV. Jennifer fell asleep about halfway through the episode."

"That's probably a good thing." Looking exhausted, he ran a hand through his hair. "What a night."

"How about something to eat?"

"Really?" He shifted to face her. "Are you sure you don't want us to leave?"

She didn't at all. She wanted to sit with Dylan, try to help him if she could . . . and yes, she would love to know what was going on. "Why don't you let your sister sleep?" she asked easily. "I mean, unless you want to go home right now."

"Honestly, I don't think I want to leave this room."

"Then come eat some supper."

He followed her obediently, like a small boy anxious for a treat. First, she heated up a portion of the casserole and set it in front of him alone with a big glass of sweet tea. After he started eating, she cleaned up a few dishes, then sliced a generous portion of pie and put it on the table.

When she noticed that he'd already drained his glass, she decided that they both needed something stronger than another cup of hot tea, she pulled out a couple of beers and opened them both.

He grinned and lightly tapped the top of his bottle with hers. "I knew I liked you."

"I don't know how well Coors goes with lemon meringue pie, but I thought you might appreciate it."

"It goes great." He finished his slice in five bites and then leaned back and took a long sip of his drink.

"Better?"

"You know? Yeah. I got busy at the station and lost track of time. I hadn't eaten since around eleven this morning."

"Oh, Dylan."

He shrugged, like it didn't matter. "No big deal."

Sitting down next to him, she said, "So . . ."

He smiled tiredly. "So, I'm not sure what's going to happen now, but I think this moment is excellent. Thanks for this."

"Anytime." And yes, she meant that. She was starting to hope that they would have a lot of moments like this. Well, the supper together after a long day, not after a crisis with his sister.

He took another sip. "I'm just sorry that we couldn't have our lesson."

She laughed. "I almost believe you mean that."

"You should. And I'm not just talking about the bet, either. There's something about dancing with you that helps me. I like that . . . for a little while I'm not thinking about anything other than that I need to count steps, remember to lead you around a room, and not step on your toes."

"I know what you mean. Dancing is good for your brain."

"We'll have to make it up soon."

Now realizing that he needed to take his mind off everything, she stood up. "You know, if you want, we could go downstairs and dance a little bit now."

He grinned. "Seriously?"

She winked. "I don't joke about dancing, Officer Lange."

"I'm not sure how good I'll be . . ."

"I wouldn't even count it as a lesson. I mean, not unless you wanted me to," she said quickly, just in case she had misread his cues. "We could dance for fun."

"For fun," he repeated. He dragged the word out, then slid a look at his sister.

Shannon felt a little burst of pleasure, knowing that he was slowly becoming a fan of dancing, too. "I could let Traci and Kimber know that we were downstairs, so if Jennifer woke up, you wouldn't have to worry about her getting scared."

A smile played on his mouth as he stood up. "All right . . . but I'm not doing anything crazy. No salsa lesson."

"I'll put on a pretty song and we'll just rumba, Dylan. Nothing crazy."

"Let's go, then. But I think I'm going to need another beer."

"Get two and meet me downstairs. I'm going to go fill in my sisters."

As he walked to the refrigerator, she peeked in Kimber's room. Traci was sitting in Kimber's incredibly comfortable blue velvet chair in the corner looking at magazines. Kimber was painting her toenails. Both looked up at her in surprise.

"Jennifer is sound asleep," Shannon said.

Traci winced. "Poor thing."

"I know. I feel so sorry for her. Anyway, Dylan doesn't want to leave her here, and we both thought it would be a shame to wake her up right now."

"It would be a real shame," Kimber said, her voice way too sweet.

Shannon knew she was undoubtedly blushing by now. "Anyway, um, we were talking. I mean, Dylan and I decided that it would be a real shame to not take advantage of our time together."

"You're right," Traci said with a nod. "You two should put it to good use."

She shifted her weight and tried to look serious. "What I'm trying to tell y'all is that he and I are going to be downstairs dancing, so if you could check on Jennifer and get us if she wakes up, I'd appreciate it."

"Don't worry. We'll look after her," Kimber assured her.

"Promise," Traci said with a nod.

Feeling a little embarrassed but excited, Shannon picked up the heels she'd slipped off earlier and quietly walked down the stairs.

Jennifer was asleep, Dylan did need his lesson, and she was too keyed up to simply sit and stare at the television.

All of those were really good reasons. True ones, too.

However, all she seemed to be able to think about was that she had a blond-haired and blue-eyed hunky cop downstairs waiting for her.

And for the first time—maybe even the first time ever—she was going to ballroom dance with a man just because she wanted to, not because he was paying her or because she had an upcoming competition to practice for.

Ignoring her racing pulse, she headed downstairs.

CHAPTER 18

"When I have bad days, I just eat lots of chocolate ice cream and dance to the 'Lion King' soundtrack. It's really odd, but it's true."
—BLAKE LIVELY

"Now, don't forget, Dylan," Shannon warned. "It's *slow*, step, step. *Slow*, step, step." She drew out the word *slow* two beats before adding a quick *step-step*.

She'd put on "Lovesong" by Adele, Dylan was holding her right hand with his left and encircling her waist with his right. Once again she was wearing a pretty dress and heels. Her brown hair was down and her brown eyes were bright and highlighted with a coat of black mascara. And, yes, she smelled good. A combination of roses and cinnamon. He hadn't known such a scent existed but now he knew he'd never forget it.

"Dylan, are you okay?"

"Hmm? Oh, yeah." He smiled down at her. "Sorry. I was just thinking about something else."

Her lips, so pretty and plump, pursed. "I'm so sorry. I bet this is one more thing to do in a really long day."

"It's not. Dancing with you doesn't seem like a chore to me at all." As Adele's perfect voice continued to float around them, he grinned down at her. "Let's rumba."

She rolled her eyes, then whispered her *slow, step-step* chant. He stumbled a bit, then his muscles seemed to pick it up like he'd been rumbaing all his life.

Shannon lifted her chin and smiled broadly. "Good job! You're getting it."

Feeling braver, he turned her a bit. Sure, it was clumsy, but she scooted closer and made it seem so easy. And then, just like that, all the stress that he'd been feeling that week—the snowstorm, Jennifer's rescue, even his new partner's idiosyncrasies, they all faded away.

Now, all he was thinking about was not losing his footing and how good she felt next to him.

"Ready to do a twirl?" she whispered.

"I'm ready to do whatever you want."

Her eyes widened. "Huh?"

He needed to focus. At least a little bit. "I mean, sure."

The line in between her brows smoothed again. "Okay, slow, step-step, release, step-step, take my hand, step-step." When she was back in place, she looked up at him and smiled. "Good job."

"Thanks, baby." Yep, the endearment had slipped out without him thinking about it.

Her smile faltered a bit but she didn't correct him. Instead, when a new song came on, she stepped a little closer and murmured the correct counts again.

Once again, his body automatically adjusted to hers, moving in sync. It was innocent, nothing too intense. But there was now an underlying tension simmering between them.

"Hey, Shannon?"

"Hmm?"

"Is it always like this with your students?"

Her eyebrows inched together. "Like what?"

"These lessons. Are they always so easy?" Of course, he wanted to say *so perfect.* Maybe *so intimate* . . . or *so good*?

She looked confused. "Hmm. Well, sometimes. But not often." She paused as he turned her again. Then, when they were facing each other, she smiled up at him. "Actually, most lessons don't feel like this."

"What do you think is the difference? My athletic prowess?" he teased.

"More like our chemistry," she said with a smile before counting off a turn again.

After he got her settled again, he murmured, "I'm glad you felt it too. I mean, you do, right?"

"Oh yes. I mean, I did. I do."

"Hmm."

She looked flustered as a Jason Mraz song began. After they did a turn around the room, this time dancing so close his hand was in the center of her back instead of politely curved around her waist, she pulled away abruptly. "You know what? That's probably enough for now."

"I'm sorry. Did I get too close?"

"No. It's just . . . well, I'm sure you're ready to get on home."

Okay. So that was how she wanted to handle things. Like they weren't really happening. When he almost reached out to her, he stuffed his hands in his pockets. "Yeah, it's been a really long day. I need a shower."

"I'm ready to put on a pair of sweats and a thick pair of socks."

"I bet." He ran a hand through is hair. "I'll go wake up Jennifer and we'll get out of your way."

She winced. "I can't believe it, but I had forgotten about her!" She looked at the clock on the wall. "It's only been a little over an hour. That's not a very good nap at all."

"She'll be all right." He knew from experience that he was going to be able to pick her up, carry her to his car, get her home, and put her into her bed without her hardly waking up. When she slept after a traumatic experience like she'd had, like this, she slept like the dead.

Shannon looked down the hall with a worried expression. "How about you let her spend the night?"

"I couldn't let you do that."

"All I'd be doing is giving her a place to sleep. When she wakes up in the morning, she can drive home, or one of us can take her."

It was tempting to take Shannon up on that. Jennifer had been a wreck—and deservedly so.

He was a wreck even thinking of one of those guys who he'd put in prison getting let out and now stalking her.

But what if she woke up and got upset? Jennifer would suffer for that . . . and so would Shannon. It wasn't easy dealing with a victim of a violent crime. Even when everything inside him kept reminding himself that Jennifer was healing, her panic attacks were difficult to watch and always made him feel completely useless.

"Shannon, there's a chance that she's going to wake up and get upset."

"We'll be here, though. I can sit with her."

"I appreciate that, but she may get agitated." Jennifer wasn't a child, of course. But her panic and pain was hard to watch. He didn't want to inadvertently make Shannon deal with something she wasn't ready for.

But she brushed aside his worries. "If that happens, I'll talk to her. And, if that doesn't work, I'll call you and you can talk her through it. Or, even come get her," she said reasonably.

"You've got an answer for everything, don't you?"

Her expression softened. "No, but I don't want you to think y'all are alone here. I want to help."

He didn't need to rely on his five years' experience in the force to know that she was being sincere. But more than that, he knew that tonight they'd made a shift in their relationship. Shannon Murphy wasn't just his dance teacher or just his partner's sister. She was important to him. "I appreciate that."

"So?" Shannon tilted her head to one side.

He couldn't help but notice the way her hair slid down her shoulder. It looked like silk. He wondered how soft it was. Yep, he was staring at Shannon like he was fascinated . . . and maybe he was.

But he also needed to trust her . . . and trust Jennifer. His sister was right—she did need him from time to time, but she had made a lot of progress. He needed to respect that. "Let me go check on Jen."

She was sprawled on the couch, one of her legs halfway off. Shannon frowned. "Let's move her into my room."

"Are you sure?" He hated to kick Shannon out of her own bed.

"Positive. It's going to be okay, Dylan."

Realizing that his worry wasn't helping anyone, he scooped up his sister.

She opened one eye. "Dylan? What's going on?"

"Moving you to a bed. Go back to sleep, everything's okay." When Jennifer's eyes drifted closed again, he looked at Shannon. "She's good. Lead the way." Shannon led him down the narrow hallway and opened the door.

Seconds later, Jennifer was on her side with a thick, soft blanket tucked around her body. Her shoes were off and she was still sound asleep. It was obvious that she wasn't going to wake up anytime soon. The night had really done a number on her.

Motioning to Shannon, he walked back out of the room.

She closed the door behind her.

"Where will you sleep?" he asked as they started down the stairs.

"With one of my sisters."

"They won't mind?"

"No." She smiled softly at him when they reached the main floor entryway. "Dylan, you're giving new meaning to the phrase 'protective older brother'."

"You might be right." He sighed. "All right, then. I guess I'll go." He pulled on his jacket and knit hat, double-checking that he had his keys and his phone with him.

"Be careful driving home."

He smiled at her. "I might be a worried older brother but you're kind of turning into a worried dance teacher."

Her eyes sparkled. "Maybe we all worry about people we care about."

Her answer hit close to home. The truth was that he did care about Shannon . . . and he was glad she cared about him, too.

Somewhere in between football bets and this moment, something had changed. There was something real between them now. Something that he couldn't wait to explore further.

Reaching out, he took hold of the tips of her fingers. "Thanks again. I'll see you soon."

"Good night, Dylan," she replied softly. Then turned and closed the door behind her.

He waited almost a full minute before he got back into his car. For some reason, even though it was cold and snowy, he felt warmer than he had in a long time.

Maybe even years.

CHAPTER 19

"It's not about the shoes.
It's what you do in them."
—MICHAEL JORDAN

The sound of her phone ringing woke Jennifer up. It actually wasn't a ring, it was a tinny version of Pharrell Williams's "Happy." A few months ago she decided to try to make everything in her life a little bit more optimistic.

As she listened to the familiar, peppy beat, she blinked and reached for her phone but drew up short when there wasn't a phone on her bedside table.

Or even a bedside table.

Jarred awake, she sat up abruptly and tried to get her bearings. When she saw a series of framed prints of dancers in various poses with inspirational phrases above them, she exhaled.

She was at the dance studio. Luckily, she remembered the

girls sharing how their bedrooms were on the top floor and that they lived a bit like they were in a college dorm.

By the looks of things, she was in Shannon's room.

Then, like a sledgehammer, the previous night's events hit her hard. The snow, the unlocked car. The envelope. The note inside. The way she'd fallen asleep on the couch and had been vaguely aware of Dylan carrying her to Shannon's room. The realization that the nightmare she'd thought was over was instead alive and well. Finally, the tears and the feeling that she was as helpless as ever. Always a victim.

That feeling was so harsh and acidic, her stomach clenched. She surged to her feet, afraid she was going to lose the contents of her stomach on Shannon's bed.

Realizing how close she was to dissolving into tears yet again, Jennifer clenched her hands.

She had to get it together. Had to.

She'd *just* gotten stronger. There was no way she was going back to that dark place. It was ugly and filled with dangerous thoughts.

She'd lost *so much* because of the attack. So had her parents. So had Dylan. They'd all lost the shine on the world and the thought that darkness would never touch them. Now she realized that not only was she not ready to go back to that place, she wasn't ready to take her family there, either.

She made a decision. Slipping her shoes back on, she decided that now she was going to have to face whatever happened next head-on. This was going to be the last time she hid from the world and dissolved into despair.

After splashing cold water on her face and swishing a bit of toothpaste around her teeth with a finger, Jennifer picked up her purse, which someone must have brought into Shannon's room, then made her way downstairs at last.

Her steps slowed when she saw that Shannon was sitting at her pretty desk near the entrance. She was wearing buff-colored leggings, an ivory fisherman's sweater, and dark-brown designer boots, the kind that Jennifer had only ever seen in a magazine before. Her hair was perfectly styled, and she had on light makeup. In short, she looked polished and pretty, while Jennifer had swollen eyes, kinky hair, and was wearing yesterday's clothes.

But, no matter, it was time to move forward. "Hi, Shannon."

She looked up and smiled. "Hey. You're up."

Jennifer nodded. "Yes. I'm so sorry. I not only took over your room, you weren't even able to get in there to get your clothes."

Shannon shook her head. "I'm so much shorter than Traci and Kimber, I'd drown in their clothes. I actually tip-toed into my bedroom about an hour ago and grabbed something of my own."

That was a surprise. Usually, the slightest noise woke her up. "Boy, I must have been really sleeping hard."

"I think you were, which is a good thing, right?" She smiled kindly as she got to her feet. "How about a cup of coffee? And don't say no. I promise, it's great," she continued in that light, chatty manner. "Kimber, Traci, and I might not be able to cook worth a darn, but all three of us are practically baristas."

Shannon looked so sincere, Jennifer couldn't help but take her up on the offer. "Thanks."

Looking pleased, Shannon clicked a couple of buttons on the thin computer on her desk. "Come on back upstairs. I don't know if you saw it, but our little kitchenette is at the far end of the hall."

As Jennifer climbed the stairs again, she said, "This is sure an interesting situation. Do you like living together?"

"Oh, yes. Well, I mean, I do. But it's new. I'm pretty sure you know about our situation, right?"

"Your situation?"

"About how I only just found out about Kimber and Traci a couple of months ago? I grew up as an only child, you see."

"Wow. That's, um, really something."

"I know! And please, you don't need to try to act like you're not shocked. My sisters and I haven't mastered that, have we, Kimber?" she asked as they walked into a really cute kitchen decorated all in white.

Traci wasn't around, but Kimber was sitting at a small bistro table eating two oranges and sipping black coffee. "Good morning," she said. "How are you doing, Jennifer?"

"I'm okay." Not eager to start talking about last night's events, she said, "Uh, Shannon was just telling me about how you guys just discovered each other."

Kimber nodded. "Amazing how life happens when you least expect it."

"You're right. I guess change can be good, though."

"This change has been very good, though every once in a while I wake up feeling confused. Bridgeport, Ohio, is a big change from New York City."

"I bet."

Shannon pulled out a pair of mugs. "We came for coffee."

"You're in luck. I just made a fresh pot."

"How do you take your coffee?" Shannon asked, still playing hostess.

"Cream and sugar, please," Jennifer said.

Shannon winked. "A girl after my own heart." After she added a generous amount of both, she placed the cup in front of Jennifer.

Jennifer took an experimental sip, sighed in appreciation, and then took another drink. Shannon hadn't lied. They might not be able to cook worth a darn, but they could sure make a mean cup of coffee.

Shannon, who was holding her own mug with two hands, smiled over the brim. "I told you. We've got a way with caffeine."

"This is great."

"We use really good beans and spoonfuls of cinnamon and cocoa," Kimber said. "They add just enough extra flavor to make things better."

"I'll have to remember that."

Kimber stretched out her long legs. "Just come over more often, girl. Anytime you want, I'll be glad to share my coffee with you."

Jennifer smiled and leaned back in her chair. It was amazing how much she was starting to relax. Here, in less than twenty minutes, she'd gone from embarrassed and scared to actually imagining sitting with these women again one day soon.

As if she sensed what Jennifer was thinking, Shannon said, "So, are you doing better now?"

"Honestly? Yes. And what's sad is that I wouldn't have thought it was possible."

"I don't think that's sad at all. What's happened to you would freak anyone out, honey," Kimber said.

Hesitantly, she said, "I don't know what Dylan shared, but I was pretty freaked out for years after my attack. Last night, when I saw that note? Well, it sent me back to that place. I really didn't want to return there, either."

"I don't blame you," Shannon said. "Not for going through such a dark time or being afraid to go back to that place."

"I don't know if this will help, but I have realized that going through bad stuff doesn't necessarily make things better . . . but it is inevitable," Kimber added. "All you can do is get through it."

"I'm trying." Jennifer took another fortifying sip, then added, "Actually, that's what I decided when I got up. I am going to try to do my best to not think the worst. My brother is a great cop, and the men and women on his team are, too. They'll figure this out."

"Good for you," Shannon said. "I know Traci was eager to help him when she left on her shift this morning."

"I wish I could do more to help."

"I think the best thing you can do is continue to get better," Shannon said.

"That's what I am going to do." Making up her mind, Jennifer said, "This probably sounds like nothing to you both, but I'm going to do my best to summon my nerve and go back to Backdoor Books."

"What's that?" Kimber asked.

"An amazing bookstore. It has everything you can imagine inside." Hearing her words, she smiled. "I mean, as far as books go."

Shannon raised her eyebrows. "You must really like books."

"I do. Well, I really like cookbooks. But it's more than that. There was the nicest lady there who owns the place. She serves coffee and tea in china teacups and never acts like you're imposing if you take your time looking around. And then there's her son."

"She's got a little boy?" Shannon smiled.

"Oh, no. He's our age. And he's so . . ." Jennifer caught herself just in time. Boy, she couldn't believe she almost started fangirling on that guy.

Kimber's light brown eyes sparkled as she leaned forward. "Come on. Don't stop now. Her son is so . . . what? Cute? Hot?" She smiled. "Amazing?"

Maybe embarrassment was overrated. "He's so . . . dreamy," she corrected. "His name is Jack."

"Jack's a good name," Shannon said.

"I thought so, too."

"When are you going to go back to this place?" Kimber asked. "I want to see him."

Shannon chuckled. "You can't go over there to ogle the owner's son."

"Sure I can."

"I'm not even sure he's going to be there. He doesn't work for his mom. He's a contractor."

"Oh, a manly man." Kimber playfully waved a hand in front of her face. "He's sounding better and better."

"Kimber, you are too much," Shannon said.

"Honey, if you've seen all the pretty boys that I have on these modeling shoots, you'd be excited to be around men who don't mind working for a living. Don't underestimate a handy man."

"Noted."

Jennifer was enjoying the sisters' teasing and their silly conversation. She really was. But as she looked at the two women—petite Shannon, with her dancer's figure and sweet personality, and Kimber, so glamorous and so gorgeous—her insecurities caught hold of her tight again.

Even though she didn't have a relationship with Jack, there was still a part of her that didn't want him to catch sight of these women. How could she not pale next to them? She had an extra twenty pounds, a scar on her cheek. Oh, and had a dozen hang-ups.

"So, want to go over there today?"

"Today?"

"Sure? Why not? I don't have a class scheduled until two o'clock, and the roads are fine. It would be nice to get out."

"I can do anything. My time is my own right now," Kimber said. "I'd love to check out this place. I'm a huge reader."

"That's really nice of both of you." Really nice, especially since she'd pretty much ruined their evening last night.

"We want to go," Shannon said as her voice gentled. "Hey, I know you're probably still shaken up from that note, but it might do you good to get your mind off of it."

Shannon had a good point. She also realized that she wanted

to be around these women some more. They were so nice, they made her feel like she didn't have to be alone anymore. Somehow, their friendliness was making her even feel like she could live her life even if things were happening that were out of her control.

"That would be nice."

"Sure it would," Kimber said.

Just as she started thinking about how much fun that would be, she looked down at herself. She had on yesterday's clothes. She'd slept in them, too. Plus, there was no telling what her hair and face looked like. Her eyes felt gritty since she'd slept in her contacts. "I can't go over there until I get cleaned up at home."

Kimber nodded like that made perfect sense. "How about you go home and get ready, and then we'll run by your house and pick you up in an hour? Is that enough time?"

"More than enough."

Kimber looked at her sister. "What about you, Shannon?"

"I can leave in an hour, no prob. Jennifer, we have a plan."

"Thanks, guys."

After saying goodbye, she walked out to her car and got in without a bit of fear. She really was doing better.

She was making friends, they were going to pick her up at her house and then all go to the bookstore not twelve hours after she had been sure she wasn't going to be able to leave the safety of a locked and alarmed house for days.

Six months ago, she wouldn't have believed such a thing was possible. God was so good.

CHAPTER 20

"If you stumble, make sit part of your dance."

You're doing WHAT?

Dylan had texted her three times that morning. The first time Shannon had gotten a message from him, she'd felt a little thrill, loving the idea that she was on his mind. He'd certainly been on her's. Dancing with him last night had been so special. It had been everything she'd ever dreamed about back when she'd first started ballroom dancing lessons in high school. Back then, she'd been sure that one day she would get to have the thrill of twirling around in a handsome man's arms. Unfortunately, that hope had faded when she'd come to realize that competitive ballroom dancing was anything but romantic. It had been stressful and exhausting. The pleasure she'd gotten from the sport had been because she and her partner had scored well or won a trophy . . . not because she'd been swept away in his arms.

But now, as she continued to receive Dylan's texts, it was becoming obvious that her warm thoughts had been one-sided. The reality was that Dylan was simply worried about his sister.

Of course. Anyone would be.

She'd texted him right back, relaying that Jennifer was still asleep but that she'd let him know when she got up. That text was followed by a quick message that said Jennifer seemed to be doing okay and that she was drinking coffee.

But as soon as she conveyed their new mission—to get Jennifer back out and about—she'd received the text she was currently staring at.

Her finger hovered over her phone's screen, debating how to respond. She didn't want to make him nervous, but she also didn't want to betray Jennifer. Not that Jennifer had asked her to keep a secret or anything . . . but Shannon was fairly certain that there was a girl code to follow, even when one was almost thirty. That code included not tattling to a girl's older brother about plans he might not agree with.

She decided to reply back with something simple.

Don't worry. Kimber and I will go with.

He replied back immediately.

That is supposed to make me feel better?

Absolutely. She went home to change. We're picking her up in 45.

You're going to my house?

She smiled. They might be both worried about Jennifer's health and emotional stability, but she couldn't deny that there was something kind of playful in their exchange. Especially since he seemed a little alarmed by her seeing his house without him there.

Taking a chance, she texted something a little more flirty.

I hope you picked up your underwear off the floor.

The moment she pressed SEND, she bit her lip. Maybe that didn't sound flirty at all. Maybe it was more in *creepy* territory.

Thirty seconds later, he texted back.

Does that mean you're going to inspect my bedroom?

Okay. He didn't sound mad. Grinning, she wrote back.

Maybe

"What has got you so smiley?" Kimber asked.

"I've been texting Dylan."

"Really?"

"Oh, yes," she replied before realizing how goofy she sounded. When Kimber gave her a look, Shannon attempted to sound like a grown woman instead of a love-struck teenager. "Dylan has been worried about Jennifer. I've been reassuring him."

"I bet."

Okay, so she wasn't fooling either herself or her sister. But that didn't really matter. She was having fun. When her phone buzzed again, signaling another incoming text, she said, "I'm ready when you are."

"Give me ten and I'll meet you at the door."

"Perfect." The minute Kimber left the room, Shannon looked at her screen again.

Stay out of my bedroom, Shannon Murphy.

I will! I was just teasing.

You know the only time I want you to see it is when I'm with you.

And . . . they had just ventured into new territory.

Feeling her cheeks burn, she let her finger hover over the screen, then wrote him back.

Don't worry about Jennifer. We'll look after her.

She breathed a sigh of relief when he didn't say a word about that.

* * *

Thirty minutes later, a breathless Jennifer met them at her door. "I'm so sorry. I'm not quite ready."

"Don't apologize. We're in no hurry," Kimber said.

"Come on in. I won't be more than five more minutes."

"Even if it's ten, that's fine. Take your time," Shannon replied. Actually, she was looking forward to seeing where Dylan lived. The minute they were alone, Shannon exchanged a look with Kimber. The interior of the house was so different than what she'd envisioned.

Shannon realized she'd been expecting something kind of bare, or maybe even more of a basic *guy's* place, with everything decorated in "bachelor"—old leather furniture and a giant television mounted on the wall.

Instead, it was a modern showplace. All the furniture was dark wood or metal. The walls were white and the floors were either covered in thick planks of dark wood or creamy carpet.

"Whoa," Kimber murmured as she walked into the living room, obviously focusing on the stone fireplace on the far wall. It was a gas fireplace and it was so tempting to flip a switch and sink into one of the beige suede couches arranged in front of it. "This place is gorgeous. Are you starting to get the feeling that we just walked into a photo spread for *Architectural Digest* magazine?"

Shannon had never thumbed through the pages of *Architectural Digest* in her life, but it sounded fancy enough to do this room justice. "I'm not sure about that, but I sure am impressed. Boy, I bet Jennifer thought my bedroom was really shabby."

"Let's go look at the kitchen."

Sure enough, it didn't disappoint. The floor was red brick and the appliances were stainless steel. There were black granite countertops and a wide butcher block–topped island. "Wow,"

Shannon murmured as she ran a hand along the smooth, cool countertop. "*I'd* even try to cook in a kitchen like this."

Kimber chuckled. "Jennifer would probably beg us not to touch even one of those fancy pots hanging from the ceiling."

Kimber was right. Those pots and pans didn't look cheap. "No doubt." She sat down on one of the black leather stools next to the island. "I wonder what Jennifer makes every night."

Kimber sat down next to her. "I don't think I want to know. I'd just be jealous and hungrier than I already am."

"Hello?" Jennifer called out.

"We're in here," Shannon said as she jumped to her feet.

When Jennifer joined them again, she had on thick black leggings, high leather boots, and a dark-gray tunic-length turtleneck sweater. Her hair was pulled into a complicated knot at the back of her neck. She also had on red lipstick and her glasses, which Shannon thought looked really cute on her.

"Wow, look at you," Shannon said. "You look amazing."

"I doubt that. I'm just hoping that I don't look like I need a long shower and a four-hour nap."

"Jack won't be thinking that at all," Kimber said. "Your glasses are cool, girl."

Jennifer grinned. "Thanks. I couldn't bear to put my contacts back in."

Kimber was still sitting on her barstool. "So, we were just sitting here, admiring your beautiful house."

"Thanks, but most of the credit goes to my brother. He's a pretty handy guy and did a lot of the work on this place himself. All I did was upgrade his kitchen a little bit."

"It's amazing," Kimber said.

"So, are you ready?" Shannon asked.

"Yep . . . if you're *sure* you don't have anything better to do?"

"We're sure. Stop worrying."

"Yes, ma'am," Jennifer teased as she locked her front door and followed them to Shannon's car. Just as they we're getting in, she said, "So, I got the strangest call from my brother."

"Oh? What did he say?"

"He told me not to bring you into his bedroom, Shannon. Do you have any idea why he would have told me such a thing?"

"I was teasing him about Kimber and me seeing his laundry on the floor," she said as they got in the car.

"Ah."

Behind her, Shannon could hear Kimber trying not to laugh.

As she drove down the street, Jennifer was grinning. "I'm beginning to think there's more to that conversation than I want to know."

"You would be right about that."

They talked about books and cookbooks and the conditions of the snowy roads and how all of them were impressed with Traci's job.

"You three are all so different," Jennifer said.

"We are, but as we're getting to know each other better, we've started to realize that we're not as different as each of us thought," Kimber said. "For example, I'm no cop, but I am scrappy."

"You? You probably weigh a hundred and ten pounds wet."

"That has nothing to do with it. I grew up in New York City. I'm scrappy as all get-out."

Shannon rolled her eyes. "Way to sound like a country girl with a New York accent, Kimber."

"My point is that I'm awesome to have in a fight. I don't back down."

Jennifer, who'd been turned around to face Kimber, looked like a believer. "Good to know. So, um, how are you like your sisters, Shannon?" she asked.

Shannon had to think about that. Suddenly, it came to her.

She wasn't exactly scrappy, but she did have something they had in spades. "I'm as stubborn as they are. When I want something, I dig my heels in."

"She's loyal, too," Kimber said. "If not for Shannon's prodding and pushing and telling me and Traci that she loved us all the time, I doubt we'd have moved here."

"That's so sweet," Jennifer said.

"It was. Shannon Murphy is a tiny thing with a big heart."

"We all have big hearts, Kimber," Shannon retorted. "We might each express ourselves differently, but I think we're more the same than we are different."

Kimber nodded. "You know what, I'm starting to think you're right about that."

Shannon let that thought settle in as she continued the drive. The snowstorm yesterday had cleared, and while it wasn't exactly blue skies, it was clear.

"Y'all, I'm really glad we did this. Maybe we could get lunch or something when we're done."

"I'm in," Kimber said.

Jennifer nodded. "Me, too."

Ten minutes later she parked in the lot just to the south of the shop. Just as she was buttoning up her coat, she received a new text from Dylan.

If you wait, I can rearrange my schedule and go with.

No need. We're already here.

His response was quick and to the point.

Jen okay?

She's fine. Stop worrying. We're at the bookstore, not cruising back alleys in downtown Cincy.

Ha-ha. Call if you need something.

She didn't know a lot, but she absolutely knew Jennifer wasn't going to want her brother around when she saw this mysterious Jack again.

I will. bye.

"Shannon, get off your phone!" Kimber said.

"I'm trying," she said as her phone buzzed yet again.

Wait.

This was almost too much fun.

Sorry. Can't. We're here and the girls are mad I'm texting so much.

When her phone started ringing, she glanced to make sure it was Dylan. When she realized it actually was, she promptly ignored it. She was beginning to think that this little trip with Jennifer was also good for Dylan and her.

"Did he finally decide to leave you alone?" Jennifer asked.

"Yes. He's really protective of you."

"He is, but I don't think I'm the only reason that he's been texting you."

"Maybe not, I don't know." Suddenly realizing that she might have overstepped herself, she said, "Hey, I wasn't even thinking. Would you like him to stop by? I can call him and ask him to join us after all."

"No. No, don't do that." Jennifer kind of wrinkled her nose. "This is good for me."

"You sure?"

"It might even be good for both of us, if you want to know the truth. I've gotten too used to being afraid of everything and Dylan's gotten too used to taking care of everything for me. I decided the other night that no matter what happens, I need to move forward."

"For what it's worth, I'm really impressed," Shannon said, and she was.

"Don't be. We've all got something, right?"

"I suppose," she said as they started walking toward the bookstore's entrance. When they neared the door, she noticed that Jennifer seemed more tense. "You okay?"

"I'm fine."

Shannon exchanged looks with Kimber. Jennifer wasn't fine at all, but if she wanted to play it that way, she supposed she could go with it. That decision made, the three of them entered the shop, ready for anything.

CHAPTER 21

"Life may not be the party we hoped for, but while we're here we may as well dance."
—JEANNE C. STEIN

"So, what do you know about these guys?" Traci asked Dylan. They were sitting at their desks in the main room at the precinct, which faced each other. They'd just finished their first meeting and got the latest reports and ongoing investigations from the lieutenant.

While two other officers went out to do patrol, Dylan had gotten permission to make some calls about the letter Jennifer received.

Now, thinking about Traci's question, he struggled to keep his composure. There was a deep part of him that just about lost it every time he even thought about the two guys who were convicted and sentenced for attacking Jennifer.

"One guy was a thug. He had a list of petty crimes and

warnings, and by the time he attacked my sister he'd served a year for a class-two burglary. The other one? He was part of a third-rate motorcycle gang and high on some crap. When we dug deeper, we uncovered a charge against him for sexual assault that had later been dropped."

"So they were scum."

Dylan didn't even bother responding. As far as he was concerned, they were worse than that. It was difficult, but he continued. "Their DNA was on her. After we tracked them down and picked them up, things went relatively smoothly. They got sentenced to five to ten."

"It's only been two years, though, right?"

"Yeah. Two years and change. They're still inside. I texted a buddy of mine late last night just to make sure."

"So . . ."

"There was a third guy."

"And he's who we're worried about."

"Yep. It's in the report, but Jennifer—whenever she does talk about it, which is pretty much never—doesn't usually mention him."

"Why not?"

"I guess he was just lurking and keeping watch. He was there but didn't put his hands on Jen. Not that she remembers, anyway." With effort, he tried to pull the emotion out of the explanation. "He was acting as their lookout."

She frowned. "I'm trying really hard not to say anything to make you angrier."

"I promise that's not possible. Anyway, this guy, this Lance, was only sixteen and looked like he was about thirteen when the DA was making his case. Since he hadn't actually touched Jennifer, he wasn't given much more than a slap on his hand—just a couple of months in juvie. I think that's who has been following my sister around."

"What do you want to do?"

He grimaced, hating that in order to be the man he needed to be he couldn't do what he ached to do, which was to find the guy and beat the crap out of him. "Let's go for a drive and see what we can find out."

"I'm game. Where do you have in mind?"

"It just so happens that Lance's parents live in Bridgeport."

She smiled as she held up the day's reports, signifying things they should be looking for. "That suits me. We'll take a visit, and while we're at it, I'll keep an eye out for anything on the lieutenant's list."

"Sounds like a plan."

Fifteen minutes later they were on their way. Traci was driving and Dylan was riding shotgun. She'd raised her eyebrows when he asked if she wanted to drive, but honestly, he wasn't one of those guys who insisted on always being behind the wheel. Today, especially, his mind was so full of details and memories that he was afraid he wouldn't have the reflexes he would need if they came across something.

Instead, he looked out the window, reported their destination to the dispatcher, and gave Traci the directions.

She pulled in front of a nondescript house in the heart of one of the largest subdivisions in town. "This is it?"

"Yep." He unbuckled his seat belt and took a deep breath. He needed to control himself and keep it together. He needed to remind himself that Lance having been the one to leave the note was only a hunch. It was a good one, but it wasn't based on evidence or facts.

Traci had unbuckled but was still staring up the house. "I'm just going to say it. This place surprises me."

"Why? Did you expect us to pull into a run-down trailer park or something?"

She shrugged. "Maybe. Probably."

He gave her a sideways look. "What's on your mind, Lucky? Maybe that it looks like the house you grew up in?"

"Uh, no." She glanced at him and quirked a brow. "You know I didn't grow up in a place half as nice as this, right?"

"I don't know much about you besides your service record, and that you didn't know about your sisters until recently."

"The three of us were separated when we were real young. Shannon and I were toddlers and Kimber was just a newborn."

"Separated by whom?"

"By the adoption agency, I guess. Back then, I guess they didn't think there was anything wrong with separating siblings."

"I know Shannon grew up in a small town in West Virginia."

"She did." Looking straight ahead, Traci added. "Kimber was adopted by a couple up in New York. I was never adopted. I grew up in a group home in Cleveland."

He knew enough that he was able to read between the lines. "That sucks."

'Yeah." She shook her head. "Sorry. I didn't mean to run us down memory lane. Let's go pay a visit to Mr. and Mrs. . . . ?"

"Wengard."

She nodded and then got out and slipped her cell phone into a pocket. He did the same and led the way up the walkway, looking around the yard as he did.

Everything seemed quiet. Not abandoned, but definitely not a lot of life. Two lights shone through the windows. One on the bottom floor in what looked like the living room. One upstairs in what was probably a bedroom. Those were sure signs that they were out of town.

Still . . . he could be wrong.

He knocked. Listened for movement. When he didn't hear anything, he knocked again.

After another minute went by, Traci looked his way. "Seems pretty quiet."

"Yeah. I was thinking the same thing."

"I'm going to take a walk around the back."

He nodded, stepping back to see what the neighbors were doing. The woman to the right looked to be watching television. The house on the other side looked quiet, but from the looks of the sports equipment on the lawn and in the driveway, it was a foregone conclusion that the kids were at school and their parents were at work.

Traci came back. "Nothing to see back there. Blinds were down. Porch needs shoveling."

"I looked at the neighbors' houses. Nothing much to see there, either. I'm guessing everyone's at school and work.

"Want to do you want to do?"

That simple question meant a lot to him. Even though Traci likely had plenty of her own reports to type up and other work to do, she was willing to put it aside for his needs. Here she was, pretty much telling him that she'd sit and stake out the property, knock on doors, do whatever he wanted. That kind of generosity in a department was rare.

He didn't want to take advantage of it, especially since they were only visiting the Wengard's place on a hunch. "Come on. Let's move on."

"All right . . . Do you want to drive now?"

"Nah. You go ahead."

She smiled at him, obviously pleased about that. "How about we visit a couple of parks?"

He laughed. "Sure." He was partial to visiting the public areas around Bridgeport a couple times a week. If a teenager was in trouble, he or she might be hanging around there. Sometimes he might even find an older person walking or sitting by themselves. He liked taking a minute to talk to folks. It was good small-town police work. Bridgeport officers were a part of the community, and the citizens appreciated them.

He believed these interactions were important, and they were. Just like a lot of other police departments, Bridgeport's motto was Protect and Serve, and he saw that as looking out for the people in small ways, too.

But Traci? Well, it was obvious she was still getting the hang of not being busy every minute of the day. Sometimes he felt the need to remind her that just because they weren't dealing with homicides, impaired drivers, and lots of domestic violence cases didn't mean their work wasn't important.

She pulled out onto the street and drove along slowly. "Freedom Park first?"

"Sure. It's right around the corner."

"I remember."

Just as he was about to ask how she was feeling, getting used to the slower pace, she spoke again. "So, I'm just going to say it. I think Shannon likes you."

Well, that little tidbit came out of nowhere. Ignoring the burst of happiness that ran through him at the news, he spoke carefully. "She told you that?"

"Not in so many words. She and I might not be super close yet, we're close enough for me to see the way she looks at you."

"And?"

"And it's affectionate. Maybe more like longing." She drew to a stop, flipped on her turn signal, and then made a right. "I think you need to take her out on a real date."

Glad he wasn't driving, he gaped at her. When she smiled, he coughed. "Are you pulling my leg?"

"No, sir, I am not." She pulled into the park. It was going on eleven thirty, overcast, and about thirty-eight degrees. The park was empty. "Want me to drive to the back?"

"Yeah." He scanned the area, hoping that they wouldn't see anyone. And, luckily, they didn't.

After Traci made a loop, she pulled out onto the street. "Palmer Park now?"

"Yep."

Just as she was turning left, a white Chevy pickup truck zipped by, going easily thirty miles over the speed limit.

"Yee-haw," Traci said with a grin. She turned on the siren and picked up speed. While she tailed the truck, Dylan pulled out the computer to enter in the plates.

Dylan shook his head in dismay, but he couldn't really disagree with the way she felt. Pulling over speeders was far easier to deal with than the ghosts that were pulling at him over Jennifer's attack.

When the pickup pulled over and they noticed that the driver was a kid who looked to be about sixteen, Traci grinned. "Looks like somebody might be loving his new driver's license just a little bit too much."

When Dylan noticed the boy had just rested his forehead on his steering wheel, he inwardly groaned. Tears and drama might be on the way.

Traci opened her door. "I'll be back."

"Go get 'em, tiger. But don't forget that you are in Bridgeport not inner-city Cleveland. Kid gloves, remember?"

She waggled her fingers. "I've got 'em on," she said as she headed toward the truck.

Deciding to join her at last, he almost smiled when he approached. Officer Traci Lucky had affected a perfect stance of all business and motherly manner while she was giving him what-for for speeding. The kid looked contrite and nervous but not scared stiff. All in all, the exchange seemed to be going as well as it could.

Dylan made a mental note to praise her for that when they

went to lunch later. A lot of cops from the big city never seemed to be able to find the right way of talking with the suburban residents of Bridgeport. Traci wasn't one of them.

Lots of things in his life were up in the air, but this new partnership? He couldn't have asked for anyone better.

CHAPTER 22

"Dancers have a very hard job. We must take our ugly, callused, blistered, and bruised feet and present them in a way so that they are mistaken as the most beautiful things on Earth."

As she headed up to the third floor of Backdoor Books, Jennifer felt a little self-conscious. She knew she was avoiding everyone, but she preferred to look at it as taking a moment to care for herself. Shannon and Kimber were nice, and their hearts were huge. She couldn't think of another pair of women willing to drop everything in order to give someone they hardly knew a few minutes of happiness.

So she was grateful to them. She really was. But her mind was in such a mess, she knew she needed a few minutes of silence or she was going to lose the last bit of composure she was clinging to.

The best way to find that was in the middle of a stack of cookbooks.

Sitting down in the chair she'd occupied just a couple of days earlier, she picked up a *Joy of Cooking* hardcover and placed it on her lap. The book was serving as her makeshift security blanket, and that was pretty sad.

What was she ever going to do with herself? When was she ever going to be normal again? Was it ever possible to be normal when one was the victim of a violent attack?

The patter of steps brought her attention to the doorway—and to Harvard. The German shepherd puppy peeked around the stacks of books, spied her, and then approached with a fierce tail wag.

She laughed as he scrambled closer, his four big paws practically tripping over each other. "Hey, buddy. Where's your owner?"

The puppy just wagged its tail again.

She leaned down and gave him another pet, then laughed when he artlessly attempted to nudge her book and hands out of the way so he could sit on her lap. Unable to resist, she did as he requested. The cookbook went back to its place. Next thing she knew, she was holding the pup in her arms, cuddling him close and inhaling that wonderful puppy smell.

Harvard wiggled with pleasure, making her chuckle.

Huh, maybe the cure for the blues wasn't a stack of cookbooks but a warm, affectionate puppy.

"Harvard? Harvard, where are you, buddy?"

When Harvard just gave her another lick on her face, she answered. "He's up here with me. In the cookbook stacks."

After she heard a couple of heavy steps on the wooden staircase, Jack appeared, looking just as gorgeous as he had the first time she'd seen him.

"Hey," he said. "Looks like you've got some company."

"I do," she said smiling at the dog. "Harvard found me."

"I can see he found your lap," he said as he strode forward. "Sorry. German shepherds are usually pretty independent dogs, but not this one. I don't know if it's because he's a mix and not a purebred, but he's as cuddly as some kind of fluffy lap dog."

"I think he's perfect." She ran a hand down Harvard's side, silently coaxing him to stay a little bit longer. After Harvard peeked at Jack, he snuggled closer to her.

Jack grinned. But instead of coaxing the pup down, Jack pulled out a chair next to her. "Would it be bad to say that I'm kind of glad he found you for me?"

"You were looking for me?"

"I got here about ten minutes ago. Mom waved me over and introduced me to your friends. They, of course, became fans of Harvard here."

"Of course." Jennifer smiled at him, loving how much he loved his dog.

Jack looked down at his thick work boots before meeting her eyes again. "Anyway, it took me a minute to put it all together. But after I realized that they were friends with you, I started trying to think of a way to ask them where you were without sounding completely rude. Or, um, stalker-like." Looking pleased, he added, "My buddy Harvard here solved that problem."

He'd been thinking about her! Hoping she didn't look as excited by this information as she felt, Jennifer kept her attention on the dog. "Well, Harvard is a pretty smart pup."

"He is, since he found you." Studying her closely, Jack said, "So, how are you doing?"

She guessed he was still thinking of her freak-out last week. "Hmm. Well, I've been better, but worse, too. So, I guess that means I'm all right. How's that for an answer?"

"Good enough." He pulled out one of the chairs and sat down. "Do you get those anxiety attacks a lot?"

"They come and go." Hearing her counselor's voice in her ear, she continued. "They're a lot better than how they used to be, which is a good thing."

"I know we hardly know each other, but I'm great at listening. Do you want to talk about it?"

Did she want to share that she'd been beaten and raped two years ago and just last night had received a note from one of the men who'd been there watching? That seeing that note in the back of her car had done such a number on her that she'd practically gone into shock?

Uh, no. No, she did not. "There's nothing really to say."

"Sure?"

"Positive." Reaching for Harvard, she ran her fingers along the scruff on his neck. "So, how are you?"

"Me? Oh, I'm good." He kicked out one denim-covered leg. "I've been working at a job site just three blocks away all morning. I came to check on my mom and then was going to grab some chili for lunch."

"Sounds good. It's cold out."

He groaned. "It's miserable and about to snow again."

"Winter."

"Yeah." He looked at her another second, then said, "Hey, how about I take you to lunch?"

"Really?" To her surprise, she was actually thinking about it. Lunch with a cute guy like Jack sounded so much better than sitting in her empty house reliving the last twenty-four hours.

"There's a Skyline Chili Parlor just a mile away, over on Snider. We could grab some lunch, and then I'll bring you back here. I'll need to take Harvard home first, but that won't take long. What do you say?"

Just as she was about to say yes, she remembered that Shannon and Kimber had picked her up. "I'm sorry. I just remembered that I didn't drive here. If I left, I wouldn't have a way to get back home."

"You just live in Bridgeport, right?" After she nodded, Jack said, "I could drop you home. It wouldn't take but a minute."

That didn't sound quite as easy. But . . . wasn't it time to do a little bit of trusting? She'd trusted Shannon and Kimber enough to go to this store with them.

Jack offered a charming smile. "What do you think, Jennifer? Ready to do something besides chat in my mother's bookshop?"

Jennifer couldn't help smiling back. He had a puppy who was a sweetheart. He checked on his mother. And even though he'd met both Shannon and Kimber the model, he'd still asked *her* to lunch.

After putting Harvard down, she stood up. "You know what? I'd love to go to lunch. Thanks."

"Thank you, Jennifer. You made my day." Bending down, he clipped a red leash to Harvard's collar. "Let's go, then. I'm starving. Are you?"

"You know what? I am. I just realized I never ate breakfast."

"I'd say this was perfect timing, then. A lunch date meant to be."

His words echoed in the passage as he led her down the stairs.

CHAPTER 23

"A star danced, and under that I was born."
—WILLIAM SHAKESPEARE, *MUCH ADO ABOUT NOTHING*

"What do you think about that?" Kimber asked as Shannon pulled out of the Backdoor Books parking lot.

Shannon laughed as she paused for traffic before pulling out. "Think about what? The fact that I just bought eighty dollars' worth of books that I hadn't budgeted for . . . or that our girl Jennifer just went on a lunch date when we were supposed to be babysitting her?"

"All of it." Kimber waved a hand. "Well, not the book-buying part. I knew I'd buy too many books the moment we stepped through the door. That's a great bookstore."

"I liked it a lot, too. It's got the best selection of romances and mysteries. And that Camille is a peach. She was so personable and made some good recommendations, too."

"What do you think Dylan is going to say about our visit?"

"I don't know." Though she feared he was going to freak out on her. Dylan really did provide a perfect example of an overprotective brother. Frowning at the light snow that had just started to fall, she continued, "I half thought that I should call him and give him a heads-up that we were taking Jennifer out, but it really isn't my place."

"It sure isn't."

"That said, I have a feeling he's not going to be happy about Jennifer going on a lunch date with Jack."

"I thought the same thing," Kimber said.

"Do you think I should call him about that?"

"Nope. Nobody is going to be happy if you decide to interfere like that. Jennifer will get mad at you for tattling on her, and Dylan will get pissed because you didn't stop them."

Shannon could see that happening. "You're right. I'm just going to keep my mouth shut. It wasn't like Jennifer asked for my opinion anyway." That was the truth and did give her some reassurance.

"I'd be surprised if she even remembered that you were in that building." Kimber gave her a sideways look. "Jennifer Lange wasn't thinking you, doll."

"You aren't wrong about that. The girl only had eyes for Jack."

"It was romantic." Kimber stretched her hands over a knee. "That guy was a hunk, and he looked like he'd just won the lotto when he walked her out the door."

"He really did, didn't he?"

"And then there was his mom," Kimber said, her voice still soft and dreamy sounding. "She looked like she was about to cry, she was so happy her son found himself a good woman."

"Hold on, now. You're making it sound like they're on their way to the altar. They're going to eat chili."

"I know. But there's something there. I know it."

Even though the snow had returned, the roads were clear and traffic was light. As they headed back toward the heart of Bridgeport, Shannon sneaked a glance at her sister. "Kimber, I had no idea you were such a romantic."

She looked affronted. "I'm not."

"Really?"

"All right," she added after a slight hesitation. "I kind of am."

Those answers hinted that there was a story there. "Have you ever been in love?"

Kimber stayed quiet for a moment, then said, "Almost."

"I knew it! When?"

"When I was just a kid. In high school."

When Kimber didn't add another detail, Shannon groaned. "Come on. You can't just leave me hanging like that."

"Calm down. It's not that exciting."

"Come on, Kimber. Give me a bone. What happened? Who was it? How long did y'all date?"

"Uh-oh. Your drawl is back."

"I'm excited. And you're hedging."

Kimber chuckled low. "Maybe I am, I don't know. I'm sure your relationships back in the day were just as filled with drama."

"They might have been, if I'd had a boyfriend in high school."

"Wait. You didn't?"

"Nope, not a one. I was too busy trying to be a famous dancer." A thought occurred to her as they drew up to the front of Dance with Me. "Wait, weren't you working all the time? I thought you started modeling when you were a little girl."

"Oh, no. I didn't start that until the middle of my senior year. Before that, I was all about trying to fit in and spend time with Tyler."

Shannon couldn't help but grin. Kimber probably didn't

realize it but even now her voice softened when she said his name. "Tyler, huh?"

Kimber rested against the headrest. "Oh, honey. He was so fine. He was the running back on the football team, and he played basketball, too."

"He sounds athletic."

"Oh, he was all that." She crossed her legs. "But more than all the sports, there was something more important that I couldn't shy away from."

"Which was?" Shannon was fully invested now.

"Tyler thought I was amazing." Kimber kind of sighed under her breath. "That counted more than anything to me."

Shannon couldn't believe that Kimber sounded so insecure. "But you are, Kimber." She not only was beautiful, she was fun, and she uprooted her whole fancy New York life to live in a run-down loft in southern Ohio.

"I didn't feel that way. I was constantly trying to figure out why my parents weren't all about me. I knew I was adopted, of course, but half the time they kind of acted like they wished they'd picked a different baby."

"I'm sure that isn't true." She really hoped not, anyway.

"Probably not, but I was a disappointment. They had goals, and I didn't meet them. I know that to be true."

"Oh, Kimber."

"Hey, now. It's time to redirect this conversation. I sure didn't want to go down that road. My point is that I had Tyler, and for a time, we were in love."

"And then you weren't?"

"And then . . . he found somebody else to love."

"Ouch," Shannon said as she parked the car.

"Yeah. I'm not gonna lie. That hurt . . . Bad." She sighed. "I swear I was the last to know. One minute I was feeling like Tyler and I were so tight we were going to plan a whole future together. Then, next thing I knew? Tyler had found Madison, and I was yesterday's bacon."

"Guys are pigs."

"Not all of them, but that boy sure hurt me bad," Kimber said as they unlocked the front door and entered the warm building.

Turning on a couple of lights, Shannon said, "I bet one day you'll meet a man worthy of you."

Kimber shrugged. "Honestly, I don't know if it really matters. I found two sisters. I'll take that."

Putting down her purse and her bag of books, Shannon let herself really take a good look around her new home. There was their Addams Family couch in the entryway. Her pretty desk in the corner of her dance studio. A stairway with carved spindles that Traci had polished the other night when she'd been bored.

Suddenly, it didn't seem like it was worn out and too small. Instead, it looked like home. Like a place to be thankful for.

"I'm glad I found you, Kimber."

Kimber leaned over and kissed Shannon's cheek. "You and me both, sister. Now, let's get inside and make some decent coffee."

As she followed Kimber up the stairs to their very fine coffee maker, she took a moment and looked up.

"Thanks," she said softly.

She didn't hear a reply, but she didn't need one. She'd had so many prayers answered already.

CHAPTER 24

"Our feet are planted in the real world, but we dance with angels and ghosts."
—JOHN CAMERON MITCHELL

By the time they'd gone four blocks, Jennifer knew that going with Jack was a mistake. It wasn't anything that he'd done, the problem lay with her. As much as she wanted to be better, she knew she still had a ways to go. The enclosed space, the feeling that she wouldn't be able to escape easily, even the sense that he was expecting something from her scratched at her nerves.

She began to feel clammy and a little ill.

When Jack pulled to a stop in front of a very pretty house near the river, she was silently giving herself a stern pep talk. She could do this. She just had to stop letting her imagination get the best of her.

As if he could tell that she wasn't doing well, Jack glanced at her warily before walking to the back seat to let the puppy out. "I need to put Harvard inside and give him some food. Do you want to come inside with me or stay out here?"

She wasn't ready to be alone with him in his house. "I'll just stay out here. The falling snow is so pretty."

He looked at snowflakes covering his windshield with a doubtful expression. "All right. I won't be long. But if you change your mind—"

"If I change my mind or get cold, I'll come inside. I promise."

"I'll stop worrying about you then. I'll be out in five minutes or so." He snapped his fingers. "Come on, Harvard."

The pup loped off the seat and onto the driveway, wagging his tail at his owner. Jack bent down and rubbed the puppy's head, then laughed when Harvard yipped.

As the puppy scampered around Jack's feet, gazing up at him with adoring eyes, Jennifer crossed her arms over her chest, loving how cute the two of them were together.

But then, right in front of them, Harvard stopped, spotted a fluffy gray rabbit at the tree line, and did an about-face and started running toward the woods.

Seconds later, he was gone.

"Harvard!" Jack yelled. "Harvard, come back here."

Jennifer got out of his truck. "Want me to help?" She scanned the area but couldn't see a thing.

Looking back at her, he shook his head. "You won't get too far with those leather flats. Might as well stay dry." With a curse, Jack started running. "I'm sorry. I've got to find him."

"Of course you do. Um, I'll wait around here in case he circles back."

"Thanks!" he called out before disappearing into the woods.

Jennifer craned her neck, hoping to hear either Jack or the rustle of leaves, signaling that Harvard had lost his quest for that rabbit.

After a couple of more minutes, she didn't hear anything from where Jack had disappeared. But she was pretty sure she spied a glimpse of the pup in the opposite direction. After hesitating a moment, she ran that way into the woods.

After she'd gone about thirty or forty feet, she heard a puppy-sized growl.

"Harvard?" she called, walking deeper into the woods. Her shoes were sliding on the snow, but they'd dry. "Harvard?" she called again. From the corner of her eye she spied him.

"Here, pup!" She picked up her pace, snagged the side of her coat on some brambles.

Harvard barked again. It actually sounded chipper . . . like he had discovered a new game—chase in the snow. Deciding she was committed, Jennifer ran after him again as the snow started to come down even harder.

Maybe five minutes had passed. Maybe only two. Maybe it had been fifteen.

Whatever the span of time, she noticed a couple of things. She was very alone, the mini German shepherd was nowhere in sight . . . and she was hopelessly lost.

Her feet were frozen, the rest of her was pretty darn cold, too, and the wind had picked up. Oh. And she had no purse or cell phone. She'd left those right by Jack's vehicle.

The only good news was that she wasn't frightened. She wasn't hiding, she was trying to help find a puppy. And, though she was in a patch of woods, it couldn't last forever—they were in Montgomery, not in the middle of the country.

She also wasn't upset about being alone. Amazing how two years of being basically afraid to see other people made a girl no longer fear walking by herself.

Yes, she'd learned that there were far worse things in life than that.

* * *

Thirty minutes later, the sky had darkened. She'd also managed to sprain her ankle slipping on a patch of ice. Jennifer knew she needed to seek shelter. The snow was getting worse, her ankle was throbbing, and she was getting tired.

She also knew from having a policeman brother that people were easier to find when they stayed put.

Though she still kept an eye out for Harvard, Jennifer also started looking for someplace to wait out the storm. She really hoped she would find that spot sooner than later.

* * *

"Hey, Dylan?" Traci asked as she approached his desk.

"What's going on?" he asked, not bothering to look up. He was typing up the last of his report about the stop they'd made at a senior citizen's home that afternoon. Once again, he wished he could not only type better but faster instead of hunting and pecking on the keyboard.

"You need to stop and listen to me."

Traci's voice sounded off. Warily, he looked up.

When he saw the expression on her face, he knew that something was seriously wrong. Had there been an accident? A fire?

Getting to his feet, he said, "What happened?"

"It's Jennifer."

"What about her?" he asked slowly. Only by reminding himself that she was with Shannon and her sister kept him from jumping out of his skin.

"Well, Shannon just called me. She's missing."

"She?" he asked, though it really wasn't a question. He was just attempting to not freak out.

"I'm talking about Jennifer, buddy. Jennifer is missing."

And just like that, his whole being went into high alert.

"Why'd she call you instead of me? And what is my sister doing missing?" Not even waiting for an answer, he fumbled for his cell phone.

Maybe Shannon had called him and he'd been so focused on that report that he hadn't heard anything?

But as he stared at the screen, realizing that Shannon hadn't even tried to call him, a dozen dark thoughts filled his head. Just as he started pressing apps on his screen, Traci put a hand on his arm.

"Hey, stop for a second."

"No. I've got to call her."

"Who? Jennifer or Shannon?"

"Jennifer. And then Shannon," he said impatiently. "Why are you asking me? Does it really matter?"

"I think so. You need to calm down and listen to me before you go off half-cocked."

Only Traci's reputation encouraged him to put down his cell and face her. "Fine. What do you know?"

"She left Backdoor Books with Jack Patterson at a quarter to twelve."

"No." No way would she have done that.

Traci ignored his protest. "Jack drove Jennifer directly to his house." She paused, flipped a page in her notebook, and recited the address.

"Why did he take her there?" Already imagining the worst, he blurted, "Did he—"

"Listen to me, Lange."

Her command pulled him back. That was hard to do, but he nodded. "I'm listening."

"Shannon said that Jennifer had looked excited. Like she

was proud of herself for overcoming her fears. She said that Jack looked like he was willing to take things real slow, too. I guess when they stopped by his house so he could put his dog inside, Jennifer had switched gears. She was looking stressed and had chosen to stay outside and wait for him."

"And?"

"And that's where the story gets hazy. Jack told Shannon that he hadn't put the puppy on a lead. He was going to let it do its business and then take him inside . . ."

"But?"

"But just as it was sniffing around, the dog saw a rabbit and took off into the woods. Jack started running. He vaguely recalls Jennifer offering to help, but he told her to stay warm.

"Then?"

"Then, maybe about five minutes later, just when he was about to give up, Harvard came running toward him," Traci relayed. "But when Jack got back to his house, Jennifer wasn't there."

"He was sure about that?"

"Sounds like it," Traci said. "From what Shannon told me, Jack said Jennifer wasn't standing on the driveway, not waiting in the vehicle, where it was warmer, not walking around the yard. She was gone."

She was gone. Three words that meant anything could have happened. Remembering the scene that had greeted him two years ago, of Jennifer hurt and broken on the ground, he felt sick to his stomach. This was his worst nightmare returning.

This Jack guy could have hurt her. Or, whoever had left that note could have snatched her. Or, she could have run off, or a neighbor could have done something.

Anything could have happened.

Grabbing his coat and a hat, he started walking. "Oh my God, Traci."

Pure sympathy filled her eyes. "I know, but you need to calm down."

"This is my sister, and she has issues." Even imagining how scared and freaked out she had to be practically made tears form in his eyes.

"I hear you, Dylan. I really do," she murmured as she kept pace. "But you need to get ahold of yourself. This might not be the worst-case scenario that you're thinking of."

Maybe there was a part of his brain that heard her and agreed, but if it was there, he couldn't access it. No, all he could do was react and remember. "I need to talk to Sergeant—"

"I've done that. He's on board and is ready to call out for additional help if it's needed," she said patiently. "We can take off now."

After taking two steps, he stared at her. "I don't remember what address you told me."

"I've got it. I already called Jack and told him to stay tight," she said as they exited the building and strode out to their cruiser.

"He better hope to God he doesn't move a muscle." Just as he was about to go to the driver's seat, Traci stepped in front of him.

"Nope. I'm driving."

He paused, prepared to arguc, then dropped the idea. It didn't matter who drove, and she was probably right. He was feeling so off-kilter he wasn't in any mind-set to drive.

But he was sure as hell ready to ask Shannon why she couldn't have looked after his sister.

He started dialing her number just as Traci sped down Main Street.

CHAPTER 25

"You dance love, and you dance joy, and you dance dreams. And I know if I can make you smile by jumping over a couple of couches or running through a rainstorm, then I'll be very glad to be a song and dance man."
—GENE KELLY

So, she was lost. Like, really lost. And, of course, it started snowing. When the wind picked up and her toes started to burn, she knew she needed to find some shelter. Wandering around in the woods was a bad decision.

"Please, God. Help me out, would you? I know my faith has been pretty faulty lately, but I'm trying to get better. And even though I know You don't bargain with people, I promise if You help me out, I'll try to do a lot better."

She took a breath, thinking that as far as prayers went, that one was pretty lame.

Just as she was about to sound more faithful and maybe a lot more needy and desperate, she spied an old deer blind.

It had to be several decades old, from back in the day when

Bridgeport was only about a fourth of the size and the outskirts were either county property or one of the ranchers' big plots of land.

At the moment, though, she decided she couldn't care less about why it was there. All that mattered was that it was.

Walking to the ladder, she pressed her palm against the first rung, thinking that a little test of its strength would be a good idea.

So far, so good, though. The rung didn't budge. She looked up. It was pretty high up there, and there was a good chance that some critter could have taken refuge inside it, too.

Just then a gust of wind carrying a handful of snow hit her face.

Sure, it might have been a coincidence or simply the elements getting the best of her. But given the way things were, Jennifer decided it was a sign from God to stop standing around and take advantage of the shelter He'd provided.

"I hear you," she murmured, stepping up onto the bottom rung, then slowly climbing up the rest of them. Putting weight on her sprained ankle hurt like crazy, but she ignored the pain and continued on.

When the eighth rung broke in half under her weight, she grabbed hold of the edge of the blind and pulled herself in. The first thing she noticed was that thc wood might bc old and that it had chinks in between the slats, but it was also a whole lot more sound than it looked. The old tarp that someone had left covering one of the top corners prevented the snow from falling on her head.

It was a struggle, but when she was sitting in the center of an empty—and thankfully critter-free—deer blind, Jennifer realized two things. She was now blissfully protected from the worst of the wind. And it was going to be really hard to get back down.

She curled herself into a ball and decided to sit tight. It wasn't a great option, but it wasn't the worst one.

But even though she was sitting in the corner in a ball, she couldn't help but kind of raise her hands in triumph. Like Rocky. She was cold and lost and irritated at herself for getting so lost. But she wasn't afraid.

As far as successes went, this was a big one. Maybe, just maybe, she was going to be okay one day. Maybe she was going to stop being afraid of things going wrong and start remembering that life wasn't about being safe, it was about living.

Perhaps she'd even remember this day and her prayers and how God had provided. Or at the very least, she'd remember this day because she had remained calm throughout this storm.

Boy, she liked that idea. Liked that after two years of being frozen in the past, she had actually made progress. Go, her!

She closed her eyes and smiled. And for the first time in twenty-four hours, relaxed. When Dylan saw her and heard her story, he was going to be so proud.

And so was she.

* * *

Shannon picked up the call the second Dylan's name flashed on the screen. "Dylan, oh, thank goodness!" she blurted before he even had a second to say hello. "I've been so worried. Is Jennifer okay?"

"What the hell were you thinking?"

"I'm sorry?"

"You heard me."

His voice was so hard, she was taken off guard. His tone didn't sound like him at all—nothing like the sweet guy who'd held her in his arms and danced with her last night.

After taking a second to recover from her shock, she said, "I have no idea what you're talking about. How about we try this again? How are you? How is Jennifer?"

But he ignored every one of her efforts to ease him up. "You know I didn't want her going anywhere but home, but you insisted on taking her out to some bookstore. And then you couldn't even follow through? You just let her go off with some random guy?"

With a random guy? "I think you are mistaken about what happened. See—"

"You know what? I don't even want to hear it. You had better hope that we find Jennifer soon and that she's okay. If she even has a scratch, I'm going to hold you accountable."

She'd never had anyone talk to her like this before. Her hand started shaking. "Dylan, wait. You need to listen to me—"

"Do you have anything to say that might help me find her?" he bit out. "Anything of worth?"

Anything of worth. All the things she'd been about to tell him now sounded trite.

What could she tell him? The truth was that she really didn't know either his sister or the man she left with. She'd known Jennifer had received a creepy note and had been so scared that she'd been afraid to get out of her car.

Maybe Shannon was accountable, at least to a small extent.

And he sounded furious. Like he hated her.

She knew he was with Traci. Now that she thought of it, when she'd told Traci about Jack's panicked phone call, her sister hadn't said much. What if she hated her too?

What if they both blamed her for Jennifer going missing? And what if something really bad had happened to Dylan's sister? What would happen then?

"Do you?" he asked, sounding even more impatient.

"No," she said at last, feeling even worse. "I don't have any additional information to give you. Though, I'd love to help."

"Help do what?"

He sounded so mean! "I . . . I could help look for Jennifer," she sputtered. "I'm sure Kimber would want to help, too. Where are you? I could meet y'all."

"Don't bother. I think you've done enough."

Those tears, the ones that she'd been trying so hard to hold at bay, filled her eyes. "I see," she whispered. "Well, if you could let me know what happens, I'd really appreciated it."

Then she realized that she was talking to air. He'd hung up on her.

Staring at the blank screen of her cell phone, she tossed it on her bed.

She'd really messed up, at least it seemed she had. Suddenly, all she could seem to do was replay his terrible words over and over in her head and compare it to those last months of her dancing career. Back when she'd gotten all the way to nationals and then realized that while she might have been "all that" in Spartan, West Virginia, she didn't have anything on those East Coast girls. She hadn't even come close.

She wasn't as polished, didn't have the dresses and costumes they did, didn't have their connections, and certainly didn't have their confidence. She'd felt like the most naive fool around.

Then, when one of the judges had made a pass at her in a dark hallway, she'd been so shocked and embarrassed, she hadn't told a soul. But it had settled and stewed deep inside her. She'd gone out on the floor to perform, had taken one look at the judge, and completely forgot everything.

In the span of three minutes, she'd ruined five years of hard work and put to waste thousands of dollars that her parents had forked out for that dream.

The crowd had been stunned. Her coach had been full of questions. The other girls had smirked, and she'd hung her head in shame. And her parents? Oh, they'd been so disappointed in her.

It had been the lowest point in her life—even worse than discovering that she'd had sisters that no one had told her about—because that moment, that failure in front of all those people, had felt like her fault.

Even though she'd been a kid, and she knew it was the judge's fault and not hers, she had *felt* responsible.

And that was exactly the same way she felt now. Like she'd been accosted for no reason and she was being left to flounder and find excuses when there really weren't any to give.

"Shannon?" Kimber rapped lightly on the door. "Hey, Shan?"

She pulled open the door. "Yes?"

"I talked to Traci a couple of minutes ago," she said, her worried expression surely mirroring her own. "Have you talked to her?"

"I did. She called me right before Dylan did."

"He called you, too?" Hope shined in her eyes. "Did he have any news?"

"No."

Kimber blinked. "Oh. Well, listen, I told Traci that we'd be happy to help. She said she'd get back to us, but if they can't find her soon, they might start forming a search party. What do you think? Are you up for it?"

"I'm up for it, but I don't think Dylan would want me to be there."

"What are you talking about?"

"As you can imagine, he's pretty worried." He was angry at her, too, but Shannon didn't want to share that with Kimber yet.

"I bet he's worried out of his mind. But I tell you what, I think we need to think positive."

"Positive? How?"

"There's always a chance that everybody's getting all riled up for no reason." She shrugged. "Maybe Jennifer just decided to go hang out at the movies or something." She blinked. "Or . . . she got an Uber home and is taking a nap. Now, wouldn't that be something?"

She chuckled, though she reckoned it sounded as dry and forced as it felt. "It surely would."

"Hey, what's going on? You're really taking this hard, aren't you? Chin up, now. It'll be okay."

Shannon nodded. Part of her wanted to share what Dylan said to her, but it hurt too much. And, perhaps, she couldn't bring herself to say it because she knew his words might have been close to the truth. Then, for some reason, she felt protective over her new siblings. She didn't want to cause things to be worse or cause them pain. "I guess I'm just rattled," she said. "I'm sure you're right."

"It's too bad we can't cook, huh?"

"Why do you say that?"

"If we could make a plate of brownies worth a darn, we could whip some up and take them over to the police station. Traci sounded so stressed, she needs chocolate."

"Chocolate?"

"Chocolate helps everything. Everyone knows that."

"For a stick-thin model, you sure think a lot about food."

"You would, too, if you'd had to deny yourself all the good stuff that I have." Her smile faltered as her call phone rang. After scanning the screen, she groaned. "Sorry, it's the photographer for the shoot. I've gotta get this."

Kimber rushed down to the hall toward her bedroom, leaving Shannon's door open in her wake.

Looking at that open door, Shannon contemplated the merits of closing it tight and curling into a ball on her bed.

Then, reality settled back in.

She had new a couple to teach to swing dance and her class of tap-dancing high school girls after that.

Even though she was worried sick and her heart was breaking, she sat down at the dressing table, pinned her hair up, and pulled out a pair of nylons and her favorite dancing shoes. It was time to do her job and do it well.

For the moment, she didn't have a choice.

CHAPTER 26

"If you believe that your best years are behind you, you've guaranteed they are; I'm going to dance into that good night, with the oldies turned up loud."
—GINA BARRECA

"Were you actually talking to my sister that way?" Traci asked as she continued to race down the street in their cruiser.

Dylan was already regretting some of his choices of words. Okay, a lot of them. But that didn't mean he regretted his anger toward Shannon. He'd trusted her with his sister, and she'd let him down.

But he wasn't going to start explaining himself to his new partner. "That call wasn't your business, Lucky."

"Uh, yeah, it was. You just reamed her a new one for no reason." She glanced his way, practically shooting daggers. "And you're my partner."

The frustration that he was barely holding in check erupted again. "We're partners, but that doesn't give you the right to start telling me what to do or how to talk to people."

She swerved around a garbage truck and honked her horn at an Oldsmobile that looked like it was about to pull out in front of them. "That's a bunch of crap, and you know it."

"Now isn't the time, Traci."

"We're stuck in a car together. I'm thinking it's a great time."

He looked at their GPS. "We're five minutes out. You need to focus and get your head together."

"Hold on. I might be new to this department, but I guarantee I have more experience than you do. I know I've seen a hell of a lot more nastiness than you can even imagine."

"So?"

"So, don't you start talking down to me, Lange." Her voice hardened. "Or is this some male-gotta-talk-down-to-the-female-cop thing and I'm just learning about it?"

"Oh, for Pete's sake. My sister is missing. After being brutally raped two years ago, she was last seen with a guy I never met. Plus, she received a threatening note from one of the men that attacked her. I'm freaking out, wondering what's happened to her. And wondering, if something has happened, how I'm going to be able to tell our parents that I wasn't able to protect her. Isn't that enough right now?"

Her lips pursed. After a second's pause, she said, "It's enough."

"Turn."

"On it." She turned the wheel sharply into a subdivision, then slowed way down. After he read her the address, she parked in front of the house. He'd already unbuckled. "Hold on. You're too emotional. Let me talk to this guy."

"No."

"Lange, stop being such a jerk and calm down. You're freaking out about way too much, and you know I'm right about this. Right?"

Maybe it was her tone, her experience, or simply that she was right, but altogether it was enough to make him calm down. And to make him realize that he was taking out his frustration on all the wrong people. "Right. Sorry."

She stiffened but didn't say anything as she opened her door and joined him outside the car.

Just as he was about to tell Traci that she could take the lead, the front door of the house opened and Jack Patterson appeared. He raised a hand in greeting.

Dylan merely stared back.

Traci, on the other hand, nodded. "Hi there. I'm Officer Lucky. We talked on the phone?"

"Yes. It's good to see you. Jack Patterson." His expression softened for a moment before looking at Dylan who was just walking up on the stoop to join them.

"I'm Dylan Lange," he said.

"All right, now that we've met. Do you want to come in and talk? It's pretty cold."

Traci stepped forward. "Lead the way."

Jack guided them into a small living room that looked like something out of a home design magazine. Just by glancing around, Dylan could tell that the area rug, television mounted on the wall, and couch were all on the high-end side. In the background he heard the faint bark of the guy's dog. "What do you do again?" he asked.

Jack stopped in front of one of the chairs. "I'm a building contractor. Mainly commercial, but every so often I work on high-end residential properties."

"It looks like it's working out for you."

He shrugged. "Well enough." After gesturing in a vague way toward the couches, Jack sat down and faced Traci. "Officer Lucky, when we talked on the phone, I told you everything I know. I'm not sure how else I can help. What can I do for you?"

"You can tell us everything one more time," Traci said.

Jack's expression turned wary. "Right. Well, like I said, I invited Jennifer to lunch, she said yes, which I was glad about."

Traci smiled, just like they were standing around the water cooler in an office building. "You really liked her, huh?"

Jack's posture relaxed. "Well, yeah. I mean, I thought I did. I don't know her."

"If you don't know her, why'd you ask her out?" Dylan asked, ignoring Traci's arched eyebrow.

"Why? Well, because I thought she was beautiful, she seemed sweet, and what I did know about her, I liked."

Though the guy's words were sweet, Dylan didn't actually trust him. "So, do you do this often?"

"Do what?"

"Ask out women you hardly know?"

"What? No!" Looking at them both, Jack inhaled sharply. "Wait, are you two interrogating me or something?"

"We're just getting information," Traci replied smoothly. "That's all. Now, getting back to what happened, you said that you drove her from the bookstore to your property in your truck?"

"No, I *did* take her from the store to here. Backdoor Books is my mother's shop. I stop over there a couple of times a week to make sure she's doing all right." He paused, as if choosing his words with care. "Anyway, Jennifer and I got to talking. She was there with two other women and seemed more relaxed than she had the last time I saw her. Since she seemed more comfortable, I figured it was a good time to ask her to grab some lunch, especially since she told me that she'd forgotten to eat breakfast. She said yes."

"And then?" Dylan asked.

Jack shrugged. "And then I did about what you'd expect. I waited for her, then grabbed my dog and walked her out to my truck. I had told her earlier that I needed to drop off Harvard before we could grab chili. She'd seemed okay with it."

Traci grinned. "Just to make sure I have everything right, Harvard is your dog's name?"

"Yes. He's a twelve-week-old German shepherd mix."

"So then . . ."

"Then I drove us over here in my truck."

It all sounded so normal. And this guy? Well, he seemed normal, too. He could see why Jennifer had unbent enough to say yes when he asked her out to lunch.

Dylan started to wonder if maybe Lance had found her or had texted her or something. He knew that might be grasping at straws, but a lot of things that were unexpected happened. "When you were driving, did she seem different or anything?" he asked.

Jack pressed his palms together and seemed to think about it for a moment. "I think maybe she did? Maybe a little bit. She got pretty quiet and seemed a little more distant. I started wondering if she was getting second thoughts. So, when I parked, I asked her if she would rather I take her home instead."

"And what did she say to that?" Traci asked.

"She said she still wanted to go out to lunch, so I didn't worry about it." Jack shot Dylan a look. "Look, I guess there are some guys who have to use tricks or something to get a date, but I'm not that guy. If she had wanted to go back home, I would've taken her, no problem."

As much as Dylan wanted to believe that the guy was lying, he didn't. He felt the same way about Jack as he had after the first time he'd seen his sister gaze at him. Jack was a decent guy. He may not be keen on his sister dating, but he believed the guy was harmless—especially after he'd run a background check on him.

Traci glanced his way, paused, and then cleared her throat. "So . . . you let the dog out of the car and it ran off?"

"Yeah." He stuffed his hands in his pockets. "He ran into the woods and I took off after him. I'm not going to lie, it kind of freaked me out. After I finally found him, I carried him back. But she was gone."

"What did you do?"

"I put Harvard in the house and started calling Jennifer's name. I walked around the outside of the house and even looked for footprints." He ran a hand through his hair. "But I didn't hear a word. She was gone."

"What did you do then?"

"Well, after I stood outside for about another ten minutes, I went in and waited."

Dylan was incredulous. "That's it?"

"Yeah. I thought maybe she went for a walk or something."

"I'm having a hard time believing that."

"Why?"

"It was snowing. Don't you think it was kind of bad weather for a lone woman to decide to go for a walk?"

"How would I know? My mother likes to go for walks in the rain. It doesn't make sense to me, but I've stopped questioning it." He took a deep breath. "Look, I'm going to be real honest here. I was freaked out, but there was a part of me that thought she called for an Uber and took off."

"Because that's what girls do thirty minutes after they say yes to a lunch date," Traci said, her voice thick with sarcasm.

"You're sounding like she was a kid or a teenager. She isn't. She has to be at least twenty-three."

"She's twenty-one," Dylan supplied. "Only twenty-one."

Jack raised his hands. "See? She's a grown woman. I don't want to sound like a jerk, but I don't think I'm the one who had a problem here."

Dylan glared. "If you didn't think there was a problem, then why did you call your mom?"

"Because after an hour I started worrying about her, so I went out and looked some more. And that's when I saw that her purse had gotten blown under one of my truck's wheels. I hadn't noticed it earlier, because it was covered in snow. That's when I realized that she hadn't Ubered anywhere." He swallowed. "I remembered that my mom had gotten Jennifer's contact information as well as the two other women's phone numbers for some book club she was starting. I got the number, and called Shannon to ask if she'd heard from Jennifer."

"And then Shannon called me because she's my sister," Traci reminded him.

Tired of talking, Dylan stood up. "Let's go do another sweep around the area. If we don't see anything, I'll call in more help."

Jack stood up as well. "I'll be happy to help you search."

"No. Stay here," Traci said as she handed him her card. "If you hear from her before we get back, call my cell."

"Let's go," Dylan said.

Still holding Traci's card, Jack walked them to his front door. "No offense, but is there a reason you seem so angry at me?"

"Jennifer is my little sister."

Jack raised his eyebrows a little nodded. "Oh, okay. I get it now. Well, if you change your mind about me giving you a hand, just let me know. I'm worried about her, too."

If the guy said anything more, Dylan missed it. All he could think about was his sister and how he'd somehow made a mistake over the last couple of months. He'd been sure she was much better, but it was starting to look like that wasn't the case at all.

CHAPTER 27

"You live as long as you dance."
—RUDOLF NUREYEV

She'd fallen asleep. That was the second thing Jennifer had become aware of. The first was that she was really cold. She could see faint splinters of sunlight slipping through the slats of the shed she was in—no, the stranger's deer blind that she'd gone inside and then fallen asleep in.

Looking out, she saw that night hadn't fallen, but it was on the way. Dylan was probably worried sick.

Feeling stiff and sore, she gingerly got to her feet, wincing when she tried to put much weight on her left foot. Looking down, her foot looked a little fat, squished into her black flat. If her foot looked that bad, her ankle was probably in real bad shape.

Leaning against the wall, she grimaced. Boy, what a mess. Her good-deed attempt had been a disaster, and now she was stuck in a broken-down deer blind.

Now it was getting dark and even colder. She was out of options. She was going to have to figure out a way to climb down and find someone to help her. Otherwise, she was going to freeze.

After clapping her hands together a couple of times in an effort to get the circulation flowing again, she put her right foot out, felt for the rung, and then started praying that it would hold her weight. Then she did the same with her left, biting her lip when sharp needles traipsed up her calf.

Then she did the process again.

By the time Jennifer reached the ground, she was panting, colder than ever, and seriously hating her cute black flats.

At least the snow had stopped.

She looked around, wished she'd thought to look out of the slats of the blind on all four sides to get her bearings. But since she hadn't, she decided to retrace her steps as best she could.

It was a slow journey, filled with a lot of stops for rest, a lot of pep talks to herself, and even more prayer.

Then, ironically, she started thinking about her recovery two years before. To say it had been difficult was an understatement. But as the days went by, she'd begun to see small slivers of hope in otherwise dark days. She'd started cooking more. She'd discovered that it was okay to be alone. She'd started journaling. She'd even begun to pray.

Each of those activities had started in small ways—her first journal attempt had consisted of one sentence.

But she hadn't given up.

She was stronger now.

Just as she was giving herself another pep talk, she spied a pair of women. "Hello?" she called out.

They turned, revealing that it was a woman in her thirties

or forties and her daughter. They looked at her curiously as she hobbled closer.

"Can you help me? I was chasing a dog and I got so lost."

The woman eyed her with sympathy. "You poor thing. You're hurt."

Jennifer nodded. "I think I hurt my ankle and my phone . . . it's . . . it's at someone's house. I don't even remember that address. Do either of you have a cell phone I can use to call my brother?"

The teenager looked at her mother. After she nodded, she handed it to Jennifer. "Here."

"Thank you so much." With the girl helping her get to the right screen, she dialed Dylan.

He answered on the first ring. "Lange."

"Dylan, it's me."

"Jennifer? Oh, thank God." He continued, barely pausing for breath, "Are you okay? Please, are you okay?"

Even though her getting lost had been an accident, shame poured through her. His voice sounded so strained. "I'm okay. It's a long story, but I ended up seeking shelter in an old deer blind. I must have fallen asleep for an hour or two."

"Where are you now?"

"I just came upon two ladies." Smiling at the teen, she added, "One of them is letting me use her phone."

She heard him murmur something to whomever he was with before he got back on the phone. "Where exactly are you now?"

"Hold on. Um, ma'am," she asked the mom, "do you know where we are?"

"Sure, honey. We're about a ten-minute walk from our house."

She couldn't believe it. She'd been that close to a house and she'd had no idea. "Did you hear that Dylan?"

"Sure did. Let me speak to her, okay?"

"Ma'am. My brother wants to talk to you. He's a cop," she explained.

The lady took the phone, obviously listened to Dylan introduce himself, and then said, "Yes. We live off of Gilbert. Yes, Gilbert Circle, right off of Columbia. Fifteen Eighty-Nine Gilbert Circle. Yes. Of course. Bye." As she handed the phone to her daughter, she said, "My name is Marianne, and this is my daughter Vanessa. We're going to walk you to our house, and your brother's going to meet us there." She smiled.

"Thank you so much. I'm Jennifer."

"It's real nice to meet you, dear. Now, how about the three of us get you over there quick?"

Jennifer laughed. "I think that sounds like a great idea."

"Me, too." Her smile got wider. "I tell you what, your brother sounded like a very worried young man."

"I'm sure he was. He's a really good brother."

"My brother is twelve," Vanessa said. "He's a pain."

"Mine was, too, at twelve. They get better," Jennifer promised as the three of them continued along.

It took longer than ten minutes—maybe double that time—but eventually they ended up on a gravel path that ended next to a driveway.

Practically the moment they arrived, a blue and white Bridgeport Police cruiser pulled up. It had barely come to a stop before Dylan climbed out of the passenger-side door. "Jennifer."

She walked right into his arms and hugged him tight. "I'm so sorry I got so lost. I'm even more sorry for worrying you."

"It's okay," he soothed, rubbing a hand down her spine. "I don't know what happened, but we'll get through it, okay?"

She turned to Marianne and Vanessa. "Here are my saviors," she said. After introducing them, Dylan shook their hands.

"I'm indebted to you," he said. "We've all been worried sick."

"We're just glad we were there to help," Marianne said.

After hugging them both and thanking them again, Jennifer limped into the back seat of the cruiser. As soon as the door closed, she leaned back and sighed. She'd done it! She was safe again.

Traci, who was behind the wheel, turned around and smiled at her. "You are a sight for sore eyes, girl."

"I'm sorry for all the trouble I caused. I can't even believe it."

"Hey, you livened up a pretty boring day. I'm glad we weren't just out and about today trying to catch speeding soccer moms."

"Speak for yourself," Dylan said with a dry laugh as he buckled up.

When Traci started heading to their house, Jennifer realized that she'd forgotten all about her purse. "Dylan, my purse is still over at Jack's."

"No, it's not. I've got it. Remind me to give it to you when we get you home."

"All right . . ." Realizing that if Dylan had her purse, he'd been at Jack's, she said, "So you went by Jack's house?"

"Oh, yeah. Traci and I talked with him for a while."

For a while. Dylan's cop-speak for interrogating him. She could only imagine how that had gone. "When I get home, I should call him and explain what happened." Boy, she bet he was really confused. The last thing he'd known was that she was going to stay in his truck. She'd be lucky if he didn't hate her for the rest of his life.

"I'm sure he has a pretty good idea by now," Dylan said.

Did he, though?

"I'm thinking you've got some time," Traci said in a teasing tone. "You were outside for a while. We need to get you home and warm."

"All right," she replied. She looked at Dylan's back. He looked tense, and no wonder. It took everything she had not to press her palms to her eyes and attempt to block everything out.

When they pulled up to the house, she and Dylan got out. Without a word, he went to the cruiser's trunk, pulled out her purse, and handed it back to her.

"Thanks. Are you coming in, too?"

"Yeah. I will for a second, but then I'm going to have to get back to the station." He leaned into the open door. "I'll be right back, Lucky."

"Take your time," Traci said, holding up her phone. "I need to look through these emails."

"Come on, Jennifer," he murmured, as he helped her walk to the door.

Feeling like a little kid, she kept her mouth shut and stood there while he unlocked the door and helped her enter.

She'd expected him to help her upstairs and convey that they'd talk later.

Instead, he closed the door and leaned against it. "So," he said.

This was awful. Though all she wanted to do was get some water, go to the bathroom, and then soak in a hot bathtub, Jennifer knew she needed to clear things up for both their sakes. Setting her purse on the floor, she said, "I guess you'd like to talk right now?"

"Yeah. We better."

She noticed that he looked both apprehensive and resigned. Neither was a welcome sign. Determined to at least sound normal, she said, "Let's go into the kitchen. I'll make a pot of coffee, and you can take some out to Traci."

"Sounds good, but I don't have much time."

He was hardly looking at her. "I understand." Half hopping to the kitchen, she rinsed out the morning's dregs in the coffee pot and then pushed a button on her industrial-sized grinder to start the beans.

Since it was that easy, she sat down in one of their chairs next to the kitchen table and waited. Dylan sat down, too. But though her day had had a happy ending, he looked weary. Absolutely exhausted.

This was her fault. She needed to clear the air and try to get them back on the right track. "Dylan, I don't know how to apologize to you enough."

"Just tell me what happened, Jen."

"All right. Well, um, I guess you know that Jack invited me to lunch."

"I heard about that. And I heard how you accepted and went to his house."

Each word he said sounded like it was getting torn out of him. "I did. And though I was feeling a little panicked, I was determined to go through with it."

"But then you took off?"

"Well, kind of. I mean, I meant to stay there, but then—"

"But then you couldn't take it and got scared?"

How had he put that together? "Uh, no."

But before she could explain about Harvard, Dylan stood up and stared pacing. "I thought you were dead," he said.

"No. Dylan—"

"I thought that guy had found you and kidnapped you. I thought that Jack guy had raped you. I thought about a dozen scenarios and each one was worse than the other." He stopped and stared at her. "I pretty much lost my mind."

"I'm sorry. If I would have known what was going to happen, you know I wouldn't have left the truck." She shook her head. "Or the bookstore."

"Or the house?" he added. Still looking haunted, he said, "Jennifer, I think we might need to look at other options for you."

A tremor zipped up her spine. "What do you mean?"

"I mean that I love you, but I don't know if I'm the best person to take care of you."

"I don't need anyone to take care of me." When he raised his eyebrows, she lifted her chin. "I'm not a child."

"No, you're not. But today was bad. It's obvious that you're not all right. Not anywhere close to being all right. I'm no counselor, Jen."

She didn't need him to be one, either.

So many emotions were pulsing through her, she could hardly contain herself. She wanted to argue, try to explain herself. She wanted to do a lot of things and offer a bunch of excuses . . . but she knew he was in such a dark place that he wouldn't believe them anyway.

"I understand," she finally replied. Turning to the kitchen that she'd perfectly arranged, she limped to a small cupboard and got out two ceramic to-go cups. As Dylan watched, she filled the cups, opened the refrigerator, and pulled out the cream. "Traci likes cream, I think," she murmured.

"You don't have to do this."

"But I already am." She poured a couple of tablespoons into one of the cups, fastened lids onto both and handed them to her brother. "Here you go. I'll see you later."

He took both. Looked like he was about to say something, but in the end simply turned around and walked out.

When the door closed, she carefully locked it and then got herself her own cup of coffee. Then she sat down and pulled out her cell phone. She thought about Jack and how she owed him a call, about their parents—she needed to talk to them before they heard about this latest drama from Dylan. She thought about Melissa, her counselor.

But instead of calling anyone, she simply sat and sipped a whole cup of coffee. And then she slowly made her way upstairs, turned on the bathtub faucet, and took a very long, very hot bath.

CHAPTER 28

"I try to dress classy and dance cheesy."
—PSY

Had she ever been more thankful for dance? Shannon doubted it. After learning that Jennifer was fine and that Traci was back at the precinct with Dylan, Shannon had been so relieved that tears had filled her eyes.

Then, on its heels, were all the things that Dylan had told her. How he'd trusted her and she'd let him down. How she'd failed Jennifer.

How Dylan no longer had anything to say to her.

And . . . how she'd felt about all of that.

She'd been so torn up, both with his words and the knowledge that she'd been unable to move.

And then she'd gotten angry.

Knowing that yelling or calling him back and giving him a

piece of her mind wasn't going to happen, Shannon had walked down the stairs, double-checked her schedule, and taught that private swing class and the high school girls' tap class.

When the last girl went on her way, she went upstairs, pulled off her dress, and put on something a whole lot more comfortable.

Then she walked back into her dance studio and closed the door behind her.

And at last, in the privacy of her favorite space, Shannon reached for her iPad, bypassed all the ballroom songs she played for students, and went straight to the music that was good for her soul. Country, plain and simple. Old-school Garth Brooks and Brooks and Dunn. Keith Urban and Jason Aldean. Eric Church and Dierks Bentley. Singers that had gotten her through bad days and self-doubts and hours of practice until her body hurt as much as her feet.

After two more clicks and an adjustment in volume, the piercing strum of an electric guitar filled the room, and the familiar twang fed her soul.

Her body reacted the same way it had when she'd been twelve and eighteen and twenty-two. She might be living in Ohio now, might be trying to keep up with a whole lot of people who'd been more places and had more schooling, but at the end of the day, she was still who she was. Shannon was a small-town West Virginia girl with a fondness for music that talked about trucks and farms and Friday night lights.

More importantly, she was okay with that.

Already feeling better, she opened a small closet nestled in the corner of the room. On the top shelf was a clear plastic container filled to the brim. It took a minute, but eventually she was able to stand on her tiptoes and coax it down. When she got it on the floor, she crouched down and pulled off the lid.

The faint scent of peonies wafted out—the remnants of her

favorite drugstore cologne when she'd been fifteen. It brought back memories of big dreams and early morning Sunday church services wearing one of the many dresses her mother had bought for her that Shannon had always been *sure* were too old-fashioned and plain.

Shaking off the memories, she pushed aside the extra pair of tap shoes and the pair of heels that she'd worn for her first ballroom competition. After digging some more, she at last found her goal: an old pair of pale-pink satin toe shoes.

Holding them up, she made sure the ribbons were still secure, then dug back in that box for some cotton for the toe box.

Brooks and Dunn started singing "My Maria," making her grin. It was time. She took a chair and at last put them on. Her toes protested for a few seconds but settled down when she stood up and lightly stretched and tried out a couple of almost-forgotten steps.

Then, feeling like she was looking at a stranger, she walked to the center of the room and stared at her reflection.

And perhaps she really was staring at a stranger. The woman looking back at her wasn't the girl she'd once been. Instead of pink tights, she had on tight black leggings. Instead of one of her many black leotards, she was wearing a fitted aqua tank top. Her hair was in a ponytail, not the bun that was so tight she used to swear it made her eyebrows rise a quarter inch.

But maybe—just maybe—there was still that look of determination in her brown eyes. Back in the day, she'd refused to listen to anyone who said she hadn't started dance classes early enough, wasn't tall enough, wasn't talented enough. She'd just worked harder.

Now, her body was bigger than it used to be. And, maybe her steps weren't as steady and her legs and core weren't nearly as strong.

But, even as she stared at this almost-stranger in the mirror, Shannon realized that everything that she'd been focusing on for the last six months had been a mistake.

No, she wasn't an only child. She wasn't from West Virginia, and she wasn't even much like her mom.

But that said, she wasn't all that different from the girl she used to be, either. She was still Shannon. She still liked to dance. She still liked her country music. She still loved her parents and would never think of them as anything other than "Momma" and "Daddy."

She was still so grateful for her life and the blessings she'd been given.

And looking at herself—at this older version of herself, with her long brown hair, same long arms, full lips, and faint scar on her eyebrow from a fall when she'd been a toddler—she wasn't perfect, but she'd never been. More importantly, she'd never needed to be perfect.

Which was okay.

As the songs changed and she heard Garth singing about the river, she walked to the barre and lightly rested her hand on it. And then went through the exercises and warm-up steps she'd done so many times it was as if her muscles were leading her brain. Maybe they were.

Pliés and *relevés* slid into *jetés* and *sautés*. A faint sheen of sweat formed on her forehead and back. She welcomed it as she pirouetted then arched her back.

And at last, she leapt into the air.

The music switched, singers as familiar as high school memories filled the room, encouraging her to remember old recital pieces, favorite combinations, different times.

An hour later, just as Eric Church was singing about memories, perspiration was running down her back, and her toes and ankles were protesting, Shannon at last drew to a stop.

When she looked at her reflection again, she couldn't help but smile. She was a sweaty mess, but something had returned to her eyes that she hadn't seen in far too long: satisfaction.

She could still do something that she'd worked hard to do. Could still encourage her body to perform in a way that was pleasing. But, more importantly, she'd found herself again.

"Welcome back, girl," she whispered. "I've missed you."

* * *

Two hours later, she had showered and was sitting at The Works with Traci and Kimber. The pizza place was in the old train depot in downtown Bridgeport. There was a large stone fireplace taking up one of the walls and worn red brick under their feet.

Shannon was dressed in a pair of skinny jeans, an oversized sweater, and her favorite pair of duck boots. Her sisters were wearing much the same thing, though Traci was wearing a pair of Sorrels and Kimber was looking as fashionable as ever in her sleek black leggings, fitted turtleneck, and flats.

One thing they all had in common were glasses of red wine in front of them.

After they ordered two large pizzas—guaranteeing leftovers—each of them seemed to practically dissolve into their chairs.

"Has any day ever been worse?" Traci said. "I thought I'd seen everything there was to see back in Cleveland, but today's been awful." Picking up her beer, she took a long sip. "I need a two-week vacation."

Shannon grinned. "Any chance of that happening?"

"Not unless I want to get fired."

"It was awful for me, and I wasn't even out hunting for Jennifer with Dylan," Kimber said. "I can't imagine how stressed you were."

"I wasn't as much stressed as worried," Traci explained. "I hate feeling out of control, and that was definitely how I felt this afternoon."

"You had reason," Kimber said. "It had to be hard."

"But Dylan hung in there," Shannon said.

"He was doing his best, but to be honest, he was a real mess and I kind of was, too. I've walked into some really bad situations over the years, but spending the day with a cop who is dwelling on every awful scenario that could have happened to his sister? It was bad."

Shannon gulped. "How did it go when y'all found her?"

"Honestly, I think by that time we were all so wrecked, I didn't feel anything but relief."

"And Dylan?" Kimber asked.

"Poor guy. I think he was trying not to dissolve into a pool of tears."

Kimber patted Traci's arm. "Hey, you did it though, right? She's okay. That's something."

Traci's frown slipped into a half smile. "Yeah. It was a good day. It could have been so much worse." Raising a glass, she said, "Here's to happy endings on stressful days."

Kimber chuckled. "I need to remember this toast."

Shannon clicked her glass and attempted to feel more optimistic. Of course she was very thankful that Jennifer was okay, but Dylan's blame was still weighing heavy on her heart. She'd thought that after her workout she was better . . . but maybe not.

"Hey, what's wrong?" Traci asked.

"Me? Oh, nothing."

"Okay. So . . . Kimber told me about your country music ballet."

"What?" Horrified, she glanced at Kimber. "What did you see?"

"Only you in a pair of toe shoes doing things that I've only seen at the Kennedy Center. You, girl, have been holding out on us."

Still trying to get over the idea that Kimber had watched her dance and she hadn't realized she'd had an audience, Shannon shook her head in dismay. "Come on, you knew I was a dancer."

"I knew you fox-trotted around your studio to boring music. I didn't know you were a ballerina."

"I can't believe I missed the show," Traci said. "Tell me when you do an encore."

"You didn't miss anything," Shannon said quickly. "I was just messing around."

"You were leaping and twirling on one foot to a bunch of country songs. It was amazing," Kimber said as she sipped her wine.

It was official. She was embarrassed. "Whatever. I don't do ballet much anymore. Just when I'm having a tough day," she added as their server brought over two huge pizzas and placed them in the center of the table.

After placing a thick slice of pepperoni and mushroom pizza on her plate, Kimber said, "What happened with you?"

Did she really want to go there? She wasn't sure. "Something happened with Dylan."

"What?" Kimber asked.

"I'm not sure I want to talk about it."

"I think you should," Traci said. "I wasn't going to mention it, but I heard Dylan's part of the conversation."

That made her feel even worse. "If you heard what he said, then you probably have a good idea about why I don't want to talk about it." *Like, ever.*

"For what it's worth, I told Dylan he was wrong to chew you out like that."

"What did he say?" Kimber asked, her voice a full octave higher.

"He, um, he pretty much said it was my fault that Jennifer was missing."

Traci dabbed her mouth with the paper napkin. "I could say that he had a good reason for freaking out and saying something so stupid, but I don't know."

"How was it your fault?" Kimber asked, her voice outraged.

"Because I didn't try to keep her from going to have lunch with that guy."

"But you aren't her mom. And besides, he was really nice. I would've had lunch with him, too."

Shannon shrugged. "I thought the same thing. Plus his mom was so nice. That means something, don't you think?"

Kimber nodded. Traci just looked sympathetic. "When we saw Jack he was as upset as the rest of us. This wasn't on him."

"What are you going to do when he calls to apologize?" Kimber asked.

After a momentary burst of hope, she tamped it down fast. "I don't know if Dylan will do that."

Kimber pursed her lips. "But Shannon, what if he does?"

"If he does call, I don't know if I'll answer." She cast a glance at Traci. "Sorry if this puts you in a bad spot."

Traci shrugged off her comment. "Don't worry about me. Like I said, I told him what I thought about him talking to you that way."

After finishing her second piece of pizza, Shannon decided to go ahead and say what she was thinking. "Y'all, this year—discovering I had sisters, starting my business, moving . . . all of it—well, I've given a lot up and made a lot of changes. It's been hard." She looked at both of her sisters. "At least it has been for me."

"You aren't lying, it's been real hard." Kimber agreed.

"That's what makes me think I don't need to get into a relationship like that."

"Like what?" Kimber countered. "Shannon, you really like him."

"I know." But did she want to fall in love with a man who could blame her so easily? And had she *really* just thought about loving Dylan Lange?

Oh, for Pete's sake. Did she even know what love was?

"Listen to me, sister. You don't have to decide anything right now."

"Kimber's right," Traci said. "Guys are fine, but they can be a pain in the rear even on their best days. Try not to think about Dylan."

After motioning for the server to bring her a second glass of wine, Shannon smiled. "As far as I'm concerned, he's already out of my life."

After sharing a look with Kimber, Traci raised her glass. "Cheers to that."

As their drinks clinked, Shannon realized right then and there that she actually did know what love was.

Love was when her sisters didn't point out that she was lying through her teeth.

CHAPTER 29

"When a body moves, it's the most revealing thing.
Dance for me a minute,
and I'll tell you who you are."
—MIKHAIL BARYSHNIKOV

Dylan had stayed late at work. He'd had a report to type. Paperwork was an essential part of his job, but this report had taken a really long time, especially since he'd been called into the lieutenant's office for a lengthy meeting to discuss how he and Traci had handled the day.

Though Dylan had known his report, written in the most factual, impersonal way, had been correct, it still left a bad taste in his mouth. Because while he and Traci had performed well enough to receive praise from his lieutenant, he'd done so many other things wrong. He might know how to keep his emotions in check when summarizing police procedures, but he had a long way to go before he was able to keep cool when it came to his personal life.

In the span of a few hours, he'd managed to hurt his sister, irritate his partner, and surely tick off Shannon.

Now, as he walked into his house, Dylan knew he was going to have to apologize profusely to Jennifer. He'd said some words that he really regretted. While he did believe that his sister needed more help when it came to dealing with the trauma that she'd endured, he realized that he'd been letting his hurt and frustration show. He'd hurt her instead of helped, which was always his greatest fear.

Well, all he could do was apologize and try to make amends. It wasn't like he could change the past.

"Sorry I'm so late, Jen!" he called out as he walked into the kitchen. "You wouldn't believe how long the report was that I had to write. I didn't think I'd ever finish it."

But as he looked around the space, with its modern appliances and granite countertops, it was obvious that Jennifer hadn't been cooking. Actually, it didn't look like she'd even set foot in the room, which was a rarity. Even though he knew better—and that he'd just chided himself for doing the very same thing—the fear that was his constant companion where she was concerned loomed large.

"Jennifer?" he called a little louder.

One second passed. Then two. He walked into the hallway, peeked into the living room for her coat and boots that she always took off and left scattered around.

But the room was immaculate.

Just as he was about to start searching the house, she appeared at the top of the stairs.

"Dylan?"

She was dressed in soft looking corduroys and a lavender sweater. She looked rested. That was good. "Hey."

Leaning over the bannister, she frowned. "Dylan, is everything all right?"

"Yeah. I, um, I wasn't sure where you were." That was a little better than admitting he'd been afraid something had happened to her again.

She pointed to her hair, which he hadn't noticed was wet. "I was in the shower."

"Oh." Well, now he felt stupid. Looking for something to say, he said, "You didn't make supper."

Her eyes narrowed. "You're right, I didn't." Her voice hardened. "I thought I'd order a pizza or order something in tonight."

"There's no need for you to do that." Eager to be of help, he pulled out his phone. "What would you like? I'll order it for you."

"I can order a pizza."

"I know that," he said quickly. "I didn't mean you couldn't. I just want to help." No, what he really wanted to do was apologize but he wasn't sure how to get started on that.

Looking resigned, she walked down the stairs. Her feet were bare and her hair was still streaming down her back in wet waves. Thanks to the plummeting temperatures outside, their house was cold. On another day, he might suggest she go put on some socks or maybe dry her hair a little bit. Tonight, he didn't dare.

After she stopped a couple feet from him and folded her arms in front of her chest. "Dylan, I think we need to talk."

"Okay . . ." He looked around. "Do you want to go sit down?"

"No, I don't want to sit."

"All right. So, what's up?" And yes, he realized that he was sounding like had nothing in between his ears except a lot of hot air.

"Well, I've been doing a lot of thinking about everything, and I've decided something. You were right. We are in a rut. You are used to looking out for me, and I'm used to asking you for help. I need to start doing more things on my own. A lot more things."

Relief poured through him. She wasn't going to be mad at him forever. "That's fine," he said with a smile.

"No, Dylan. You don't get it," she countered impatiently. "What I'm trying to tell you is that I'm going to move out."

Move out? Move out when she still got rattled by big crowds? Move out when that Lance guy was still at large? "Jennifer, don't you think you're overreacting?"

"Stop being so condescending!"

"I'm really trying here. But—"

"You wouldn't even listen to me when I tried to tell you that I was looking for a dog today. I wasn't freaking out. I wasn't running from an imagined person. I got lost in the woods and the snow while looking for Harvard."

"I realize that." *Now.*

"It sure didn't sound like it."

She wasn't wrong. "You're right, and I'm real sorry about that. I shouldn't have gotten so freaked out that I took it out everything on you. I'm so sorry for the things I said."

She sighed. "I'm not looking for an apology," she said softly. "I'm saying, that this is the right time for me to move forward. It's the right time for both of us."

"Where do you plan to go?" Maybe she was headed to their parents? That might be best. They could take care—

"I'm going to ask Shannon, Traci, and Kimber if I can move in with them."

She wanted to room with his partner and the woman he was dating? He couldn't think of a more uncomfortable situation for himself. "Jen . . . you can't do that."

"Why not? Shannon told me that her money situation is tight. Plus, they have an extra room. It sounds like an answer to a prayer."

"You don't need to move," he said in a rush. " If you want more space, I'll give it to you."

Her expression softened. "Dylan, I really do think living with those girls is going to be better." She smiled. "Not a one of them can cook, they need me."

Just as he took a deep breath, one word that she said resonated with him. *Need.* Jennifer needed to be needed. That was something he could understand. Hell, hadn't that been half the reason he'd become a cop in the first place? He'd liked helping others in the community. "Are you sure?"

"I'm very sure." As if she realized that he finally got what she was saying, she smiled softly. "I need to stop standing still and start dancing a bit."

Dancing. His sister turned before he could ask if she meant that literally or figuratively. After all, she was about to be living on the upper floor of a dance studio.

Jennifer was back upstairs before he realized that it didn't matter.

CHAPTER 30

"Thanks to dance, I can change my hair, costume, and makeup in five minutes."

How had everything gotten so mixed up? It wasn't that Shannon wasn't happy to have Jennifer move in with them—she was. Jennifer was nice, her rent was going to take the edge off of their money troubles, and she was even going to cook for them. Traci, especially, was thrilled about that.

But, it was all quite a surprise.

Luckily, she was beginning to realize that unexpected developments were a part of life. People were imperfect, and life wasn't supposed to be so simple, so cut and dried.

She reckoned it made things more flavorful and rich.

Now, showing Jennifer her small room in their loft, which happened to be located right next to the kitchen, Shannon wondered if it was Jennifer who was having second thoughts.

Not that she would blame her. The room didn't look like much, not even after she, Traci, and Kimber had cleaned it out last night.

"What do you think?" she asked Jennifer. "I know it's not much, but at least you have a pretty window seat."

Jennifer was standing right in front of the little alcove. Honestly, it was every teenage-girl's dream. It already had a pretty set of cushions in coordinated blues and green paisley patterns. A perfect place to sit and read or even just to enjoy sitting in the sun and watching the world go by below.

Turning around, Jennifer smiled. "I love this window seat. It's cozy. I think the rest of the room is going to be just fine, too. It's big enough for my double bed and dresser."

"There's no closet," she warned.

"I noticed that, but I'll make do. I'll get one of those portable closets from the discount store."

"And you're going to have to share a bathroom with three of us."

A hint of a smile played on her lips. "I can share a bathroom."

Thinking of her classes, she added, "Also, this room is right above my dance studio. That means you'll sometimes be hearing the music float up. Especially when I have my teenage girls. They can be loud."

Jennifer looked even more amused. "Shannon, are you trying to encourage me to move in or stay out?"

Feeling foolish, Shannon shrugged. "Sorry. I guess I don't want you to get moved in and then realize that this situation is a far cry from your beautiful house."

"I knew that it was going to be different." She bit her bottom lip, then added, "Honestly, this might be a better situation for me than living with Dylan. He was gone a lot, both with work and his social activities. There were times when I got kind of scared, being so alone."

"You definitely won't be alone here. Between the three of us and my classes, there's always something going on."

"I'll be fine. The price is more than fair, too."

They'd agreed to a rent of three hundred dollars a month. It included utilities and food . . . but Jennifer also agreed to cook that food four nights a week. Shannon had told her that she and her sisters didn't care what nights she chose to cook—just to let them know.

"We're so excited to experience your cooking, Jen. Things have been pretty slim pickings around here."

"Believe me, I'm excited to cook for you. It gives me good practice for the business I'm starting."

Glad that all the nuts and bolts were getting organized, Shannon finally brought up the part of Jennifer's move-in that had been weighing on her mind. "So, how are you going to get your furniture and other things over here?"

"Dylan and a couple guys from the police department are going to bring them over sometime today."

"That's good." She tried to smile, though her insides were pinching. She really wasn't ready to see him anytime soon.

Some of the confidence that had been shining in Jennifer's eyes dimmed. "Shannon, I know the two of you were getting close. I feel terrible that my personal problems interfered with that."

"This isn't on you." She shrugged. "I'm sure you know as well as I do that not every relationship works out."

"Maybe it isn't over yet."

She didn't want to hurt Jennifer's feelings. Dylan was her brother and they were close. "You're right. Never say never."

Jennifer sat down on the window seat. "For what it's worth, I think you should know that Dylan had almost as hard a time with my attack as I did." She paused to take a fortifying breath before continuing. "He not only found me right, um, after, but caught the guys. He also had to testify, not only on the crime scene, but on what they said when they were being interrogated."

"I didn't know that."

Jennifer turned to face the window. "It was bad, Shannon. Not just my attack, but the things they said. I wasn't the first woman they'd done this to. Dylan was haunted by it all . . . and scared to death that I wasn't going to be able to recover and that somehow they were going to get off."

"But they did go to prison, right?"

"Only two out of three of them went. The third was sixteen, and his lawyer made him sound like a choir boy. Almost as much of a victim as I was. He was put in a juvenile rehabilitation center."

"And now he's writing you notes."

She turned back to Shannon. "We think so. Some of what he wrote me was so close to what the other guys said during the attack, I can't imagine that it would be anyone else." She exhaled. "I'm telling you all of this not to change your mind as much as to give you an idea of how freaked out he would have been when I got lost in the woods. Even though all this time has passed, the memory of it all is still fresh."

Shannon's mouth felt dry. Jennifer hadn't been wrong. That information did give her a new sense of what Dylan had been feeling when he'd lashed out at her.

But did that mean that she needed to give him a pass for the things he said? She wasn't sure.

"I appreciate you sharing that with me."

Jennifer stood up again. "And I appreciate you opening up your home to me. No matter how bad that experience was, I need to keep moving forward. That means that I need to keep getting stronger." Looking even more assured, she lifted her chin. "Moving out of Dylan's place is the right thing to do."

"We're really glad you're here," Shannon said, crossing the room to give her a quick hug. "Let us know if you need help getting settled, okay? I've got to go get ready for a class."

* * *

Looking at her watch, she hurried down the stairs. She had a brand-new client arriving in fifteen minutes. It was another private lesson, this one last-minute. The man had contacted her via email, asking if she could teach him how to swing dance. After she'd given him the standard information about classes and fees, he'd asked for her first available slot.

Though they'd only exchanged a couple of emails, his notes were polite and formal, and she imagined him to be in his sixties or seventies. Honestly, after all the tension she'd been feeling with Dylan, she was looking forward to an easy class with someone her grandfather's age.

She also didn't want him to be disappointed with his decision to contact her. Luckily, she was already in her dress and two-inch heels. She scurried into her studio, turned on lights in there and in the front entryway, and opened up her new file, now neatly filled with blank contracts and forms.

As soon as she wrote down Mr. Emerson DiAngelo's name and the date on the form, she turned on her stereo system and double-checked the swing dances she had marked on her Ballroom Beats program.

She'd just sat down at her little desk—with five minutes to spare—when the front door opened.

Shannon stood up, happy to greet her little old gentleman, and came face-to-face with someone completely different.

She was looking at a young guy in faded jeans and a dark gray T-shirt with some kind of snowboard emblem on it. He had short dark hair, a couple of tattoos on his arms, and the best pair of cheek bones she'd ever seen.

She stood up. "Hi. May I help you?"

"I hope so," he replied in a deep voice that wasn't displeasing. "I'm looking for Shannon Murphy."

"That's me."

He walked toward her with an outstretched hand. "Good to meet you. I'm Emerson DiAngelo."

"Good to meet you, too," she said as his hand covered hers. When he smiled at her, she smiled back.

But inside? Her stomach was churning. Honestly, how come no one was who she expected them to be?

CHAPTER 31

"Yes, I dance in my car.
Yes, I can see you staring at me.
No, I don't care."

"I really appreciate you fitting me in," Emerson said after they'd filled out his paperwork and he'd smiled when he'd shared that he was in "real good" health and didn't have any physical problems preventing him from learning to swing dance.

Shannon had blushed like a thirteen-year-old with a first crush—or at least a gal who hadn't given hours and hours of dancing lessons to relative strangers.

Now they were standing in the middle of the studio and holding hands while she was attempting to get him to listen to the beat of the music.

Emerson might have been a gorgeous twenty-seven-year-old man, but a dancer he was not.

When he stumbled for the fourth or fifth time, he laughed. "Am I helpless?"

"Of course not. We'll get this."

"I hope so. What am I going to say to my grandma if I can't dance at her wedding?"

And . . . that was yet another part of his dreaminess factor. Emerson might look like he was heading out to surf or join a biker club or something, but he was as kind as can be and loved his family. Especially his Grandma Marie, who was about to get married after spending ten years in widowhood.

Looking up into his eyes, she said, "I promise that you'll be dancing."

"You sound confident."

"I am. I'm good at what I do, you know," she said lightly.

"Oh, of that I have no doubt," he replied, looking at her in an appreciative way. "You look like a princess."

After encouraging him to lead her around the room in his lurching gait, she grinned. "Emerson, you just made this girl's day. Not too many people compare a hick like me to royalty."

"Hick, huh? Where are you from?"

"Spartan, West Virginia."

Worry filled his eyes. "I'm sorry. I've never heard of it."

"I'd be surprised if you had. Yes, that's it. Now I'm going to show you how to twirl me."

Looking doubtful, he watched her, holding her right hand lightly like she showed him.

"Ready?"

"Yep. Well, not really, but I'm game."

"There you go." She started counting, as she turned and grabbed hold of his hand again.

"Shannon—damn."

"First time for everything. Come on. Let's do it again." She counted slowly and did a respectable turn, twirling enough so that the hem of her dress floated around her knees.

He smiled slowly. "We did it."

"We did. Good job." Releasing his hands, she said, "And that concludes our first class."

"It's already been an hour?" When she nodded, he said, "Boy, fastest hour of my day."

"It was fun." Walking to her calendar, she said, "What do you think? Did I scare you off, or are you up for another class?"

"I'm up for another one." After he paid her and they marked their next session on her calendar, he paused. "Hey, not to be a creeper, but are you seeing anyone?"

Dylan flashed into her head . . . and so did the way he'd yelled at her. "Not really."

"Does 'not really' mean that you'd consider going out with me?" While she blinked, he said, 'Don't say no. I promise, just dinner. Or lunch, if you'd rather."

"Well . . ."

"I'm taking dance lessons, and I love my grandma. I'm a good guy." His eyes sparkled.

She supposed he probably was. Then, there was the fact that he was nice and respectful, had shown up on time, and had even asked about her. He was also handsome. *Very* handsome. "Okay?"

He cocked an eyebrow. "Is that a question? Do I need to give you some references?"

She shook her head but couldn't resist teasing him. "Do you really have dating references?"

"No, but I'm willing to do whatever it takes for you to give me the time of day. Heck, you could even talk to my grandma if that would help."

She chuckled. Everything about the last couple of minutes

had been flattering. And she was a lot of things but unfortunately not immune to that. "I'd love to go out with you."

"Yeah?"

She nodded.

"Great. Okay, give me your phone number and I'll text you as soon as I look at my schedule. Okay?"

"Okay." After she gave him her number, she looked at him more closely. "You didn't plan on this, did you?"

"No." He looked sheepish as he reached for his coat. "Honestly, I thought you would be close to my grandmother's age. All day I was preparing myself not to get creeped out when I put my hand on your waist."

"And here we just held hands."

He shrugged on his coat. "I'm thinking maybe I would've liked holding your waist just fine, Shannon Murphy. I'll call you. Promise."

She smiled at him as he walked out the door. Then, as soon as she was alone again, she sat down and breathed deep. Whew. She sure hadn't seen that coming.

CHAPTER 32

"No one dances sober, unless he is insane."
—CICERO

Looking skeptical, Jennifer walked backwards ahead of Dylan, Ace, and Kurt on the narrow flight of stairs leading up to the third floor. "I guess this is a pretty tight fit," she said. "I didn't even think to measure the size of the dresser before asking you to carry it upstairs."

Since his arms were burning, his back was about to send out an SOS signal, and they still had half a flight to go, Dylan didn't say anything.

"This ain't no big deal," Ace called out. "All in a day's work, yeah?"

"Thank you again." She stopped.

"Keep walking, Jennifer," Dylan called out. "We've got this."

Realizing she was blocking them, Jennifer scurried forward. "Oh. I'll just go make sure my door is still open."

"Thanks, darlin'," Kurt said.

As soon as Jennifer trotted off, they climbed another two steps. Ace was leading the way, and Dylan was supporting the bottom half of the dresser next to Kurt Holland.

"You guys with your Southern charm," Dylan teased. "The minute you pull out those drawls and 'darlin's,' girls turn to putty."

"What's wrong with that?" Kurt asked as they lifted the dresser and pulled it up another few steps.

"Not a damn thing. I'm just wondering where you learned it."

"From the best sweet-talker I know—my pa," Ace said. "He could sweet-talk my momma into doing just about anything."

"Huh."

"Oh-oh," Ace teased. "Are you thinking it's time you adopted some of that charm for yourself?"

Maybe. Not that he was going to admit it to his buddies, though. "I'm just surprised, is all. I hadn't ever had the privilege of seeing it in action."

"For what it's worth, sweet-talking doesn't do much for Emily," Kurt said. "She just kind of rolls her eyes and asks me to listen to her."

"Noted." Three steps later, they were on the landing. After they set the dresser down on the wood, Ace stretched his arms. "This place is really is nice up here. Way cooler than I thought. That Shannon knows what she's doing."

"She always did though. Right?" Kurt murmured. Reminding Dylan once again that Shannon might be a new resident, but she wasn't without a support system. She had her sisters and a trio of guys from Spartan, West Virginia, to lean back on. Whenever they mentioned things like that, he was reminded that they all knew her far better than he did—and had known her for years.

"What was Shannon like?" Dylan asked.

"When?"

"I don't know. When you all were growing up."

"She was younger than us. Jackson knew her better—I didn't know her real well," Kurt said. "But she was a star."

Ace nodded. "We were all real proud of her. Still are." There was a slight edge to his voice now. Almost as if he was making sure that Dylan knew Shannon Murphy wasn't without friends in Bridgeport.

"Good to know." Raising his voice, he said, "Jennifer, we got your dresser. You ready?"

The door flew open. "Yes! Sorry, I was on the phone and the reception was a little shaky."

The words were out before she could stop them. "Everything okay?"

"Hmm? Oh, yes. It was Jack. He's taking me out for coffee." Before he could say anything about that, she pointed to an empty wall. "Could you guys put it right here?"

"No problem," Kurt said bending down to pick up the beast again.

After it was exactly where she wanted it, Jennifer thanked them, and Ace and Kurt took off.

Dylan stayed a moment to look at Jennifer's room. He couldn't deny that it was shaping up real nice. "This is pretty, Jen."

"I think so, too. To be honest, I wasn't sure how everything was going to look together, but now I know it's going to be just fine."

"It's quiet back at home. I already miss you."

"I bet you're missing your hot dinners."

"That, too. Maybe one day soon we can go out to lunch or dinner? My treat."

"I'd like that."

Feeling awkward but not altogether bad, he nodded. "Okay then, it's a date. Now, I better go check in with Shannon. I've got my class in twenty minutes."

"Have fun."

He rolled his eyes, but in truth he was looking forward to his hour-long lesson. He had a lot of making up to do and, though there was a lot to talk about, he knew that the two of them had some chemistry that couldn't be denied. Surely that had to count for something.

* * *

When he walked into the studio ten minutes later, Shannon was already there.

She was wearing another pretty dress. Her hair was in a complicated-looking kind of ponytail, too. And she had more makeup on than usual. He thought she was just as beautiful in leggings and a T-shirt with her face freshly washed.

But he couldn't deny that she looked flat-out gorgeous right now. He suddenly wished he had put on something other than faded Levi's and a worn flannel shirt.

"Hey," he said.

She was texting on her phone. She looked up at him in surprise. "Hey." Setting her phone down, she stood up and walked over. "Did you get Jennifer all settled?"

"I think so. That dresser of hers weighed a ton."

She laughed. "I bet it gained two pounds with every step, too."

"That about covers it. I'm glad Ace and Kurt were here."

"They were? Are they still around?"

"No. They took off." Why was he disappointed that she looked disappointed? "They said something about getting home to their wives."

"Ah." She glanced at the ornate clock that now graced the wall. "I bet they're ready to go out for supper."

"There's poker tonight, so I think they were probably going to make do with a quick bite." He smiled.

She looked at him wide-eyed. "What about you?"

"Well, we have our class, right?"

"Yes. But if you want to reschedule, we could."

"I don't want to."

"Well, we only have two more to go, right?"

She sounded relieved by that. Which, he supposed, gave him a good taste of his own medicine. Boy, he'd been a real jerk at their first meeting. He knew better, too. "Right."

She walked over to the iPad. "Let's get started then." When an old song from the sixties came on, she faced him. "Shall we dance?"

"Absolutely." He placed his hand on her waist and folded her palm in his left.

"Now, one-two, three, one-two, three. Yes?"

He nodded, then started leading around the room according to her counts. After they'd made a circle, she looked up at him and smiled.

"You're doing well."

He smiled. "I've got a great teacher."

Some of the sparkle faded from her eyes. "It's time to twirl. Do you remember what to do?"

"Nope. I'm afraid you're going to have to go over it again." He grinned, showing her that he was teasing her a bit.

But she only continued to count and instruct. As he listened and positioned her and stepped back and helped her turn and caught her again, Shannon held her body in such a controlled way that it felt almost like he was dancing with a mannequin.

Though he ached to stop and hash everything out, he didn't. He had to give her the space she needed. After all, he'd done this.

But later, when the hour was over, and he was walking back to his car, Dylan realized that he'd lost something really good. And worse, he had no idea how he was going to get it back.

CHAPTER 33

"Dancing is the art of getting your feet out of the way faster than your partner can step on them."
—EVAN ESAR

One Week Later

It was Friday already. What a week it had been. First, she'd been a nervous wreck, worrying if Emerson was actually going to text her . . . and then wondering if *she* was ready to go on a date with him.

He had indeed texted her, but it had been full of apologies. He'd gotten a temporary job up in Toledo, and it paid so well he took the company up on an offer to do additional work for them. He asked for a rain check for the following week.

She had been so relieved that she feared her return message had sounded a little too pleased by his work schedule.

In other news, Jennifer had settled in with them like she was another long-lost sister. She was sweet, easy to talk to, and cleaned up after herself in the bathroom, which turned out to be a big plus for Kimber.

But the best news was her cooking. Not only was her food amazing, but her fussing in the kitchen somehow accomplished what the three of them had not been able to do. She'd made their loft a home.

Traci had verbalized it the best, saying that Jennifer's cooking and comfortable way of acting around the loft made her want to be at home, too.

So, all of that was a plus. Her dance classes were going well, too, and she'd had two more private clients—both women.

The only difficulty she'd been having was the confusion she was feeling about Dylan. Their last class hadn't felt right. And watching him leave, looking so alone, hadn't felt right either. She realized that whether or not her head had completely forgiven him, her heart had. It just wasn't in her nature to hold a grudge. And she was starting to realize that she, too, might say and do a couple of things she wasn't proud of if one of her sisters were in jeopardy.

All that was why, when the clock turned six, she was in a new dress, her good heels, and was sitting on the beautiful Addams Family couch waiting for him.

At 6:03, the door swung open and Dylan strode in. He was dressed in dark jeans, a button-down, and had his badge still fastened on his belt—the corner of which was visible when his navy blazer opened.

"Am I late?" he asked, looking worried.

She couldn't help but contrast the way he was acting with their very first meeting. She pointed to the big clock on the wall. "Not at all. You're right on time."

He tilted his head back. "Thank goodness. My sergeant wanted to talk to me about some scheduling stuff."

"If you would've been late, I would have understood."

He grinned at her, then stilled. "Look at you."

She got to her feet. "What?"

"You look like a picture. Is that a new dress? Or, do you simply have a huge supply of pretty dresses?"

"It's new." She smiled at him softly. "So, shall we dance?"

"Yeah. But wait a second." He shrugged off his blazer, folded it in two and set it on the arm of the couch. Then unfastened his shoulder holster. He pulled out his gun. "My safety is on, but I can go lock this up in my car if you'd like."

She was now used to Traci and her pistol. But that said, she didn't want it sitting out in the open where anyone could pick it up. "Would you mind if we put it in my desk drawer?"

"Not at all." He set it in the drawer she had pulled open and then shut it neatly. "Now I'm ready to dance."

"We could waltz or rumba, or I could teach you a little bit of swing dancing."

"I'd rather waltz or rumba. I don't trust myself with anything new."

"Fair enough." After turning on the music she'd chosen, this time some of her favorites, she lifted her arms to him. "Ready?"

This time, when he placed his hand on her waist, it was a little bit closer. His hand seemed a little more gentle. When she looked up at him, he wasn't smiling. Instead, he was staring down at her. His expression intent.

Before she realized what she was doing, she relaxed into him and let him lead.

And he did just fine.

It was as if something had clicked in his brain and he no longer needed her to remind him to do a thing. Almost as if they were meant to be dancing together.

It sounded cheesy even to her, but she knew if she were describing how they moved, she would have said that they were floating around the room. In sync. It was beautiful and made all the practice and focus on wins and trophies seem so empty.

Actually, maybe dancing only for points was wrong.

Dancing wasn't supposed to be about carefully controlled head tilts and extended legs and perfect posture. No, it was about moving with the music and being with a partner.

It was about simply enjoying being with someone that you cared about. And how one could convey feelings without words.

When the third song ended, Shannon realized she was slightly out of breath. Stepping back and dropping his hand, she said, "Boy. We were, um, on a roll there. Do you want a sip of water? I have an extra bottle."

"Sure." He took it from her, twisted off the cap, and drank half of it. "Thanks."

Glancing at the clock, she noticed that somehow thirty minutes had already passed. "Are you ready to rumba now?"

He grinned. "For a moment there, I thought you asked if I was ready to rumble."

"No rumbling today," she retorted, realizing that she was both joking and referencing their earlier disagreement.

"Then I'm ready, Shannon."

There it was again. That electricity between them that she'd first thought was wrong, then one-sided, then simply confusing. Now she was thankful for it—she just wasn't sure what to do about it.

He held out his hand. She took it. Gave herself a good talking to, and then Michael Bublé's "Save the Last Dance for Me" came on, and she quietly reminded Dylan of the beat.

Their pace wasn't quite so fluid, which she was grateful for. The slight awkwardness made her remember that she was the teacher and he was the student. That he was paying her for her time. That, as of right now, that was all they really had.

As Michael began singing the chorus, Dylan looked down at her face. "So, Traci told me something interesting the other day."

"What was that?"

"That you got asked out by a hot guy wearing tats."

Oh! "I didn't realize y'all talked about things like that."

"You wouldn't believe what we end up talking about. Some days when we're cruising the streets of Bridgeport, we talk about everything under the sun. And then some."

"I'm starting to get worried. Hopefully Traci isn't talking too much about what happens around here." She'd die if Traci ever shared the way they sometimes fought over the bathroom like they were teenagers instead of grown women.

"Not too much. But the news about your date was notable." She gaped at him as he guided her through a turn. When they moved forward, he murmured, "So, how was it?"

"The date? Oh, um, it hasn't happened yet."

"Yet?"

"Yes, well, Emerson had a work conflict. We're going to reschedule."

His expression was almost smug. "Is that right?"

"Yes. I mean, I think so." When he continued to look at her intently, she said, "The truth is, I might not go out with him."

"How come?"

"Because, well . . . it's a conflict of interest," she said suddenly.

"Because you're his teacher?"

She nodded. Then, for good measure, she said, "Slow down, now. The rumba has a smoother pace."

When he followed her lead, he spoke again. "Is that a thing? Are ballroom teachers not supposed to date their students?"

"I don't know if it's written down anywhere. But, it doesn't seem like a good idea."

"What about me?"

"What about you?"

"Well, we got upset with each other. It did make things difficult."

She grabbed hold of that like she had a bull by the horns. "Right. That's what I'm talking about."

"Of course, I only have one more class. So . . ." His voice drifted off.

And she felt that the tension between them was starting to go far beyond mere attraction and into something bordering on lust. She shook her head. "Well, our situation is kind of a moot point, you know."

"Because?"

"Because we aren't dating." Namely, he hadn't asked her out.

"What would you say if I asked you?"

Michael Bublé's song ended. On its heels was "All of Me" by John Legend. Darn it. "I don't know if I need to answer that question. It's rhetorical, after all."

"Shannon Murphy, would you go out to dinner with me tomorrow night?"

"Yes."

His eyes warmed. "I've never been so happy to only have one more class left."

She was starting to feel that way, too. "Dylan, I'm not really sure what we're doing."

"That's why we're going to go out to dinner," he said. "I'm going to pick you up, hold your hand when you walk down your front steps and help you into my car. And then I'm going to drive you someplace quiet and dark and expensive."

"And then?"

"And then I'm going to help you into your chair, encourage you to order whatever you want, and maybe even get us a bottle of wine." He paused. "How am I doing so far?"

She had to find her voice. "Pretty good."

Looking pleased, he continued. "While we're sipping wine and eating dinner I'm going to tell you about me, and you're going to talk about whatever you want." He pulled her closer. "And then . . ."

"Yes?"

"I'm going to ask if you want dessert."

She laughed. "Sounds like the way to a girl's heart."

"The dessert part?"

All of it. "Especially the dessert part," she said with a smile. Just as she realized they weren't dancing anymore. They were simply standing in the middle of the floor with John Legend's voice drifting around them.

"Shannon, I was going to wait to do this tomorrow night, but don't make me wait."

She lifted her chin so he could kiss her.

His lips were warm and firm and his breath tasted faintly like peppermint. And suddenly, she didn't care what they were supposed to be doing or if he was going to take her out for sushi or steak or hole-in-the-wall Mexican food tomorrow night. She was just glad he was going to take her out.

When he lifted his head, they were both a little breathless yet again.

"Shannon," he murmured. "That was incredible."

But before she could answer Traci was at the door. "Lange."

A chill rushed through her and they broke apart.

Looking at Traci, Dylan's expression was hard. "What happened?"

She held up a note. "I went to work out after work, so I just got home. I parked next to Jennifer's Altima and saw this under the windshield wiper."

"She got another letter."

Looking pissed off, Traci nodded. "I'm not into having rapists hanging around my house, Dylan. We need to put a stop to this."

"You'll get no argument from me." Turning to Shannon, he said, "Do you mind if I go upstairs, hon?"

Hon? "Of course." As Dylan walked by Traci, Shannon smiled at Traci's *what-just-happened* look.

As Dylan climbed the stairs, Shannon took a breath and allowed herself to take one last moment to appreciate what had just happened.

She and Dylan had changed course. There was something really good between them now. Something special worth hanging onto.

She hoped that was going to be possible.

CHAPTER 34

"Break dance, not bones."

"Hey, Jen, are you around?"

Jennifer looked up from the page she was designing for her new website. "Yep, I'm over here," she called from her bedroom. When her brother poked his head in her doorway, she waved him in. "This is perfect timing! You're exactly who I need to see. What do you think, should I mention the cooking classes I took years ago, or does that just make me seem out of date?"

Dylan walked inside but stopped against the doorframe. "Hmm?"

She moved the screen of her laptop so he could see it better. "For my website. Right now I'm calling it 'Home Cooking by Jen' until I can think of something catchier." She sighed.

"Of course, I started thinking that maybe 'catchy' doesn't

matter all that much. I mean, people want good food, not gimmicks. What do you think?"

A line formed between his brows. "I couldn't tell you."

She rolled her eyes. "That's no help."

Looking back at her screen, she said, "Anyway, I know I need some kind of bio, but it turns out that it's harder to write about oneself than I thought. So, what do you think about those classes? You never said."

"Um, I'll have to do some thinking about that." He paused. Cleared his throat. "But first, there's something we need to talk about."

Jennifer heard the words, but it was his expression that made the big impression. It was carefully blank, the one she knew he used often as a cop.

It was also the look he'd worn when he'd visited her at the hospital the day after her attack. So she knew that look, but she really wished she didn't.

Feeling like she was about to drown, she pushed her laptop to one side and stood up. "What happened?"

"You got another note."

That just about took her breath away. "When?" she asked when she finally got her voice to cooperate.

"Today. Traci just found it."

"Where did she find it?" Not that it really mattered. Did it?

Dylan looked regretful. "It was on the windshield of your car, honey. Traci parked next to you, saw a familiar-looking envelope stuck under one of your windshield wipers, and brought it inside."

Would this never end? Determined to not let all her fears get the better of her, Jennifer sent her brother a watery smile. "I guess it's good I'm still living with a cop, huh?"

Dylan just looked at her. "We need to see what it says, Jen. Are you ready for that?"

The question caught her off guard. "You don't already know?"

He shook his head. "Traci thought since you were here, you should get the honors."

For some reason, that made some of her muscles relax. She didn't know if it was because it was empowering or simply because she knew that giving up control was never easy for her big brother. "What did you think about that?"

He shifted, looking almost boyish for a moment. "You know what I thought. If I had my way, you'd never even know it had arrived."

Walking to his side, she nudged him gently with her elbow. "You're the best brother a girl could have. Literally, I think you're going to go in some world-record book, you're so great."

"But?"

"But, I'm glad that I'm going to get to be one of the people who deals with this letter. I don't want to just be the victim."

"I never thought of it that way, but I think you're right. This is better." Looking more resigned, he nodded. "Well, come on, then. The girls are downstairs."

"Pardon me?"

"Sorry," he said as he walked down the stairs. "I meant *women*. The *women* are downstairs. Does that sound better? You know I meant no disrespect."

"Whatever, Dylan. I'm trying to figure out who you're talking about."

"Traci, Kimber, and Shannon, of course."

Of course? "All of them are here?"

He paused on the landing and looked up at her. "Jennifer, yeah. They're your roommates, honey."

Yes, they were. But had she expected them to become involved in her personal nightmare? Ah, no. No, she had not.

"Everyone's in here," Dylan said as he led the way into Shannon's dance studio.

And sure enough, sitting around Shannon's desk were her three roommates. Traci was still in her jeans and button-down for work. She even still had her holster on, with her gun in it. The only concession she'd made to being off duty was an untucked shirt.

Beside her sat Shannon, who was wearing yet another amazing dress. This one was knit in a bold shade of dark red and sported a deep V around the neckline.

Jennifer would have looked like an overripe tomato or strawberry in it. On Shannon, though, it was particularly flattering, showing off her trim figure and dancer's legs.

Rounding out the group was Kimber. For once, though, she didn't look like a famous New York fashion model. She had on glasses, no makeup, loose jeans, and a chambray shirt big enough for Dylan to wear.

They were talking quietly to each other and then stopped when Jennifer walked in at Dylan's side.

"Hi, guys," she said.

"Hi," Shannon said. She got up and hurried over to give Jennifer a hug. "I'm so sorry about that note."

She swallowed and gave them all a watery smile. "Me, too."

Kimber shifted to face her. "We wanted to be here to support you. You don't mind, do you?"

"Not at all." She spoke the truth, too. For so long, she'd been alone. Right after it happened, some of her close friends had been there for her, but it had been hard. They asked questions and got upset when Jennifer kept things from them.

Eventually, she'd drifted apart from them. They didn't have a lot in common, since they were all going out and Jennifer could barely leave the house.

That's when she'd started leaning on her parents. But soon, even their looks of pity or frustration that she wasn't *okay* had created a wedge between them.

Ever since she'd moved in with Dylan, Jennifer had tried to keep the worst of her days to herself. She had Melissa, of course. But as helpful as Melissa was as a counselor, Jennifer didn't consider her a friend.

Now though, she had all three of her roommates. They cared enough to want to be there for her. She shook her head to clear it. "Sorry, my mind drifted. I don't mind you being here at all. It's, uh, nice."

Dylan sat down in one of the empty chairs in front of the desk and motioned for Jennifer to take the other one. "Let's get this over with. Jen, Traci used gloves and opened it with a letter opener. The paper is folded, so you can open it in the ziplock bag."

"Isn't this a little bit overkill?"

"Maybe. Maybe not. Better to be safe than sorry," Traci said.

Jennifer took a calming breath and then pulled the ziplock bag toward her. She'd never wanted to do anything less . . . or more.

"I'm ready," she whispered, more to herself than the others. Then, it was just like Traci had said. It was fairly simple to manipulate the paper so it was lying flat inside the plastic.

All she had to do was read it.

She decided to read it out loud. "*We haven't forgotten. It's your fault that our lives were ruined. It's time to pay.*"

Right as she took a breath, Kimber said, "What is all this about? Are they really that whacked?"

"One of the men in prison got hurt last night," Traci said.

Dylan looked at her sharply. "Why didn't you tell me?"

"You were off duty."

"Still."

"I would've called you tonight. Or the sergeant said he would. Wasn't anything much to tell anyway. The guy got in a fight and got his jaw busted up. He'll survive."

Jennifer looked up at her brother. "There's more. Are you done?"

"Crap. Yeah. Sorry."

She held up the plastic again. "*I know where you live. I know you're putting your roommates in danger. I'll make sure you pay.*"

With shaking hands, Jennifer put it down. "That's it."

"Well, he gets points for drama," Kimber said.

"And being a dimwit," Traci added. "One of your helpless roommates carries a Glock."

She looked up at Dylan. His jaw was twitching, but he didn't look afraid. "What happens next?"

Traci smiled. "Well, this is just me, but I'm thinking this is a real threatening letter. We need to pick him up."

Dylan's eyes lit up. "I knew you were going to be perfect. Let's go to the station."

Traci was already up and trotting up the stairs. "Give me five and I'll be ready."

Jennifer was just about to do what she always did and warn Dylan to be careful, when she noticed that Dylan was looking at Shannon with concern.

"You okay?" he asked.

"Hmm? Oh, sure."

He walked to her side. "I won't let anyone hurt you. Honestly, if Traci or I had thought the first note was serious, we would've told you and taken precautionary measures."

She nodded. "I . . . well, I feel so bad for you, Jennifer. And, I know it's your job, but I'm worried about you, too, Dylan. And Traci."

Right in front of all of them, Dylan wrapped Shannon in his arms and hugged her tight—letting all of them know exactly what he felt about her.

It was obvious that they were a couple now, and he wasn't letting her go.

CHAPTER 35

"Part of the joy of dancing is conversation. Trouble is, some men can't talk and dance at the same time."
—GINGER ROGERS

After much debate with herself and having about a hundred conversations with her therapist, her roommates, and her brother, Jennifer had finally gone on her date with Jack.

It was really too bad that it was likely going to be her last, but how much drama could one guy take? And who would even call lunch in her loft kitchen—with Traci on the premises in case she was needed—a *real* date?

The only consolation was that he had eaten every bite of the meal she'd prepared and had even looked a little disappointed that he'd only had room for seconds and not thirds.

The cook in her was beaming with pride. The feminine, girly part of her, however, was wishing that she'd gone to the casual sports bar he'd suggested and they were sitting around eating burgers and having a beer.

"Tell me again how you made that soup?"

"It wasn't any big deal. Only green chicken chili."

"It was amazing. And I'd use even stronger superlatives if you weren't such a lady. And it was a big deal. You made cornbread and those . . . roll-up things."

"Pork empanadas."

"Better than any restaurant."

"I hope you have room for dessert?"

Jack grinned. "What did you make?"

"Mexican chocolate cake."

"I don't know how you don't weigh two hundred pounds." The minute the words were out of his mouth, he groaned. "Sorry. I know better than to talk about weight with a woman. Especially on a first date."

That mention—or maybe it was the way he'd complimented her so nicely—but she said, "So, you don't mind too much about not going to Champ's?"

"No. As in, not even a little bit. I was just trying to think of somewhere you might feel safe."

She'd gone ahead and told him the *Reader's Digest* version of the latest episode. It hadn't been easy to do, and she'd been practically stuttering on the phone when she'd done it. But he'd acted like women he dated got threatening notes all the time—or at least like he understood—and readily agreed to dine at her house instead.

"Jennifer, my mom is a bookseller, not a cook. I grew up with pasta and pizza and grilled hamburgers and about five other meals that were fine, but nothing to get too excited about. I don't even cook half that well. This was a real treat for me."

"Thanks." She stood up. 'Would you like dessert now?"

"How about I help you clean up first?"

"Well, I need to let the girls know that we're done."

"Because?"

"Because they're waiting for leftovers."

He laughed. "I would say that they could have joined us . . . but I'm glad they didn't."

"Me, too," she said, shyly. They'd talked. Really talked. And not about her and her past either. Jack had told her about his job as a building contractor. He'd told her about getting Harvard and the dozen "bad puppy" things he did on a daily basis. He'd laughed when she told him that she thought Harvard's fascination with Jack's slippers was cute.

She'd told him stories about growing up in Bridgeport, back when it wasn't much more than a sleepy town.

He'd grinned when she'd told him that she'd played softball when she was little and was on the golf team in high school.

It had been easy. Really easy.

"Why don't you go tell your roommates they can come up and eat?"

"But dessert . . ."

"I can eat here with them." When she was ready to protest, he looked her in the eye. "I want to get to know them, Jennifer. I need them on my side, too."

"Why?"

"Because I plan to see you as often as you'll let me." He smiled. "That means I might need their help to make it happen." He snapped his fingers. "I almost forgot—my mother wants you to call her about a job."

"Pardon me?"

"She wants you to cater an event she's been planning. It's called Murder by the Book."

"What is that?"

"My mom is bringing in three mystery writers. They're going

to chat about their books, sign them, and there's going to be all kinds of snacks and desserts to go along with it."

"Wow. It sounds like a lot of fun."

"It is, and the authors sell a lot of books, which means she keeps getting a bigger turnout every year."

"When is it?"

"Two weeks." He grinned. "And before you ask, yes, she did have the food arranged. But the owner's mother or something got sick and they had to cancel. She was really in a state until she remembered you."

"Wow." If she did a good job, it would give her business a real head start. But it also meant that she had to be ready for that.

Was she ready?

She'd gotten that letter. She'd barely made it into the store just a couple of weeks ago. Maybe it was all too fast?

But then she remembered that she wasn't alone anymore. She had her roommates and her brother and, yes, maybe even Jack. Plus, it was his mother hosting the event, and she was lovely.

"Jennifer, are you okay?"

She blinked. "I'm sorry. I guess I was already dreaming up mysterious-sounding snacks."

"So you'll do it?"

She made a decision. She was ready. She nodded. "Yep. I'll do it. It might not be perfect, but I'll do my best."

"If you do it, it will be fine. That's all you need to know." He gestured toward the stairs. "Now can we let your roommates upstairs?"

"Absolutely. Just tell them they can come eat. They'll come up in a heartbeat. They always do."

CHAPTER 36

"When I dance, people think I'm looking for my keys."
—RAY ROMANO

It turned out that Lance wasn't as stupid as they thought. He'd lawyered up practically before they could get his full legal name.

While the assistant district attorney grumbled to their captain, Dylan and Traci shared their frustrations with each other at Paxton's after their shift ended.

A couple of other men and women had joined them for a beer. Now the two of them were lingering and complaining, nursing the same drinks they'd gotten an hour before. "Sometimes I just wish we didn't always have to be the good guys," Traci grumbled.

"Me, too, but what can we do? If we bend the law to suit our needs, we're no better than guys like Lance."

"Oh, I know I'm better than a rapist. But I agree. Back in

Cleveland, I saw more than my fair share of creepiness. Someone has to do the right thing. Might as well be us."

Dylan glanced at his phone and saw he'd gotten a text from Shannon.

Are you okay?

Boy, she was a sweetheart. He quickly typed out a reply.

Okay. Finishing up with your sister. I'll call you later.

When he put his phone down, he said, "Shannon was just checking on me."

Traci's expression softened. "She texted me, too." Looking up at him, she said, "It's nice having someone around who cares, huh?"

"Yeah." Of course, he'd always had that. His parents were good people. They'd supported his wish to become a cop, even though it hadn't been what they'd wanted for him. Now he had Jennifer. Even though she wasn't making him dinner anymore, she still took time to text or call him every couple of days. "You've been alone a lot, haven't you?"

Her nod was almost imperceptible, but he saw it. "I didn't grow up like Shannon. I was in foster care and then a group home."

He knew enough about those to know that a lot of situations weren't safe or loving environments. "How bad was it?"

"Huh? Oh, not too bad."

"Really?" He didn't know why he pressed.

But instead of looking uncomfortable, she kind of half shrugged. "Ms. Henderson was real strict, but fair. And, she only kept five girls at a time. We had space, too. We only had to share a room with one other girl. Then, when I was the oldest I got a room to myself."

"Do you still keep in touch with her?"

"No." She inhaled, then murmured, "She ran a tight ship, but it wasn't like we became buddies or anything." She ran a fingertip around the rim of the glass. "Some girls got along better than me. I can see them writing to her."

"What about the other girls? Do you keep in touch with any of them?"

"I did for a while . . . but it was hard, you know? I had real good grades in high school, and I always knew I wanted to be a cop. I got a full ride to the community college and to the police academy. So, I had somewhere to go. Everyone else wasn't that lucky."

Dylan knew that the system didn't offer many choices for an eighteen-year-old. There were too many needy kids to take care of. "I'm glad you girls found each other."

She smiled faintly. "You mean Shannon found us. If not for her, I'd still be exhausted in Cleveland." Pulling a ten out of a pocket, she tossed it on the bar. "And speaking of not being alone, I'm going to head on home." She winked. "I heard Jennifer was cooking tonight."

"Don't tell me that."

"Do you want to come over? I'm sure no one would mind."

"Thanks, but I'm not quite ready to see my sister yet."

Her expression turned guarded. "If she asks about Lance, what do you want me to say?"

"I'm not going to tell you what to tell her, Tracey. Say what you want."

"But—"

He smiled tiredly. "But if she asks, let her know that I'll stop by to see her in the morning."

"I'll do that. Have a good night."

He watched her leave, realizing that she was walking home. Also that she'd lifted her badge back out over her shirt so it was visible. He wondered why until he saw that she was talking with a group of teenagers on the corner.

He grinned to himself. And that was definitely what she was doing, too. Just talking with them. Being friendly. A person to know in the community. The sight made his day a little better. She was going to be just fine in Bridgeport.

"Anything else, Dylan?" the bartender asked.

He was about to tell her no until he remembered that he had an empty refrigerator at home. "Get me a menu, would you? I need an order to go."

* * *

The next morning, not even a carefully insulated bag of lasagna was making the conversation easier. It turned out that Jennifer had gone out for ice cream with Jack, so she hadn't talked to Traci at all.

Which meant he got to share the news that Lance still wasn't behind bars, was probably cockier than ever, and that he didn't think she should cater the murder-mystery party at Camille's bookstore.

Jennifer had stayed silent while he'd talked, obviously doing her best to take in all the bad news as calmly as she was able. He'd given her that space, knowing that he'd had almost twenty hours to come to terms with what happened.

But then, she'd shaken her head. "I'm not going to do that."

"You're not going to cater the event?"

"No, I mean I'm not going to hide anymore," Jennifer said, her voice firm. "I'm doing it, Dylan."

"But it's not safe." He wasn't exaggerating, either. He could feel in his bones that something was about to happen.

"It's also not safe for me to stay home and be afraid."

"Jennifer, this is a lot to take in. I think as soon as you think about it, you'll agree with me."

"This is a lot, but I'm not going to change my mind. I need to do this event, Dylan."

"I don't want you to get hurt."

"And I don't want to get hurt. But I also really don't want to go back to where I was."

"Jen . . ."

"Why don't we *all* go?" Shannon said from the doorway.

She joined them in the loft's kitchenette. "I'm sorry for interrupting, but well, there aren't a lot of walls in here. Private conversations are hard to keep private."

He stood up. "Hey."

"Listen, I know you don't agree with Jennifer, but how about if Traci and you are there? That's two cops keeping a close eye out, right?"

He nodded but immediately had a flash of what could happen—what if Shannon got hurt, too? "I don't want anything to happen to you. To any of you."

"Dylan, I'm going to be in the kitchen. Jack will be there, too. And all of you. That's enough." Jennifer's voice was firm, her expression resolved.

He knew his sister was right. He knew Shannon's idea was a good one. Unfortunately, he knew that bad guys were good at screwing up even the best plans.

"All right," he said. "You ladies are right."

"Thanks, Dylan," Jennifer said, giving him a hug before leaving the room.

"I'm proud of you," Shannon said. "I know that wasn't easy."

"I'm starting to realize that I want to keep everyone I love in a cocoon. I'll try to not do that."

She looked at him with wonder. "Did you mean that?"

He realized what she was asking. "Yeah," he murmured. "I did. I love you, Shannon."

Her smile was brilliant right before she reached up and kissed him.

CHAPTER 37

"Dance for yourself. If someone understands, good. If not, no matter."
—LOUIS HORST

"I can't believe Kimber is on a beach right now, while we're dressed in sweaters and freezing," Traci said as she frowned at the ice forming on the windshield. Flicking on the defrost, she grumbled, "I'm so over this winter."

Though Shannon privately agreed with Traci's comment, she felt honor-bound to defend their lucky sister. "Kimber's having to wear skimpy bikinis while having to pose in the hot sun for eight hours a day. It's not like she's laying out and working on her tan."

"Well, I'm working, too," Traci said as she parked her vehicle right behind Backdoor Books. "I'm also a whole lot colder."

Watching Traci type something into her phone and check her gun before securing it in her shoulder holster, Shannon felt a rush of sympathy for her. She was only coming to the bookstore as a favor to Jennifer and Dylan.

Of the three of them, Kimber was the reader. Shannon liked to read a book on vacation or one of the bestsellers, but usually preferred to watch movies. Traci, however, didn't like to read at all. In fact, every time Kimber mentioned a new book she'd just read or recommended something from her bedside table, Traci looked like Kimber was recommending one of those low-fat, high-protein shakes she often consumed instead of real food.

Thinking of all that, Shannon murmured, "I guess this event here really is going to feel like a job to you."

"A little bit," Traci said as they got out. "But it's not the fact that we're going to be spending the next three or four hours at a bookstore." She stopped and scanned the area. "Shannon, I'm actually feeling a little off-kilter."

"Because?"

"Because I'm not used to worrying about family while I'm working. I hate that I'm going to have to be watching Jennifer, looking out for this Lance guy, and worrying about you, too."

Shannon frowned. "You don't need to worry about me. I can take care of myself."

"That may be true, but I'm still gonna worry. I can't help it. It's all the training, I guess."

Shannon smiled to herself. Traci wasn't the type of girl to gush about how much she loved her sisters, but what she had just shared was pretty close to it. "I love you, too," she said.

Traci grinned at her as they started walking.

Feeling pleased, Shannon followed. Traci once told her that she'd heard the words "I love you" more since she met Shannon and Kimber than she had in her entire life. That comment said a lot about her sister's early life. But instead of dwelling on how sad that was, Shannon liked to concentrate on how much Traci seemed to *like* hearing it. Her goal was for Traci to one day be just as comfortable saying the words as she was.

When they stepped into the foyer, Shannon noticed Dylan was already inside. He was talking with Camille and Jack but turned to greet them right away.

"Hey, you," he murmured as he bent down to kiss Shannon lightly on the lips.

"Hey back," she replied, looking up at him with a smile. He had on a light-blue oxford, dark jeans, and a dark-gray blazer that she'd never seen before. Shannon thought he looked so handsome. "How are things going around here?"

"Pretty good. Jen is in the back, frantically arranging already-perfect trays of food. Camille is a nervous wreck, and now that I've informed Jack about Lance, he looks like he's ready to be Jennifer's shadow for the night."

Shannon smiled. "That's kind of sweet."

After a slight hesitation, Dylan nodded. "I guess."

Pressing a reassuring hand on his chest, she said, "It is, I promise."

Traci shifted. "Where do you want me, Dylan?"

"Can you hang by the front door? I'm going to stay around the back."

"No problem. I can do that."

When Shannon noticed her sister and boyfriend give each other a look, she said, "Dylan, are you as stressed as Traci is about tonight?"

"Yep."

"I can help," she offered. "Do you want me to be on patrol somewhere?"

"Absolutely not," he replied. "Don't mind Traci and me. We get paranoid from time to time."

Shannon tried to look at ease, but she knew Dylan well enough by now to realize that he was worried.

"It's the drawback of being a cop, Shannon," Traci said. "We always look for the worst to happen. Don't worry."

"I'll try not to." As the door opened and a dozen or so people entered, she added, "I'll go see if I can help Jennifer."

"Good idea, hon," Dylan said.

* * *

As they watched Shannon move gracefully through the increasingly crowded rooms of the old house, Traci snorted. "Kisses and 'honey,' huh? Looks like y'all got everything patched up."

Dylan rolled his eyes, but he didn't deny it. "We made up the other night. I told her I loved her."

Traci's grin vanished. "That's awesome, boss. I'm happy for you. Happy for *both* of you."

"Me, too. She's really special. I know she's who I've been looking for all my life," he added as the door opened and another crowd of people entered. Forcing himself to focus, he said, "We better get to work. I'll head to the back."

She nodded, looking all business again. "If Lance shows up, we'll get him."

"We better," Dylan murmured as he headed into the crowd.

An hour later, the bookstore was filled with at least a hundred people. Camille looked triumphant, and every time he spied Jennifer, she looked like she was having the time of her life.

It was amazing, really. Two months ago, he would have never imagined that she would be comfortable around so many people. But something had happened to her out in the woods that day. She'd finally come into herself. Or maybe she'd simply come back to the girl she used to be. Dylan had to remind himself more than once that his sister didn't used to be nervous or scared when she was younger. All through high school and college, she'd been the more social of the two of them.

Watching how Jack was staying by her side, Dylan knew that he was part of Jennifer's transformation, too. She really liked him. And based on the way he was protectively hovering over her, it seemed Jack liked her just as much.

For his part, he was more than ready for this event to be over. There were too many people spread out through three floors and too many things going on. Camille was manning the cash register on the first floor. Three authors were up on the second floor signing books. Stragglers and book browsers were up on the third floor.

He and Traci had been in constant contact, so he knew Lance hadn't shown up. But that said, Dylan couldn't shake the feeling that something was about to go down. He'd just told himself to stop worrying, when he heard his partner shout loud enough to be heard over the din of the crowd.

"Shannon!"

He turned and ran to the front of the shop, and then stopped in his tracks. There was his girlfriend stepping in front of Jennifer.

Jack was nowhere to be found.

Lance, however, was pushing Shannon to one side as he reached for Jennifer.

Feeling like everything was happening in slow motion, Dylan watched Shannon fight back and thrust herself in front of his sister.

"No!" Dylan yelled as he surged forward. There was no way he was going to let his sister get hurt again. Or Shannon.

Just as Lance looked his way, Traci tackled the guy like she had been the offensive end of the Buckeyes.

As he fell, Lance reached inside his coat.

But that move was foiled as well, thanks to the elbow Traci had slammed into his ribs.

As the crowd gasped and Dylan went down on one knee to cuff him, Shannon wrapped her arms around Jennifer and pulled her to one side.

Lance's attempt to resist was firmly put down, and within minutes, he and Traci were escorting the guy to his cruiser at the back of the shop.

Dylan caught Jennifer's eye as he walked by and smiled at her just as Jack ran up.

"Jen, I'm so sorry," Jack said, his voice strained and out of breath. "I can't believe I fell for that guy's story and ran outside to help with an accident that wasn't even there."

"It's okay."

He ran his hands along her arms. "Are you all right?"

Jennifer's smile was bright. "I am."

Dylan thought his sister had never looked more beautiful. She was okay, proud of herself, and had made it to the other side of her depression and anxiety. He was suddenly sure that everything was going to be just fine for her.

Maybe even for all of them from now on.

CHAPTER 38

"Once a dancer, always a dancer."

Two days later, the four of them were having a girls' night. Kimber had arrived home the night before, sporting a faint tan, a suitcase of trinkets that she'd picked up from some vendors on the beach, and a big appetite.

The previous night, Shannon had stared at Kimber in shock when she'd practically eaten a whole pizza by herself. Her sister had just shrugged, saying that her next modeling job was on a runway in two weeks. In Kimber terms, that meant she could spend a few days eating everything she wanted.

That was partly why they were sitting at the new dining room table Kimber had ordered, and all eating Jennifer's latest creation: Honey-baked ham with all the fixings.

As Traci reached for another helping of mashed potatoes,

Shannon smiled at Jennifer. "This is the best meal I've had in years."

"I'm glad you like it," she replied. "I had a good time cooking all day."

"Every one of my students asked what smelled so good the minute they arrived for class," Shannon said.

"Everything smelled even better up here," Kimber said. "Since Traci had the day off, she and I kept circling the kitchen like alley cats."

"And . . . kept getting denied," Traci teased. "Especially since Jennifer would hardly let us help."

Jennifer shook her head. "I told you, this meal was my thank-you gift to you girls. If you'd helped, it wouldn't have been much of a present."

"We didn't need a present," Shannon said.

"But you all went above and beyond for me the other night. Cooking a decent meal was the least I could do."

"And I told you that there was no need to thank us," Traci said. "I'm just glad we got the guy."

Kimber shook her head. "I still can't believe I missed it all. I would have paid money to see you tackle that guy, Traci."

"It was epic," Jennifer said with a grin. "Dylan is still talking about it. He told me that the sergeant suggested you start moonlighting as a bodyguard, Traci."

Traci rolled her eyes. "Ha ha."

"I'm just glad it's all over," Shannon said. And it really was. Dylan and Traci had arrested Lance, and he was now sitting in jail awaiting trial. He had so many charges against him, from stalking to writing threatening notes to attempted murder, there was no doubt that he would be going to prison for a very long time.

"Me, too," Jennifer said. "Which reminds me . . . I have a surprise for you. I'll be right back."

Shannon looked at her sisters. "What's going on now?"

"No telling," Kimber whispered. "All I know is that we have our very own Betty Crocker, and I'm never giving her back."

Shannon's chuckle faded as Jennifer walked toward them carrying an enormous chocolate cake. "Oh, goodness, look at that."

"It's beautiful," Traci said. "I have no idea when you baked it."

"Early this morning," Jennifer said. "I wanted it to be a surprise." Looking at the three of them, she said, "This isn't a thank-you for helping me with Lance. It's for letting me live with you and making me feel so welcome."

"We like you, Jen," Kimber said. "And for the record, we'd like you living with us even if you didn't cook so well."

"Well, I really appreciate it." She smiled at Shannon. "Of course, this cake is probably for Shannon most of all."

"Why me?" Shannon asked.

"Well, you've made my brother really happy. I've never seen him so enchanted."

"*Enchanted* is a good way of putting it," Traci commented. "Dylan is always kissing and touching you every time you are together now. It's like he can't be in the same room without getting up close and personal."

Embarrassed, Shannon pressed her hands to her cheeks. "We're not that bad . . . are we?"

"Oh, stop. They're in love," Kimber said as she reached for the slice of cake Jennifer handed her. "I think it's sweet."

"I do, too," Jennifer said as she passed out more cake. "Who knows? Maybe one day in the future Dylan will be getting down on one knee."

Shannon knew she was blushing. Both from the teasing . . . and from the fact that she could actually imagine that happening. But if that did happen one day . . . everything would change with her sisters again. Struck by that, she put her fork down.

"What's wrong?" Traci asked.

"Oh, I was just thinking that if Dylan and I did get married one day, things would change for all of us again."

Traci put her fork down, too. "Change how?"

"Well, if Dylan and I married, I'd move in with him," she explained.

Looking mystified, Kimber said, "I would hope so. What's wrong with that?"

"Well, if I lived with Dylan, we wouldn't be together anymore. And . . . and we just found each other." She held her breath, half expecting Traci and Kimber to remind her how they'd just moved to Bridgeport to be with her.

But instead they laughed.

Spearing a bite of cake with her fork, Traci said, "Shannon, not even you marrying my partner and moving in with him is going to change things with the three of us."

"Sure?"

"I'm positive. We're sisters now. Forever and ever."

Leaning back, Kimber nodded. "You've always got us now, Miss West Virginia. No matter what happens in the future, Traci and I will be there for you. We love you, and we're going to love you forever and ever."

At a loss for words, Shannon smiled at them both. They really had become sisters. No matter what happened, that's what they would be.

EPILOGUE

"There are shortcuts to happiness,
and dancing is one of them."
—VICKI BAUM

June

"Are you ready to go home?" Dylan asked Shannon as they crossed the Ohio River from Kentucky on the historic Brent Spence Bridge.

Looking at thc array of boats on the river, the expanse of trees along the banks, and the bright blue sky, Shannon smiled. She was beginning to like everything about her new hometown. She loved the quaintness of Bridgeport, the vibrancy of living near Cincinnati, even the novelty of flying into Northern Kentucky in order to get home. There was something about seeing that Welcome to Ohio sign posted on the bridge that tugged at her heart every time.

"I can't wait," she said at last. "It feels like we've been gone for a month."

"Only ten days, Mrs. Lange."

Shannon bit her lip so she wouldn't start grinning hard enough to beat the band. "It felt longer."

"I wished it had lasted longer." Continuing to drive along I-275 toward Bridgeport, Dylan chuckled. "Only you would complain about a honeymoon in Florida."

Their honeymoon had been wonderful. They'd elected to stay away from the fancy resorts in Sarasota and had instead stayed in a house Shannon had found through Airbnb. The house had been right on Siesta Key and had had its own pool. After the craziness of the last two months—with Dylan's sudden proposal and their decision to have a small ceremony two months later in a tiny church in Bridgeport instead of back in Spartan, which had been stressful—they had both needed a break.

At first her mother had been upset—she'd hoped to hold a big wedding with half of their hometown in attendance. But she'd eventually understood . . . and then had helped Shannon plan the intimate ceremony with her usual precision and flair.

"I loved our honeymoon," she murmured. "And I loved our wedding, you know that."

"I know you looked beautiful in that white lacey gown."

"You keep saying that, Dylan." Not that she minded. She, too, kept remembering their sweet, intimate ceremony. Dylan had worn a dark-navy suit. And she? Well, she'd worn her dream gown—a confection of white satin, tulle, and lace that was the most beautiful thing she'd ever seen. Walking down the aisle on her father's arm, she'd only seen Dylan. He'd smiled at her in a way that made her feel like she was the only woman in the room.

"I keep saying that because it's still true. You were a beautiful bride."

She smiled at him. "Now, we get to go to your house and relax. I'm excited to be finally get settled and do nothing."

"It's *our* house now, hon."

The move had been another source of exhaustion over the weeks before the ceremony. She had moved most of her things from her room so Jennifer could move into it easily. But though moving those things had been easy enough, it had been a little traumatic. Jennifer had been *officially* moving on with her life, and Shannon had been *officially* moving away from the two sisters she'd just gotten close to.

Kimber had been the one to finally stop all her tears, relaying that Shannon was still going to be on the first floor every day, so it wasn't like they were going to be getting rid of her at all.

But instead of saying something sweet about how happy he was that she was moving in with him, Dylan looked a little worried. "Shannon, about that the house . . ."

"Yes?"

"I need to warn you that everything there might not be like you hoped."

"How come?" She'd just about gotten all of her possessions put away at Dylan's house before their wedding day.

Putting on his turning signal, he exited the highway and turned onto Main Street. Now they were less than ten minutes from his house. From their house.

He drummed his fingertips on the steering wheel. "Well, you know there was that bad storm that ran through town."

"I know." A severe thunderstorm had passed through Bridgeport, bringing with it hail, flooding, and a tornado on the outskirts. She frowned. "Did something happen to the house?"

"Nothing like that. It's just that Traci was working the whole time. And a lot of our buddies had to deal with flooded offices and basements." He sighed. "But because of that, I don't think anyone cleaned up the house or went to the store or anything. It's going to be a mess."

She looked at him strangely. "You know I don't care about that, Dylan."

"I know. I just wanted to warn you that everything might not be like you expect," he said as he parked the car in the driveway.

She got out before he could come around and help her. "Pop the trunk, Dylan. Let's get everything inside."

"Let's wait a minute." He took her hand and walked her to the front door. "I can't do this if my hands are full of luggage."

"Do what?" she asked, just as he swept her up into his arms. Of course, she squealed and looped her arms around his neck.

"This," he said as he opened the door with a free hand and carried her across the threshold.

Just as she was reaching up to give him a welcome-home kiss, the whole house erupted.

In cheers.

Putting her down on her feet, Shannon stared at the crowd of all their friends and family in the living room. "What . . ."

"Welcome home, Mr. and Mrs. Lange!" Traci said as she ran up to her, Kimber right by her side.

Shannon hugged her sisters tight, then reached out and pulled Jennifer into their group hug. "This is the best," she said. "I love y'all so much."

Kimber laughed. "Your accent's back. You must be pleased."

She was. Looking up at her husband, she shook her head. "I can't believe you planned this."

He looked delighted. "I wanted something special to begin our new life together." He winked. "I told you the house wasn't going to be like you expected."

Just as someone put on music, champagne corks were popped, and all their friends started talking quickly and giving them hugs, Shannon looked at her sisters, her husband, all their friends. Everything.

And something settled deep in her chest that was so sure that the rest of her finally felt complete. She had sisters. She had a wealth of people she loved and cared about. She had Dylan.

Finally, at last, she was home.

The End

An Excerpt from

Take the Lead

"If you've got nothing to dance about,
find a reason to sing."
—MELODY CARSTAIRS

CHAPTER 1

"Let us read and let us waltz—two amusements that will never do any harm to the world."
—VOLTAIRE

"I need some help, here!" Officer Traci Lucky announced as she wrapped her arm around Gwen—a skinny woman in her late twenties who looked closer to forty. She had big blue eyes, long black hair, pale skin, and a sizable baby bump.

Traci had found her curled in a ball on the floor in one of the back rooms of a house that she and her partner had just raided on suspicion of being a meth lab. That tip turned out to be wrong, but they'd found enough drug paraphernalia for Dylan to call in reinforcements.

Just as Traci got on the phone to call for an ambulance, Gwen had gotten to her feet and started freaking out. She seemed even hopped up, and Gwen managed to convey that she didn't want to touch the expense of an ambulance. After a couple of minutes arguing, they compromised. Gwen agreed to go to the hospital if Traci agreed to escort her.

That was how Traci now found herself walking into Bridgeport Hospital's emergency room with one of her hands wrapped around Gwen's upper arm so she wouldn't collapse or run off. The poor woman really did need some help.

Unfortunately, Traci's call for assistance was being ignored. That was something of note.

Bridgeport's usually sleepy emergency room was currently a hotbed of action. Twenty people were in the waiting area—nurses, attendants, and support staff were running around like they were in the middle of downtown Cincinnati. Emerson, another officer from Bridgeport was standing off to the side talking on his phone.

After waiting two seconds, Gwen pulled on her arm. "Can I go now?"

"No. You're getting seen."

Gwen rolled her eyes. "Can I at least sit down?"

"Are you ready to listen to me and sit where I tell you?"

Gwen's already disgruntled expression darkened. "I told you I don't need to be here."

"And I told you that you need to get checked out. Your baby needs to be seen to." Yes, her voice was wickedly sharp and her tone brooked no argument. But this girl was beginning to get on her last nerve.

It took a second, but Traci's words eventually settled in. "Oh," she said. A little bit after, Gwen got that vacant look on her face that Traci knew too well. This momma-to-be was either high as a kite or coming off of something and about to crash.

Traci gritted her teeth. She loved being a cop. Loved it. Few things—the hours, the craziness, or even the paperwork—got to her anymore. But, out of everything she saw in her line of work—and in all the years in Cleveland, she'd seen a lot—pregnant mothers who also happened to be drug addicts was her kryptonite. She hated it. Hated it.

Though she knew the reason why—her mother had taken a fair share of drugs when she'd been pregnant with Traci—trying to take her personal feelings out of the equation didn't help. All she saw were babies in need of care and women who were either incapable or couldn't be bothered to do anything different.

Still afraid to leave Gwen in a chair, Traci approached the crowded reception desk. The receptionist, Sharon, looked up, immediately took in Traci's uniform and Gwen's condition, and froze.

"Yes?"

"We need some assistance. This woman needs an obstetrician."

Sharon looked over Gwen curiously. "Is she in labor?"

"No," said Gwen.

"What's the emergency, then?" Sharon asked.

"I'm afraid that's a private matter." Putting a bit more force into her voice, Traci continued. "Look, we need to see someone as soon as possible. Where can I take her? You got an empty room back there?" Traci asked, gesturing toward the triage area.

The dark-haired woman looked skeptical. "Well . . ."

"She can't just come in here and take a spot. We've been waiting for an hour," a man standing on her right interrupted.

In another life, Traci might have agreed with him. She knew she was absolutely using her uniform to get her way. But she knew that if she didn't push this, Gwen would disappear back into the woodwork of the town, and that baby would be born without a lick of care. And, well, if that happened? Traci didn't know if she would be able to handle that.

"She needs to be seen stat. I have to get back to work."

The man folded his arms over his chest. "I do, too."

"Sharon? Where can we go?"

Looking as if she knew she was fighting a battle she couldn't win, Sharon sighed. "Fine. Take this woman to five," she said to an orderly. "I think it just opened up."

"Thanks," Traci said.

"Hey, wait!" the man grumbled. "That's not fair."

Traci ignored him as she shuttled Gwen through the electronic gate and to a set of double doors. The doors swung open, revealing a beehive of well-organized activity.

Gwen got quieter with each step, and almost seemed to grow younger as well. Her eyes widened as she took in the area. Within seconds, two nurses took charge of Gwen. After getting her weight, they escorted Gwen to a curtained room.

Traci stood outside the curtain, half listening to the nurses' questions and Gwen's mumbled half-coherent replies. Everything she heard made her cringe and ache to leave. Why had she gotten saddled with this girl, anyway? It felt too personal and too hard.

"Who are you here for?"

Traci looked up and blinked. There, standing right in front of her, was a movie-star handsome man in light-blue scrubs and a white lab coat. A stethoscope was around his neck.

Getting to her feet, Traci pointed to the closed curtain. "I escorted that woman."

He pulled down the chart. "Gwen Osbourne?"

"Yep. She's pregnant and looks to be in bad shape." She held out her hand. "Traci Lucky."

"Good to meet you, Officer," he replied as they shook hands. "I'm Matt Rossi."

"Good to meet you." She lowered her voice. "I found Gwen on the floor of a crack house. She's not exactly here willingly."

Worry instead of disdain filled the doctor's eyes, which made Traci feel even more terrible. She should be feeling something more for the woman. Where was her compassion? Obviously something had happened to put Gwen in the situation that she was in.

"Are you going to be here for a while?"

She nodded. "I'm staying until you give me an idea of what I should do with her. I'm pretty certain if I walked out now she'd run." Plus, she'd promised Gwen that she wouldn't leave her.

"Okay, then." He turned and walked through the curtain, greeting Gwen as he did.

Not wanting to hear anything more, Traci took a couple of steps to the right, finally ending up leaning against the closed door of a supply closet. And as the orderlies and nurses and patients passed by, she reminded herself that Gwen's life was not her mother's. Gwen's baby was not going to be Traci.

Every child born into such a heartbreaking situation didn't end up growing up in a group home like she had. Some, no doubt, did just fine.

And then, because she was alone and no one could see, she closed her eyes and said a little prayer for that baby.

Twenty minutes later, the doctor came out.

"How is she?"

"Struggling." He sighed. "Her skin looked a little sallow and her eyes yellow. I'm worried she might have hepatitis."

"Hepatitis." She knew Gwen could have gotten it from dirty needles. Was that what had happened?

The doctor continued. "We took some blood and ran a couple of tests. Her baby's heartbeat seems strong, but I'd still like to know what's in her system before we release her." He ran a hand through his hair, making the short strands stand up on end. "I'm going to go ahead and admit Gwen. We need to see if she is hep positive. In addition, we'll need to get her cleaned up and safe, until you can get her someplace better."

Until she did that. Though she knew it could happen, the

responsibility hit her hard. For the near future, she was in charge of Gwen.

She nodded. "Thank you for seeing her so quickly, Dr. Rossi."

"It's what I'm here for." His gaze was warm as he suddenly smiled. "Hey, good job on getting her here."

Maybe it was because he was so nice. Or he cared so much and was making her want to be better, too. But whatever the reason, she found herself smiling back. And, feeling a little bit better about the world.

"I've got to go. I'll say goodbye but be back tomorrow."

He looked surprised. "Really? Do you do that for everyone you bring in?"

"No, but I'm committed now. Plus, I've got some personal reasons for getting so involved."

"Maybe I'll see you tomorrow, then."

"I hope so," she replied before she caught herself. After all, this wasn't some meet-cute. She was doing her job and so was he. They were working.

"Dr. Rossi, we need you," a nurse called out.

"I've got to go. See you, Officer Lucky." He smiled again before walking down the hall.

Traci stayed where she was and watched him disappear. But as she turned to walk back to Gwen, she realized that the future didn't feel as bleak as it had just an hour ago.

Huh.

Acknowledgments

It occurs to me that the process of publishing a book is rather like a complicated dance. From writing the first blurbs and story line, to sending it to my agent, to the editors' and publication board's approval, a book has to jump through many hoops. After that comes the many people who work on the manuscript and the book's layout, design, and cover. Finally, a great number of people work on the book's marketing and sales plans. Sometimes there are even a couple of missteps and falls before the book arrives on the bookshelf all polished and pretty.

With that in mind, I'd like to be sure to thank both Vikki Warner for seeing the possibilities of this series and editor Ember Hood for her help and expertise. Just as important are the other members of my Blackstone family: Alenka for the cover design, Jeff, Greg, Lauren, and Robin for their tireless efforts to package and promote my books and eventually get them on shelves. I'm blessed to work with you all.

As always, I am so grateful for my agent, Nicole Resciniti, who both manages to talk me up and calm me down, sometimes at the same time. I'm also grateful for Evette at Best of Ballroom for patiently answering many questions about teaching ballroom dancing and to Officer Alex Napier for his very kind advice about the day-to-day life of being both a big-city and small-town cop.

Finally, no note of appreciation would be complete without mentioning my husband, Tom. For this book, he not only listened to me ramble on about plots and problems but also learned to rumba at ballroom dance class. Every author should be so blessed to have a spouse like him.

Thank you all so much for giving this book a try. I'm forever grateful for your support.

1. I loved writing about three sisters who were just beginning to know each other. If you have a sibling, how has your relationship changed and grown over the years?

2. What do you think will happen to the women after their one year together officially ends?

3. Echoing the sisters' journey was Dylan and Jennifer's relationship. How did you see Dylan and Jennifer's relationship grow during the novel?

4. One of my favorite parts of the novel was Shannon's love of dance. Do you have a longtime hobby that has given you joy?

5. I enjoyed finding quotations about dancing and was surprised by how many of them could be applied to all sorts of things in life. Was there a particular quotation that spoke to you? Why?

6. My favorite character in the novel was Jennifer. I loved showing her growth and watching her get stronger. She also just happens to love cookbooks as much as I do. I had a good

time writing about that. Did you connect with any of the characters in particular? Why?

7. I ended up taking quite a few ballroom dance lessons for this book. It was fun to tackle a brand-new hobby at fifty years old! What new hobby would you like to try out one day?

8. *Shall We Dance?* is the first novel in a series, but it's also loosely connected with the first novels in the Bridgeport Social Club: *Take a Chance*, *All In*, and *Hold on Tight*. I, personally, love to read books in a series. Do you? What elements do you think make for a good series?